FOR A GOODE TIME CALL...

GOODE GIRLS

Jasinda Wilder

FOR A GOODE
TIME CALL...

ONE

Ink

SUCH A TINY LITTLE THING, THIS GIRL. I COULD PICK HER up one-handed. Toss her over my shoulder and climb up a ladder and barely even feel her weight. If I was gonna put numbers to her, I'd say she stood no more than five-five, but likely that's generous by a few inches. Weight? Ehh, I ain't really the type to care or know much about such things, but put a gun to my head and tell me to guess and I'd peg her at about a hundred pounds. Course, I could be off a bit simply because she didn't look frail or slight despite being so short—she looked *tight*. That's the only word for it. Hard. Strong. She moved, despite the limp, as if she is a powerhouse…smooth, lithe, strong.

Hard to tell much about her build beyond her obvious height and leanness—she was wearing a baggy hooded sweatshirt that hung past her booty and it hid her whole torso. She was wearing those black leggings girls like so much these days, and damn me if I didn't find myself wishing that sweatshirt was a little shorter, because I had a feeling she was hiding a mighty fine backside under it.

But I shook off those thoughts like a dog shaking its fur dry. Every instinct I had told me loud and clear that this girl was in need of a friend, not someone hitting on her and staring at her body.

I'd been ambling down the docks, watching the waters of the Ketchikan channel chuck against the pylons, thinking about my next piece—a spray of butterflies turning into sparrows flying up a woman's ribcage to cover a mastectomy scar. Lost in thought, working out details mentally, preparing for the first session, outlining, which would begin after my lunch. For which I was headed to my cousin Juneau's boyfriend's cousins' bar—Badd's Bar and Grille. Sounds like a more complicated relationship than it is. I'm pretty good friends with all the Badds, and I frequently took my lunch break at the bar. Today, I had been angling away from the channel, about to head for the opposite side of the street and the bar when I noticed a girl. Young, beautiful. About my age, short, with long platinum blonde hair—and she was powerwalking as if she was raging about something in her head.

None of my never mind, right? Just keep walking, leave her to her mental rant.

Course, it became my business when I realized she was so lost in her thoughts that she didn't seem to realize the street she was walking down was about to come to an end—in the frigid waters of the Ketchikan channel. Which, even in summer, were cold enough to be life-threatening if you were in it for too long. And she was seconds from taking a very unexpected dip.

I had hesitated another moment, hoping she'd glance up, but her gaze was on her feet, hands shoved into the pocket of her sweatshirt. Stomping angrily right for the water.

Nope, she wasn't stopping.

Crap.

I had darted forward, lunged, and caught her by the sweatshirt literally as she was falling forward into the water. Held her nearly horizontal, feet planted partially on the edge of the pier. Solidified my grip and my balance, and then I'd hauled her up. Turned her around, setting her firmly on her feet.

And had caught my first glimpse at the most fiery, expressive hazel eyes I'd ever seen in my damned life.

I hadn't gotten much of a story out of her, only that she'd undergone a recent and life-changing trauma of some kind—a car accident, maybe? Something. And she was struggling with it. So, I'd suggested Badd's, and she'd agreed, saying she needed to get blackout drunk, and comfort food. So, here we were, heading for Badd's, and I was setting myself up to babysit a five-foot-nothing angry blonde beautiful girl I'd only just met moments ago, and I was wondering what the hell I'd gotten myself into.

I wouldn't say I'd saved her life, really, but had definitely saved her from a nasty spill in the channel. I should've been done with her after yanking her back from the channel. So why was I inviting myself into her life? Into being her blackout drunk babysitter?

Something.

Something about her. Not sure what, but I just knew I couldn't walk away yet. If I didn't watch over her, if nothing else, I knew no one else would. I mean, the Badd clan would make sure nothing horrible happened to her, but some gut reaction was screaming that this girl just needed a friend, and that I was it.

I wanted to be it.

Why, I wasn't sure, and didn't care to think too closely about. But I did, so here we were, together.

We reached the front entrance of Badd's Bar and Grille, and I reached past her to yank open the heavy wooden door. She eyed me like I'd shot her cat.

I frowned down at her as she sidled inside, letting her eyes adjust to the dim lighting within. "The hell was that look for?"

She scanned the interior of the bar which was mostly wood—worn, squeaky, weathered wood planks on the floor, heavy tables and chairs, and a long wooden bar running the length of the building on the right side, the top of it polished to a shine despite the pits and scars and grooves. TVs played SportsCenter highlight reels, old football games, and talking head type shows. The house speakers played Delta Blues— Muddy Waters by the sound of it.

I saw Bast behind the bar pulling a beer, and Kitty at a table taking an order from a foursome of biker types. At six feet four, Bast was tall, only three inches shy of my own height, with arms covered in tattoos, wearing a plain white T-shirt stretched around a physique most athletes ten years his junior would be envious of. His brown hair was longish and left messy over his dark eyes, and he had the beginning of a beard—new for him who tended to cultivate a heavy stubble most of the time.

Kitty was on the taller end for a girl, brunette, a beautiful smile that lit up her face, dressed in blue jeans and a black V-neck T-shirt embroidered with "Badd's Bar & Grille."

The bar was fairly busy for this time in the morning, albeit most of the clientele was here for an early lunch rather than anything like real drinking.

"Which one is your cousin?" she asked.

I pointed at Bast. "Cousin-in-law, not cousin." I grunted noncommittally. "Well, sort of cousin-in-law. My cousin is serious with his cousin."

She blinked up at me. "Wait, what?"

I chuckled. "Confusing, I guess. I got a cousin, Juneau. She's dating a guy named Remington Badd, who is the cousin of the guy with the tats behind the bar." I pointed at Kitty. "And *she's* dating my cousin's boyfriend's identical triplet brother."

She blinked at me again. "Wait. Wait, wait, wait." She indicated Kitty. "That's Kitty, girlfriend of Roman Badd, son of Lucas Badd?"

I nodded. "Yeah. Why, you know 'em?"

She tipped her head side to side. "I know Lucas. My mom is dating him."

"Ahh, now it all comes together," I said. "So, your mom is dating my cousin's boyfriend's dad."

She laughed, an unexpectedly beautiful sound, light and merry and energetic, like a small handbell. "Does that make us related?"

I hummed. "No...I don't believe so, no. Not even

by law, since they ain't married." I laughed again. "Well, they might be. None of these folk make too big a deal about the difference between being legally married and married in all but the legal sense."

"So, you don't know." She rolled her eyes. "Good to know."

I waved a hand. "Don't much matter to me, and it ain't my business. They love each other, they're happy, and that's all that really matters." I pressed my hand as gently as I knew how against the small of her back. "Come on. Bast may look like a scary-ass mo-fo, but he's nice as anything."

She arched her back just slightly; enough to relate to me the fact that she didn't want me touching her. So, I withdrew my hand and headed for the bar. We took seats near the service bar, where close friends and family tended to hang out.

Bast saw me, dropped off the four beers he'd pulled on the service bar, and extended a closed fist to me. "Ink, how's it goin', big guy?"

I tapped his fist with mine. "All right. You?"

Bast nodded. "Can't complain. Wife is down on the mainland with her dad for the weekend, so I'm batchin' it." He glanced at my companion. "You resemble someone I know. Related to Liv Goode, by any chance?"

She nodded. "She's my mom."

Bast took a thick stack of cocktail napkins, laid the stack flat on his open palm, and twisted his knuckles into them to spin them into a fan. "You could be her, except for the blonde hair." He stuck out his hand. "You can call me Bast."

"I'm Cassie," she said. "And the resemblance is in the eyes and the jawline."

Bast just nodded, and eyed us, one and then the other. "Well, pleased to meet you. What can I get you?"

I looked to Cassie, who eyed the line of tap handles. "A light beer," she said. "Light, but good."

Bast nodded, glanced at me. "For you, Ink?"

I shrugged—I wasn't much of drinker, but the situation seemed to call for a beer or two. "Surprise me, long as it ain't that black shit you could stand a fork up in."

Bast laughed. "Guinness is amazing. You just gotta drink a whole pint to really get the flavor."

Within a minute, we both had pints of beer in front of us, and Cassie was eying the single-page laminated menu. "I'll have…the entire appetizer section."

Bast blinked. "Really?" When Cassie just stared at him silently, Bast shrugged. "Okay." A glance at me. "The usual?"

I nodded. "Sounds good. Thanks."

A few moments of silence ensued as Bast left to

ring in our orders, during which time Cassie focused entirely on her beer, ignoring me completely.

"You're judging me," she finally said, without looking at me.

I sipped my beer—Bast had brought me something red and malty and rich. "Nope."

"I just ordered the entire appetizer section."

I took another sip, and then wiped the foam off my mustache with the back of my hand. "Must be hungry, is all."

She eyed me, then. Her eyes were hazel—put gray, brown, and green on a Venn diagram and her eye color would be where the circles met. "Yeah, that's it. I'm just hungry." She tossed back her beer, finishing the pint in a startlingly short time.

I laughed. "If I was gonna judge you, it'd be for how fast you just downed that beer. But, you did tell me at the outset that you plan on getting blackout." I figured I'd help her out, finishing mine just as fast. "There. Now we're even."

She just fixed those hazel eyes on me with unwavering intensity. "You don't have to keep up, you know. Or babysit me. I can hold my own."

I swirled the last bit of red beer and creamy foam around the bottom of the glass. "Cassie, darlin', look at me. I can drink an almighty, unholy amount of liquor. Between my size and a freak accident of genetics, it's damned near impossible for me to drink enough to get more'n nicely buzzed."

"You *are* a freak accident of genetics," she muttered.

I nodded. "True enough. But my tolerance is bananas, even for a guy my size."

"What's that look like? How much would you have to drink to get blackout?"

I bobbed my head to one side, running my fingers down through my beard. "This one time, me, Fox, Andrew, and Royal were out in the deep bush, hunting moose."

"Clearly I know none of these people, but no matter. Carry on."

"Just friends of mine. Fox is the only one you may ever see in town, though. Andrew and Royal stay as far from cities as they can get. Anyway. We were way the hell out there, couple days' hike from where we'd left Royal's floatplane, which was the only way you could even get close to where we were. Far as fuck from any damned thing. Course, Andrew bein' Andrew, had packed a whole damn crate of booze with him. We'd hike out from the plane, which we were using as our base camp. We'd hunt and hike and camp, come back to base camp to resupply, drop off our kills, and then head back out."

"How many moose did you kill?"

I laughed. "Well, you go out for moose, come back with deer, rabbits, turkeys, grouse, whatever."

"Isn't there some sort of law about what you can hunt and when?" Cassie asked. "I mean, I know literally nothing about hunting, but I just have that impression."

"We're all indigenous, and Fox, Royal and Andrew all have subsistence hunting licenses."

"I don't know what that is."

"Well, you gotta know what subsistence means, yeah?"

Cassie nodded. "Sure."

"There's still rules and regulations to it, but basically it exempts us from those wider regulations about hunting, provided we are only hunting to provide for our families, which this was, by the way."

"Hunting for survival, rather than mere sport."

"Yep. Fox is a trapper by trade, and Andrew and Royal both hunt as their primary means of providing food for their wives and kids. I was just along for fun, although I do keep my license up to date."

"When does this answer my question about you drinking?"

Bast came by and refilled our beers.

"Gettin' there," I said. "We'd been out there for about a week by this time, and we'd only indulged a little bit around the fire, but I'd heard a telltale clinking and rattling coming from Andrew's bags, and I knew he was packing something with him, just biding his time to break it out."

I paused to remember.

"Well, one night, we'd gone the whole damn day without seein' a single animal worth shooting, and we was all frustrated. So Andrew says, 'boys, I think it's time we test the upper limits of Ink's tolerance for booze.'"

Cassie grinned. "Oh boy."

"Yeah," I said. "Especially if you take into consideration that Andrew is famous, or maybe it's better said he's *in*famous—for his moonshine."

"Homemade moonshine?"

I nodded. "Ohhh yeah. The most potent white lightning you'll ever taste. It'll sear the taste buds right off your tongue. I've seen grown men, hard-drinking boozers at that, get hammered off a handful of shots of Andrew's shine." I sighed. "Now, don't go repeating this, since it ain't exactly a legal operation, mind you."

"Can't moonshine make you go blind?"

I shrugged. "Sure, if you're an asshole or an idiot. Andrew is neither—his shine is on par with some of the best in the country. It's a real operation, with real equipment…it just ain't legal, as he don't have a proper permit. Point being, his hooch is *powerful*."

"How much did you drink?"

I shrugged. "Lost track after about an hour. I wasn't trying to chug it, as I ain't interested in dying. All I remember is Andrew would refill my cup whenever it emptied. I know I saw him uncork a new bottle more than once, but they was all drinkin' too. When I came to, there was three empty bottles, and Andrew, Fox, and Royal stayed passed out for a whole day. We were all sick as hell for three days. Wonder of it was that none of us were the worse for wear, but I know after that, Andrew never bugged me about drinking again. Said what he saw me do that night, in terms of the amount I drank, was just purely terrifying to behold." I shook my head. "Don't remember much, but when I woke up, my whole body hurt worse than the time I got hit by a truck. None of my buddies would tell me what I done, but there was a whole hell of a lotta broken shit at the camp, so I figure…well, I figure it wasn't pretty."

Cassie frowned up at me. "That's crazy. Charlie and I did a moonshine tasting during a vacation to Tennessee, and it only took us a little bit to get crazy drunk."

"Who's Charlie?" I asked.

"My older sister," Cassie said. "Real name is Charlotte but, like me not wanting to be called Cassandra, you just don't do it. I don't think even

Mom has called Charlie Charlotte except maybe once or twice in the last…shoot, ten years? I think the last time Mom called her Charlotte was when she was sixteen and I was fourteen. We were out with some of Charlie's friends, one of whom had a license and a car."

"Oh boy, that spells trouble," I said.

She laughed, nodding. "No kidding. So I talked Charlie into letting me tag along with her and her friends. Six of us, I think? Wasn't even supposed to be more than one person in the car with the driver in the first place, but there we were, all six of us. Eleven at night, all of us out past our curfews. And our one friend says 'hey, I know where my dad keeps his liquor. Wanna try some?'"

I chuckled. "Ohhh dear."

"Oh dear is right. None of us had a clue about alcohol. All we knew was it was forbidden and illegal, and therefore exciting. So we snuck into Katie's house, into her basement, and we started taking swigs right from the bottle."

I eyed her. "Swigs of what?"

"We didn't know. An old dusty bottle is all we knew. Figured, if it was old and dusty, it must mean her dad didn't like it, so he wouldn't notice any missing."

I palmed my forehead. "Oh shit. It was something rare, wasn't it?"

She nodded. "Rare, meaning a bottle of hundred-year-old scotch worth hundreds if not thousands of dollars, handed down to him by his grandfather."

"Oh no. Oh man, you must've gotten in so much trouble."

"You don't even know. He found us, so drunk off a few sips each, that we were cackling in the basement, on the floor, at two in the morning. He drove each of us home, chewed out our parents and us, then pressed theft charges…"

"He did not."

"He did. Theft." She shrugged, sighing. "He only pushed it enough to scare us all stupid. We didn't get any lasting records out of it, but we did get community service hours, on top of having to do yardwork for Mr. McClellan every Saturday morning for six months."

"And your parents?"

"Mom was fucking apoplectic. Like, so mad she couldn't even shout. She was just white and silent with absolute rage. Didn't speak to either of us for three days. Called us each by our full names every time she spoke to us for a week after that, which was to assign us all the chores in the entire house for a month, and then send us to our rooms as soon as we were done. Charlie got it the worst, though, because as the older sister, she was responsible for me and should've known better."

"Wow." I eyed her. "How many sisters do you have?"

"Four. I'm second oldest, Charlie is the oldest. After me is Lexie, then Torie, and Poppy is the baby."

"Charlie, Cassie, Lexie, Torie, and Poppy."

She nodded. "Charlotte, Cassandra, Alexandra, Victoria, and…Poppy. The only one whose name isn't short for anything." Cassie swirled her beer, swigged. "You? Any brothers or sisters?"

I shook my head. "Nah. Just me. I got a shitload of cousins, though. Mostly second cousins or first cousins once removed."

"I've never understood how that works."

I laughed. "I'm an expert. My mom's sister's child is my cousin, Juneau. My Mom's sister—my aunt, has grandchildren—those grandchildren, my mother's sister's children's children, are my first cousins once removed. My mom is the baby of her family of four brothers and three sisters, and her next oldest sister—Juneau's mom—is way older than her and has six kids, of whom June-bug is the youngest by several years."

She blinked at me. "Wow, so…you have a *big* family."

"A big, complicated family. Most of whom live far away from here, far from anything you might understand as civilization. Most of 'em live, for all intents and purposes, the way our family has lived for hundreds of years. We got electricity and plumbing, cell phones and satellite TV and laptops, but that's all just...gravy. Day to day life is all pretty much the same as it's been for...well, generations."

She gazed at me for a moment. "Wow. That's... it's really cool, actually."

"Not when you're a teenage kid who just wants to feel normal, it ain't." I took a sip. "I feel different about it now, but only because I sorta walked away from it all and did my own thing."

"Which is what?"

I tapped my forearm. "This."

"Tattoos?"

I nodded. "Yep. I own a tattoo shop. I've been doing tattoos for years. Taught myself, and then apprenticed to the best tattoo artist in Ketchikan, worked for him from the time I was fifteen doing tattoos the traditional way out of his trailer until I was old enough to get a license and do modern tattoos using a special gun, you know? Did that for a few more years, saved every penny I made, and bought my shop."

"Did your family not approve?"

I shrugged. "Not really. I mean...it's complicated. It was obvious from the time I could hold on to things with my hands that I'm the type of person who's meant to do one thing, know what I mean? Like some people are just...created by whatever you want to believe in, for one specific person. Like God or the universe or nature just looked at unformed me and went, 'This kid, he's a tattoo artist. That's his thing, his only thing. But he's gonna be the *best* at it.'"

She was silent, staring into the bubbling tan liquid in her glass. "Yeah," she whispered. "I know all about that."

I stared at her, letting the silence open up. Clearly, a sore subject. Something to do with her anger, her limp, and her stated desire to get blackout drunk today. But I knew enough not to pry, not to push. If I just held my counsel and my tongue, chances were, she'd start talking eventually.

Bast brought our food over—a giant oval tray cluttered with paper baskets of food: mozzarella sticks, steak fries covered in melted cheese and house-made chili, deep-fried pickles, fried green tomatoes, chicken wings with a bunch of dipping sauces, onion rings, melted brie cheese with triangles of toasted pita and slices of green apple, and my usual, a triple-decker cheeseburger with fries, and a cup of chili.

I eyed the mountain of food in front of Cassie. "I suppose it's worth mentioning that the Badd boys don't skimp on the portions."

She eyed me, and then the food—each basket held enough food for two or three people to share. "Yeah, you could've mentioned that." She laughed, rubbing her forehead with a knuckle. "There's enough food here for fifteen people."

I shrugged. "You seemed to know what you were about."

She sighed. Eyed me, the food, and a bemused Bast. Then, she tugged over the chili cheese fries, the fried green tomatoes, and the brie. "Give the rest away, so it doesn't go to waste," she said. "I'll pay for it all, either way."

Bast just chuckled. "You're family, Cassie. No charge."

She shook her head. "You're kidding."

Bast refilled her beer without being asked. "Your mom is dating my uncle. Makes you family even if you weren't here with Ink, and family eats and drinks for free, always."

"But...that's like, seventy bucks worth of food."

Bast shrugged. "Family is family." He winked at her. "I'll keep the beer coming until you cry uncle."

She nodded. "Thank you." A pause. "I need it."

"Been a bartender my whole life," he said. "I know when a person just needs to drink themself into oblivion." He gestured at me. "And there ain't nobody better to have around you in times like that than Ink."

She rolled her eyes. "I'm a big girl. I can take care of myself, but thanks."

Bast just laughed. "You do you, boo."

She stared hard at Bast. "Yeah, don't call me boo. Ever."

Bast quirked an eyebrow. "Just jokes."

Cassie turned her attention to the food. "Shitty day, shitty week, shitty month. Shitty couple of months. Shitty life as of..." she pretended to check a nonexistent watch, "...two months, two weeks, and six days ago." Another pause as she pulled out her phone to actually look at the time. "And...eight hours."

Bast and I exchanged looks, and then Bast gave me a look that said *that's all you, buddy, and good luck*, and then walked away to take a beer order from the other end of the bar.

A long silence unrolled between Cassie and me as I dug into my lunch and Cassie hers. After about twenty minutes of silence between us, she glanced at me.

"Not gonna ask?"

I just shrugged. "You wanna tell me what happened two months, two weeks, six days, and eight hours ago, you'll tell me. You don't wanna tell me, that's fine too."

"So you don't want to know."

I set my burger down and turned sideways in my chair to face her. "I'm sittin' here, ain't I?"

"Yeah, so?"

"I ain't a social sorta guy, Cassie. I like my solitude. I do my tattoos, I hang out with my cousin when she has time to visit me, and that's about it. Shit like this," I waved between her and myself, "ain't how I live. Me sittin' here, talking to you, spending my lunch hour with you, that's me interested in what you got to say, and if you don't got nothin' to say, I'll listen to that too." I leaned forward, gave her a long hard stare. "You need a friend, Cassandra Goode. That much is real fuckin' obvious."

She frowned, swallowing hard. "Why is it so fucking obvious, Ink?"

"Well, you damn near walking off the pier into the channel was the first clue."

She didn't answer for a minute or two. "And you're offering to be that friend, are you?"

Against my better judgment, I wanted to do just that. This girl was high octane, high maintenance. All fire and fury one minute, and then acting like everything was fine the next. Made me dizzy.

But there was something about her that intrigued me. The intensity in her changeable, hazel eyes…stormy gray one minute, and then fiery green the next, and then a muted roiling brown another, depending on her mood, which seemed to change with every breath—they drew me in, made me curious. Curious about her as a person, about how she got here, to Ketchikan, curious about the emotional reasons behind the blinding pain that nearly caused her to walk off the pier and into a channel which would still, even at this time of year, be so cold as to induce hypothermia if you stayed in too long.

I realized I'd been staring at her for a while without answering her question. I just nodded and said, "Yes, I am."

"And if I don't tell you what happened, you're not going to ask?" She sounded outright disbelieving.

I nodded. "Ain't my business unless you make it my business."

"You're weird." She said this without looking at me, tossing back her third or fourth beer in half an hour.

"Been called worse," I said, and then finished off my burger and my beer.

"Like?"

I wiped my hands on a napkin. Hesitated. "Jumbo. Dumb ass. Fat ass. Filthy Eskimo. Stinky Inky. Useless. Illiterate."

"Illiterate?"

I snorted. "Figured you'd fix on that one."

"Are you?"

I rolled a shoulder. "No, I can read alright. Just…not super well. I grew up in the bush, off-grid. Homeschooled, by which I mean if we finished our chores around the homestead, we were *allowed* to do schoolwork, which was ratty old textbooks that were probably outdated in the seventies. I mostly taught myself to read, write, and add and subtract." I sighed. "My family is just weird, reclusive, distrustful, and backward."

She gazed at me. "And you taught yourself how to do tattoos, too?"

"More or less. I was always drawing on myself. As a little baby, just learning to crawl, I'd get my hands on anything that would mark my skin and just go to town. Pens, pencils, food, pieces of ash from the fireplace. Ketchup was my favorite. They couldn't stop me. They'd lock up everything and anything, but I'd find something. Shit, if I couldn't find anything else, I'd just go outside and make mud and use that to mark up my skin."

"But your name, Ink, was what they named you when you were born? It's not a nickname?"

I nodded. "My folks've been asked about my name as often as you'd imagine, and all my dad'll say is, 'sounded like an interesting name at the time.' No deeper meaning or reason behind it than he thought it sounded cool, I guess. Never heard him or Mom say anything different my whole life. So did my name inform what I do? Maybe. I didn't know what ink was as a kid. I just knew I liked how my skin looked when I made marks on it."

"It's just a compulsion for you, then?"

I shrugged, nodded. "Started off that way. Just me, and Juneau, who lived near me and was my best and only friend. She was the same way. We'd steal pens and hide them in our secret fort in the woods behind our trailers, and we'd sneak out there and draw on each other for hours."

"So she's a tattoo artist, too?"

"She is now, but it was a bit of a journey for her to get there." I ran a thumbnail along a groove in the bar top. "That's her story, though, so you'll have to get her to tell it."

"Fair enough."

"Eventually my folks realized there was no stopping me from drawing, from art, from tattooing. So they stopped trying to make me be something else. They didn't like it, but I didn't know how to be anything other than who and what I am. Eventually, I connected with John Thomas and he was the first person to let me do a real tattoo on him. I was hooked then, boy, let me tell you. A hell of a rush. Like, when you finally do something for the first time that you've been dreaming of for forever, and when you do, it's like…you're *home*, you know? Something just clicks in your soul, and you *know* this is *it*, this is what you're supposed to do, forever. This one thing—"

I glanced at Cassie, and she was silent,

unblinking, staring down at the top of the bar. Her posture was turtled—shoulders hunched, head drawn down on her neck, chin tucked in, breathing hard and fast. Biting her lip so hard I was worried she'd bite straight through it.

"Cassie?" I said, my voice low and hesitant.

She shook her head, all she seemed capable of.

"Hit a nerve, huh?" I turned away, giving her privacy to gather herself.

A nod, a subtle, almost-missed-it jerk of her head.

I raised a hand, and Bast came over. "Shot of whiskey for our friend here."

"Vodka," Cassie whispered. "Please."

Bast filled a shot glass with Grey Goose, and Cassie threw it back. Shoved the glass toward Bast, who filled it again, and then left the bottle. Cassie tossed back another shot, hissing.

"Aren't you going to tell me that getting shit-faced isn't going to solve anything?" she muttered.

I shook my head. "Nah. You're an adult. And the fact that you're asking me that tells me you already know it."

"Sometimes you just...you just need to get blitzed, you know?"

I nodded. "I do." I laughed. "That can be tricky when you're physically incapable of getting blitzed."

She twisted her head sideways to look at me without lifting up. "Why are you being so nice to me?" She frowned. "I'm not going to fuck you."

I sighed. "I had no expectations that you would."

She frowned harder. "What's that mean?"

Dangerous ground. "Nothing. I'm not being nice to you for any reason other than sometimes you just need one person to be nice for no reason. I've been on the other end of that, so I know."

Her eyes were cloudy, by now. Woozy. Looking me up and down. "You're complicated."

"I know."

"I'm getting tipsy."

I laughed. "I know."

She stared at the food in front of her—she'd done a hell of a number on it, but there was still a lot left. "I can't eat any more." The bottle of vodka. "He left the whole bottle?"

"Bast don't fuck around," I said.

Cassie carefully poured herself more, threw it back. "Mmm. Goose. I love Goose." Another shot. "I don't suppose you happen to know where my mom lives, do you?"

I laughed. "No, I do not."

Cassie shrugged. "I don't want to go back there anyway. She'll just irate me—um. I mean. *Be*-rate me, I mean, for drinking so much." She shoved a mozzarella stick into her mouth defiantly. "And for eating…" her voice dropped to a conspiratorial whisper. "*Junk food.*"

Another shot.

"Maybe you oughta slow down just a teeny bit, huh?" I eyed her drink. "Those are gonna catch up and hit you like a truck."

"Already been hit by a truck. That's the whole fucking problem with my life." She poured yet another shot, tossed it back, and now I physically removed the bottle and pushed it away before she gave herself alcohol poisoning. "A fucking truck. They called it a—a lorry. But it was a truck. Like a semi. Had fish in it. Lots of fish. Tuna fish and salmon, and lots and lots of fish. Ran right into us. Fish everywhere."

"Cassie…"

"I told you. I told you I was gonna get blackout. I just had to warm up to it, okay? Some beer, some food. So I'd have something to throw up, later. And because I haven't eaten junk food since I was…since I was thirteen. I had a piece of strawberry cheesecake from Juniors in Times Square on my thirteenth birthday. It had four big strawberries on it, and it was the size of my head. They sang Happy Birthday to me, but it was the wrong tune. Just me and Mom and Dad. We went to Broadway shows and a ballet and they took me shopping, and I got a piece of strawberry cheesecake all to myself. Ate the whole thing." A long pause. "I haven't had any junk food of any kind ever since. A few alcoholic drinks here and there, like when I went to Tennessee with Charlie last year. It was my twenty-first birthday so I could legally drink in the US. Of course, the drinking age in most of Europe is eighteen, so I'd been drinking with my troupe now and then for years. But. *But*. Alcohol is not junk food. You know what I eat?"

She peered at me, pointing a finger at me.

"Do you know what I eat? Every day?" She tapped the bar top with an angry finger. "Rabbit food. All day. Salads. Egg white omelets. A handful of almonds. More salad. Veggies. So, so, so many vegetables. White meat, as lean as possible, in very small amounts. And you know what I do all day? I dance! All day. Practice starts at seven in the fucking morning. Dance all fucking day on an empty stomach. Probably burn a thousand calories by lunch, and then eat like a fucking baby bird, and then dance until dark. Past dinner. More bird food and rabbit food. For years I've done this. Fucking *years*. You know I haven't had a fucking French fry since fourth grade? First French fry I've had since fourth grade." She picked a fry off the pile of fries, which she hadn't gotten to until then.

"So you're a dancer?"

"Was? Am? I was, I am. I was-am." She blinked hard. "But the truck. The truck took it away."

Shit, the vodka was hitting her.

"The truck took dance away?"

She peered into the empty shot glass. "Empty. Damn. Empty glasses are stupid." She slid the glass away with a morose gesture. "Truck took dance. Took Rick. Took me. Took me away from me."

"Who's Rick?"

"Fiancé. Ex-fiancé. He was brain damaged by the wreck. Made him not love me anymore. He knew me, remembered us, everything. Just didn't love me anymore." She paused. "Fuck him, though, right? Without dance, why would he love me? He can dance. I can't dance. No dance, no us."

"That's fucked up."

She cackled. "Right? So fucked up. He was just like," and here, her voice dropped to a gruff approximation of a male voice, "'...sorry, Cass. I just need time to process things. That accident really messed me up. It wouldn't be fair to you for us to stay together. I don't know who I am anymore. I wish I could explain it better, but I can't. I'm sorry. I just don't love you anymore.'"

I frowned. "He said that to you?"

She nodded sloppily. "Oh yes. I couldn't forget that conversation in a million years. I remember his stupid, beautiful face. Those stupid, beautiful blue eyes. His stupid, beautiful cheekbones. His stupid, beautiful, perfect blond hair. Of course, it wasn't perfect hair anymore because they had to shave half of it to put his brain back in or whatever the hell they did to fix him. But he was still stupid and beautiful. And by stupid, I mean perfect." She closed her eyes, remembering. "He looked at me with those big blue eyes the color of the ocean, and he told me he wasn't in love with me anymore, and he needed to be alone. He needed to process who he was. I don't know what the fuck that means. He had his memory, he didn't have any broken bones. Didn't need weeks of physical therapy just to be able to walk again. Didn't lose anything. But the doctors were all like, brains are *so* mysterious. Brain injuries can cause breaks and changes in personality. It's not his fault, and it's very real."

"Wow."

"Yeah." She stood up abruptly, chair legs scraping loudly against the floor. "Pee. I have to pee."

"You, uh, you need help getting there?" I asked, standing up and moving to catch her if need be.

She shook her head, took two fierce, determined steps toward the back, and promptly tipped sideways.

"Ooh boy," she murmured, catching the service bar. "Wheee. Maybe I do."

I grabbed her bicep—tiny, thin, but hard as nails.

Hauled her upright, and wrapped my arm around shoulders, tucking her against my side. "Come on, Cassie. This way."

She pushed me away. "Too close. Too, too, too close." She sniffed. "You smell good. But too close." She peered up at me. "Jesus, you're big. Like, tall. Really, super, a lot tall."

"Six-seven," I told her. I held out my hand, and she grabbed it. "Now come on. Let me help you."

"But you're not just tall," Cassie said, grabbing my hand and using it for balance as she wove her way toward the back hall where the bathrooms were. "You ever see *Brave*?"

I shrugged. "The little Irish girl, and the mom who turns into a bear?"

She giggled, a snort and a tinkle of laughter. "Scottish, but yeah."

I laughed. "I'm the bear?"

"The big mean one. Just, you know, you're not mean."

"Try not to be."

She stopped at the bathrooms—peered at the door. "I have to pee."

I guided her one more door down. "That was the men's. This is yours."

She blinked. "Oh. I'm a woman. Gotta use the little women's potty."

I sighed. "Yeah, you are, and yeah, you do."

She looked at me over her shoulder. "You noticed, did you?"

I met her eyes. "Yes, Cassandra. I noticed."

She wiggled her hips side to side in a sultry shimmy, eyebrows dancing suggestively. "Ooh, I got the full name. You must really like me."

"Go pee."

She widened her eyes. "Oohhhh boy. Yeah, I'm about to leak."

I pushed the door open for her, and she carefully wobbled in. I let the door close, and only moments later I heard a slam, as her body hit a bathroom stall divider.

"I'm okay!" I heard her yell. "I'm fine!"

I grimaced. That was loud.

Another loud sound.

A stream of curses.

"Dammit," I muttered. Another crash. "Fuck it."

I pushed into the bathroom, and found Cassie clinging to the outside of the stall, trying to pull the door open—it was a push, which was her problem.

I wrapped my arm around her waist again, holding her up. "Come on, let me help."

She looked down at my hand, on her waist—carefully placed in a nonthreatening location, above her hip. Touched her hand to the top of mine.

"You have big hands." She grabbed my hand, held her palm against mine—her hand was dwarfed by mine—the top of her fingers only reaching the first crease at my mid-knuckle. I could fit her entire fist into my palm. "Really, really, really big."

"Yes, I do." I used my toe to nudge the stall door open, guided her in. "Here you go. Can you manage from here, or should I get Kitty to help?"

She snorted. "I can manage my own pants, I think." I let the door close. "I think."

I rested my head against the stall. "You think?"

"Whoops," she said, and I saw her feet slip, and then a thud as she landed on the toilet. "I've got it."

"You're sure?"

"Yep." A pause. "Go away. I don't want you to hear my pee noises."

I laughed. "Fine, but yell and I'll come help you back out."

"Yeah, yeah, yeah."

I exited the women's bathroom and waited outside. A couple of minutes later Bast came by.

"Someone's going through some shit, huh?" he said, carrying a fresh case of beer back toward the bar.

"No kidding."

"Kitty was talking about how Roman's dad was worried about her."

"I can see why." I pushed open the door an inch. "Cassie? You okay?"

Silence.

Bast just laughed. "Go get her. She'll need a friend when she wakes up."

"You know where she lives?" I asked.

"With her mom," Bast said. "Kitty can tell you, I think."

"Cool."

When I went in, I found Cassie in the stall, passed out.

I made sure her clothing was all in the right places, and then lifted her in my arms and carried her out. Kitty gave me directions to her mom's house, but I remembered Cassie saying her mom would give her a hard time. I debated, and then figured she'd rather deal with her mom on her own after she'd sobered up.

So, I carried her back to my place.

Tiny little thing. Barely weighed anything at all.

But damn, she carried a lot of hurt inside.

TWO

Cassie

OHHH GOD. OH GOD.

Oh...fuck my entire skull.

Nope. Not time to be alive yet. Too soon. Wayyy too soon.

How about now?

Nope. Still hurts to be alive. Even the thought of opening my eyes sounded like agony.

"Cassie?" A voice, whispering as quietly as possible, but still a deep, powerful, bone-rattling bass rumble.

Who? Familiar, and comforting, somehow.

"Ng. Gah. Nnnng."

A blast of air through nostrils—a laugh. "Here.

I've got you." A paw, so big it cradled my entire skull, lifted me gently. I sighed, sinking into the paw, letting it support me. My head tipped forward. "Open your mouth, darlin'."

I couldn't even formulate a protest against being called darling. I opened my mouth, and felt pills touch my tongue. A plastic rim touched my lips, and I gingerly allowed the cool wetness into my mouth.

I swallowed hesitantly—my throat was on fire, raspy, bitter, rough. My mouth hurt, and the water felt nice. My stomach didn't agree, though.

"Now this." A different something was being held to my lips, and I let him pour something into my mouth, tasted it, swallowed it. Sweet, but not too sweet.

"It's water with electrolytes. Keeps you from getting too dehydrated."

"Nggg." It was all I could manage, and I wasn't sure what it was even supposed to mean. I wasn't even really conscious. I wasn't a person. Just a puddle of poison and agony.

"Sleep."

"Mmm."

Back under the sweet, blessed veil of nothingness.

Personhood washed over me, slowly. Being alive was hot and painful.

My body ached. My soul felt…bitter, razed into coals.

My eyelids felt like they'd been duct-taped to my eyeballs and then the duct tape had been ripped off. Opening them hurt so bad I wanted to cry, because maybe the tears would soothe the burn.

Where was I? I didn't recognize anything; I was in a loft, something like eight feet wide and square, the entire space taken up by beds—two queen mattresses side by side, it seemed. A steeply sloped roof overhead, with drawers in the walls all around the bed, and a dormer window at my feet, overlooking Ketchikan, mountains in the distance, green and white and brown and slate gray.

I was wrapped in blankets, cocooned in a nest of flannel and fleece. Still dressed in all my clothes, sans socks and shoes. My hair was loose, out of the ponytail.

I took stock, now that I was sort of alive: Fucked. That's how I felt. But it was more than just being hungover. I was feverish—achy, tingly skin, headache, congested…on top of being hungover.

And I had to pee worse than I've ever had to pee in my life, and I once held it for an eleven-hour high-speed train ride from Paris to Rome. My problem right now was that I hurt too bad to move. I was weak, to the point of paralysis. I summoned all my strength, and managed a hoarse whisper.

"Hello?"

"Hey, there you are." I heard the creak of a heavy tread on a wood floor, and then the same heavy tread was climbing up the ladder. A head—long, thick, raven-black hair gathered at his nape in a loose po-nytail, a massive bushy neatly trimmed beard, the end of which hung to his chest, dark skin—Native American—and tattoos, ohhh lordy, the tattoos.

Ink.

Vague memories washed through me, but his name came attached to his face, so there was that.

Piercing, deep, warm, complex, wise, compas-sionate, impossible brown eyes.

He clambered up into the loft with a lithe ease his size should've precluded; perching on the edge of the bed, one foot still on the ladder, Ink reached out and pressed the back of his hand to my forehead. "Still burning up."

I moaned. "Where am I?"

"My house." He brushed a tendril of my plati-num blonde hair away from the corner of my mouth. "Been sick for three days."

"Three days?"

He nodded. "Hungover for the first day, and

down with a brutal flu for the last two. Ran a temp of a hundred and three for forty-eight hours. Couldn't keep anything down."

"I don't..." My voice gave out, raspy, burned. "I don't remember anything."

He shook his head. "I ain't surprised. You were bombed out of your skull for the first part of it, and then the fever took you and you were just delirious after that. Threw up about a dozen times, at least."

"No wonder my throat hurts so bad."

"Yeah, well that's probably from the flu, too. You're sick as hell, girl."

I glanced out at the room—I couldn't see much besides the roof and a bit of walls, a hint of windows. "You've been taking care of me the whole time?"

He nodded. "You only started being able to keep liquids down about twelve hours ago, which is when I brought you up here. You were down on my couch while you were puking."

I closed my eyes. "I feel so stupid."

"Don't."

"But I—"

"You been through hell, that's what."

"I just...I've made a shitty impression on you. I'm not usually this girl. I don't drink like that, I don't eat like that, I don't..." I felt tears welling, and forced them back, viciously, brutally. "I'm not this girl."

"I know."

"You don't know me, though, so how can you know that?" I wiped at my face with both hands, using a gesture of exhaustion to cover my need to wipe at my eyes.

"Because sometimes you just...you just know somebody." Ink's massive presence filled the loft with heat and masculinity, but also...peace. "I may not have known you very long, but I can tell sure enough that you needed to let go a little. That's what you did. You got that freedom. Course, freedom to let go ain't gonna protect you from the consequences of whatever shit you do, but sometimes, you just gotta let go."

"I may have let go a little too much."

He fixed his eyes on me, seeing into me, deep brown wise ursine eyes seeming to know me, to see the contents of my soul so clearly that I had to look away after a moment. "Cassandra."

I frowned. "The full name. What, Ink?"

"Quit the bullshit."

"What bullshit?" I asked.

He reached out a gargantuan paw, a hand so big it could probably fit at least halfway around my waist, if not most of the way. Touched my knee with it, a momentary, hesitant touch so gentle and soothing I didn't know how to process how it made me feel.

"Give yourself a little grace, little sparrow." His

voice was deep and wild, a rumble of waterfalls and avalanches and thunder in the mountains, the growl of bison on the plains, the murmur of a Kodiak bear. "You're too hard on yourself. Be kind."

I swallowed hard. "Little sparrow?" I snorted. "More of a badger, most days."

He shook his head. "No. You hide behind the badger, but that's not you."

My heart pattered, thumped. His hand was still on my knee and it was sucking in all my focus, all my attention. His hand was heavy, warm, and absolutely monstrously huge. Each of his fingers was more than twice the size of mine in length and width. I placed my hand over top of his; he turned his hand over and my little hand was lost, engulfed in his.

"I'm not hiding behind anything," I said. He just snorted, and I knew he didn't believe me. I sighed. "Ink, it's still me. It *is* who I am. I'm a fierce, and determined person. I made lead dancer at one of the most highly competitive professional dance troupes in the world. You don't get there without a certain amount of ruthlessness and determination."

"Didn't say you was pretending to be anything you're not. I said you're hiding behind that."

I shook my head. "You're wrong."

"I'm not." His gaze remained level, imperturbable. "It's who you are, sure. But it's not everything.

It's all you've let yourself be, because it served you. Got you where you wanted to be." A pause, a thick silence. "Now, you're lost, because that part of you doesn't serve you anymore and it's all you've let yourself be."

"How the hell do you think you know this shit about me?" I demanded, yanking my hand free, anger boiling through me. "You don't know the first thing about me."

He let out a slow soft breath; his eyes were thoughtful, his jaw working as if he was literally chewing on what to say, making the tip of his beard waggle. "You talked a lot, both when you were drunk and when you were delirious. The shit you said when you were delirious, half of it was just fever delirium nonsense, but the other half was…" He shrugged. "Shit, you probably would rather have not said."

I lay back on the bed, letting myself slip back down. "Shit."

"It's okay. It's just me, and I'm the best secret keeper there is."

I closed my eyes, suddenly weaker than I'd ever felt, exhausted beyond all comprehension. "I can't handle this conversation right now."

He reached into the pocket of his shorts—the only article of clothing he was wearing, a pair of loose, shimmery pale blue basketball shorts which hung to his knees—and pulled out my cell phone. "Your mama been callin' you like crazy. I sent word through Juneau to your mom that you was sick and being taken care of, but I guess she's gotta put eyes on her baby girl, or at least hear your voice."

My heart seized—three days in the world of a worrying mother was an eternity. I took the phone, unlocked it, and glanced at my notifications: sixty-three text messages, fourteen missed calls, seven voicemails. "Damn, Mom. You have *no* chill," I muttered to myself. I dialed her number, and it rang precisely half a ring.

I was too tired to hold the phone so, with a brief, apologetic glance at Ink, I put it on speaker and set the phone on my chest.

"Cassandra Danielle Goode!" she yelled. "Where the *hell* have you been?"

"Did you not get the message?" I asked, letting my voice sound as raspy and weak as I really did feel. "Ink said he passed a message to you that I've been sick."

She sighed, a pained, irritated, complicated sound. "Yes, yes. Lucas called and told me that, and I quote, Roman told him that Remington was told by Juneau, who was told by Kitty, who was told by I'm not sure who, that you were very sick and that you were being *taken care of*, whatever that means, by someone named

Ink, whomever that is." Her voice rose again. "But that's just a big game of telephone tag. Doesn't tell me where you are, who you're with, how you got sick, why you left without telling me—"

"Mom—"

"Cassandra, I know you're an adult, but you can't just run off without—"

"Mom!" I shouted, making my head pound. "Fuck, that hurts."

"Cassandra, language! I raised you better than that."

"God, could you *please* not be Captain America for ten seconds, Mother!"

"I don't even know what that means," Mom muttered.

"Could you just…not yell?" I rested my forearm over my eyes. "I'm really sick, Mom."

"What kind of sick?"

I sighed. "You know what? I'm a grown woman, *mother*."

"I know that, I just—"

"I got hammered, if you must know. Obliterated. Drunk beyond all reason. Completely and totally fucking shit-faced."

"Cassandra—"

"If you warn me about my language one more time, I swear I'll hang up on you."

A tight, tense silence. "Fine."

"So, yes, it started out as a severe hangover. And then, apparently, I developed the flu."

"Well, overindulgence in alcohol can compromise your immune system," Mom said.

"You don't say?" I sniped.

"Sarcasm is unwarranted, Cassandra. I'm worried about you."

"I'm fine, Mom."

"I don't mean worried about not knowing where you were. If the men and women of the Badd clan say you're being taken care of, I know I can trust them to be telling me the absolute truth." A pause, and this one extended for nearly many seconds. "My worry for you goes much, much deeper than that, sweetheart."

"Mom, come on," I moaned. "Not now. Please."

"Cassie, honey. I'm your mother. You've been through a lot and you're not really dealing with it. And then you go and get drunk, disappear, and I don't hear from you for three days. I get that you were sick, but it's all just wrapped up in the whole big messy ball that is—"

"That is my fucking life," I finished for her.

"Cassandra, really. I don't like your language."

"Mom! I can curse if I want to! I'll never dance again! Rick dumped me! I'm stuck in fucking Alaska with no future! And you're obsessing over me cursing?"

"I'm not obsessing, I just raised you to find more sophisticated and emotionally mature ways of expressing yourself than crude vulgarity." Her voice softened. "Rick may have seemed fine, in that he didn't have any lasting memory loss, but he still suffered severe cranial trauma. And I know it sounds like baloney, but such injuries can have bizarre and unpredictable effects."

"Whose side are you—?"

She spoke over my protests. "Your side, Cass. *Always*. I know he hurt you. I know it hurts. You're allowed to be angry. You're allowed to be scared. But you have to *deal* with it. Actually deal with it." A soft pause. "Going out on a bender is understandable, Cassie. Really, I get it."

"But?"

"But nothing. I get it. I'm just worried, and I tend to overreact when I'm worried."

"No kidding."

Another silence. "Where are you, anyway?"

"Honestly, I don't know."

"You don't know where you are?"

Ink shifted toward me, and the phone. "Mrs. Goode? My name is Ink Isaac. Juneau Isaac is my cousin. Cassie is at my home. She was real sick for the last few days, but she's on the mend now. I'd suggest she rest awhile longer, but I'll do my best to get her home to you soon as possible."

"Your name is…Ink?"

"Yes ma'am. Ink. Like pen and ink. It's my real, given name."

"I see. And where is your home, Ink?" Mom had her mom voice on, the authoritative, interrogative one.

Ink gave her directions to his house, which, since I didn't know Ketchikan at all, was useless to me, but Mom seemed to understand.

"I know where that is. I don't mean to invite myself over, but I would very much like to check on my daughter." It was, essentially, a politely phrased statement of intent rather than a request.

"Sure thing, ma'am. I'd've brought her home to you in the first place, but she was really, really sick and my place was closer, and then she was in no shape to be moved."

After goodbyes were said, with a promise from Mom that she'd see me soon, the call ended and I tossed the phone aside.

"She's so exhausting sometimes," I muttered.

"She loves you like crazy," Ink said. "You're lucky to have her, Cassie."

I groaned something like an affirmative. "I know. But she's still exhausting."

Ink gently nudged my arm away and rested his wrist on my forehead. "You need sleep. Still runnin' a fever. Not as bad as it was, but still."

"Have I had anything for the fever?" I asked.

"Nope. Don't believe in it unless it's life-threatening."

"Don't believe in what? Medicine?" I asked, meaning it sarcastically.

"Yeah, Western medicine. Best to just let it run its course—how my people have done things for thousands of years. These days, we'll take something if it gets bad enough that it could kill you, but short of that, we let nature do what it does."

"So you don't take medicine? Ever, at all, unless you're about to die from?"

He nodded. "Never taken so much as an aspirin in my life." A shrug, mountainous shoulders lifting their impossible weight.

"So you never get sick?"

"I get sick like anybody else," he answered, sounding bemused. "I just…deal with it. Work through it if I can, stay home and ride it out if I can't."

"You gave me a pill or something, though. I remember that."

He nodded. "Yeah, but that was more to help you deal with the bitch of a hangover, and it was just one little Motrin, along with a shitload of liquids. At least until you started horking."

"Don't call it that, please. God. It's undignified." I squeezed my eyes shut, but those vague memories of last night—or rather, three days ago—seemed to be choosing now to make themselves available for review. "Did…did I pass out in the bathroom?"

He laughed, nodded. "Yep."

I groaned. "Please tell me I at least got my pants up?"

He nodded again. "You did."

"Speaking of which…" I opened my eyes and looked at him. "I really, really, *really* have to go to the bathroom."

He swung around and descended the ladder. "Come on down," he said, from the bottom.

"Easier said than done," I said, but it was under my breath.

Moving slowly, I extricated myself from the nest of blankets and turned around to face the ladder. One foot on the top rung, I gingerly lowered myself to the next rung down. And even that was too much effort. I shook all over, bones aching, a coughing fit building up in the back of my throat. Nauseated. Head pounding. Stuck on the ladder, too weak to haul myself back up, too shaky to go any further.

"Um." Asking for help goes against the grain, rubs hard against everything I stand for as a person. But I was about to fall off the damn ladder. "Help?"

He wrapped his hands around my waist, both hands easily spanning all the way around. He lifted me off the ladder, holding me as effortlessly as if I were a child. Brought me to his chest, my back to his front, and lowered me to my feet, and held me there. I didn't even come up to his chin—barely to his chest. His hands remained resting on my waist, just above my hips. His presence behind me occluded the world. Made me feel...

Safe.

I rested my head against his chest to catch my breath—I was winded from even that. Scary as hell for someone used to being able to dance at max intensity for hours at a time.

His home, despite his own personal enormity, was a tiny house. Two hundred and fifty square feet at the most, it was simplicity at its finest. Under the loft, on the main floor, was an old, sagging, green suede couch, the kind that only gets more comfortable as it gets older. A single light was built into the underside of the loft, providing soft light. Each wall supporting either end of the loft featured built-in bookshelves, crammed with books—mostly art books, art history, tattoo history from Polynesia and Alaska, photography, technique guides and textbooks, and a handful of dog-eared fantasy paperbacks.

To the left of the loft, if you were standing with your back to it as we were, was the kitchen. Induction range and oven, refrigerator, and a few cabinets above and below the counter. Opposite was a big window above the sink, and more cabinets with a back door between; a low coffee table in front of the couch that must serve as an eating area. I didn't see a bathroom, though.

"Bathroom?" I asked.

He let go of me and took two steps across the room, pushed at a section of wall—what had looked like a space of bare wall between the loft and the front door was actually the door to the bathroom.

Without his support, I wobbled and swayed. He caught me, pulled me up, and helped me into the bathroom.

I braced myself against the wall, looking at him over my shoulder. "You're really seeing me at my worst, you know."

He just laughed. "It'll make seeing you at your best all the better."

I shook my head, snorted a laugh. "Nice."

I shut the door, took care of business with an audible sigh of relief, not even caring if he heard or not. Then, I just had to summon the energy to stand up, pull my pants up, and get out of the bathroom. By the time I'd done this, I was panting. Absolutely zapped.

I sagged in the open doorway, sweating, and feeling like I could collapse at any moment. Ink was in the kitchen, doing something at the stove, humming under his breath—making soup, it smelled like.

I just watched him for a moment.

Why did my chest feel tight? Why did my palms feel tingly? The dull ache way down low didn't bode well either.

He'd taken care of me, and had been kind, nonjudgmental. He didn't know me from Eve, but he had brought me to his house, gave me his bed, cleaned up my vomit, made sure I didn't get dehydrated.

Gah.

Gratitude, that's all I needed to feel. That's it.

So, when he turned and saw me, and when his eyes seemed to burn a little brighter at the sight of me, why did that make the tingle at the apex of my thighs shift even worse?

"You look done in," he said.

"I've never felt so weak in my life," I murmured.

"Bad flu'll do that to you. I got it real bad one time, couple'a years back. Couldn't even get out of bed for damned near a week. Juneau was out of town that week; don't have a phone, no neighbors, and no employees. Thought for sure I was gonna die alone in this fuckin' thing."

"Obviously you didn't."

"Naw. I basically, just unintentionally, fell out

the bed, hit the floor hard enough that I had to replace a few floorboards, and bruised a couple ribs
in the process. All that was super awesome with the
nasty cough I had, which was bad enough I'd nearly
cracked a rib from coughing. I managed to get myself some water, and passed out on the floor. It took
two weeks before I could leave the trailer."

"Trailer?" I looked around. "This is a trailer?"

He nodded. "Yep. Mind, I don't have a truck to
pull it, but I could, if I did. I will, someday. Just pull
on out of here, see what there is to see of the world
outside of Ketchikan."

I frowned. "You've never left?"

He shrugged. "Been all over Alaska, hunted
and fished and hiked and camped and canoed and
flown in, on, and over most of the state, but never
anywhere else." He waggled his beard, head tipped
to one side. "Well, this one time, when I was maybe
sixteen, my uncle and I took his charter fishing boat,
one o'those deep-sea ones, and we went way out.
Fished our way west over several days. I guess ol'
Uncle Billy was a little in the bottle most of the time,
and wasn't really paying attention to where we were
going, and I was just a kid, you know? Suddenly,
there was land in view, and big old battleships or cut-
ters or something surrounding us, two of 'em. They
were spoutin' off at us in Russian."

"You accidentally sailed to Russia?" I asked, with a laugh.

He nodded. "Yep. Got in a hell of a lot of trouble, too."

"Can't they, like, arrest you and take your boat and stuff? Like, really bad, bad trouble?"

"Oh yeah, they can. They were gonna, too. Turns out it was fortunate for me that Billy was blasted off his ass. I could just claim truthfully that I didn't know where I was going, and he was bombed. Talked 'em into letting me turn the boat around and sail back the way we came."

"That's crazy!" I took a step forward, wobbled, meaning to try for the ladder, mere feet away. "I'm gonna fall!"

Ink caught me, burly warm arms cradling me. "Gotcha."

A moment in time, a pause in reality. His eyes, warm and brown. They made the tingling worse. I'd never felt such a tingle, ever. Like a burn, but all over. Centered down low, between my thighs. A tangible, intense, physical ache, but with a boiling core of emotion. His hands held me, his arms surrounded me. I had to cling to him—my arms around his neck. He lifted me, one-armed, and just held me. My heart thumped, pattered, pounded.

My mouth was fused closed, my tongue seared

to the roof of my mouth. I couldn't speak, but even if I could have, what would I have said?

"Up we go," Ink murmured.

And he carried me up the ladder. I laughed, burying my face in the side of his neck to hide the laughter—but that was worse, because he smelled *good*. Cedar and pine from his beard, layered over a subtle hint of something that was just male. His skin was warm, radiating heat.

Flushed at my unexpectedly idiotic behavior, I pulled away, embarrassed, but was dizzy from the scent and the feel of him. Just from the way he'd carried me. I mean, I've done pair dances with strong male dancers before, done my share of getting thrown and lifted and spun and all that, in the name of dance. But that was always choreographed. Planned. Even when it was Rick and me, when we were dancing, it wasn't sexual. It was *dance*. The dance was sacred. We channeled our emotions and each and every touch was always planned and purposeful.

This…this was something else.

He just picked me up, because he was strong enough that my hundred and ten pounds was nothing to him. He picked me up and carried me up a ladder because he could, and because I was too weak to do so myself.

This was different.

It made my palms itch like crazy, as if the only thing that could soothe the itch was to find out if those tattoos felt as beautiful under my hands as they looked.

My thighs ached, my core.

No, no, no.

I didn't feel this way for Ink.

I didn't. I couldn't.

It was dumb.

He wasn't my type. My type was Rick—tall and lean, strong, clean-cut, sophisticated, educated, worldly. Cultured. European.

Ink was…the opposite. Not just tall—*giant*. Heavy with muscle, powerful. That beard…thick and long, but combed and oiled and well-kept. Long hair, shiny black, bound into a loose ponytail. Not educated, but still intelligent. Not sophisticated, but *real*. Honest. Down-to-earth. Wise.

Nothing like Rick at all.

Rick had dumped me, unceremoniously. Sure, sure, medical reasons, inexplicable and unexplainable aftereffects of brain trauma. He'd been rude, brusque, uncaring.

And, if I was being honest with myself, he'd always been that way, to a degree. He'd just hidden it around me. Or I'd overlooked it. Either way, it had come out full force after the accident, and it cut me to pieces.

Something told me Ink would never, could never, treat a person that way, no matter what the circumstances.

We were sitting in the loft, him cross-legged, and me on his lap. As if I belonged on his lap. I felt myself frowning. Felt panic rifle through me. I couldn't let this happen, not now. Too soon. Too soon.

"What're you thinkin', little sparrow?" Ink's voice washed over me, low and quiet and deep.

I shook my head. "I...I—I don't know." I crawled off of him, lay on the bed, on my side. Facing away from him. "I'm tired."

He was silent a moment, but I felt him there, felt his presence, his warmth. Then, his hand rested briefly on my shoulder. "Rest."

I felt the mattress rise as his weight left it, heard him descend the ladder. Floorboards creaked, a pot rattled on the stove, liquid poured, and then silence, except for the occasional clink of a spoon against a bowl.

Eventually, I slept. Fitfully, though, and full of dreams—of the accident, the huge grill of the semi smashing into my window, crushing my leg, spinning and rolling, and then darkness; of Rick telling me he wasn't in love with me anymore, the dead light in his eyes as he slashed my heart into ribbons with those seven words ("I'm not in love with you anymore."); of Ink, cradling me in his massive arms, eyes on mine, inquisitive and knowing and warm and...boiling with deeply buried desire.

THREE

Ink

S HE SLEPT ANOTHER TWELVE HOURS WITHOUT STIRRING. I left a note at the top of the stairs on the morning of the fourth day: *Have clients I cannot reschedule. Shop is just out the front door. Call shop phone if you need me.* And I left my shop phone number at the bottom of the note, along with my scrawled signature.

I did three sessions, and took a break for lunch to check on her—still asleep, sweating now with the blankets tossed off: good news, because it meant the fever had broken. Set more soup to simmering, with another note to help herself. I returned to the shop and did four more sessions. I was finishing the aftercare spiel for my last client when a woman came through the door. Not unusual, obviously, except she was dressed to kill in a business professional sense, a knee-length skirt, white shirt, blazer, heels, expensive purse. No visible tattoos, and just didn't seem like the type. Then I looked her over once more, as my client examined his nearly finished sleeve in the mirror. She was tall, slender but curvy, fine glossy black hair, and vibrant hazel eyes that I recognized immediately.

"Mrs. Goode," I said, lifting off my rolling stool and stripping off my gloves. "I'm Ink."

She peered up at me, eyes assessing me, looking me over critically but not judgmentally. "Call me Liv." She shook my hand, her eyes flicking over my bare upper body and its canvas of interwoven tattoos. "How is Cassie?"

I cashed out my client, scheduled him for the final session, and flipped the sign from open to closed. "Still sleepin', last I checked. Her fever had broken when I checked in on her around lunchtime." I gestured for Liv to follow me through the back door. "Come on, this way. I live out behind the shop."

I'd chosen the shop location primarily because it was close enough to the main drag of Ketchikan that I'd get decent traffic, but mostly from serious tattoo lovers rather than cruise ship tourists looking for butterflies and barbed wire cheap and quick. The other main reason for the location was the fact that there was a bit of a yard behind it, just big enough to allow me to put a tiny house down.

Liv followed me out back, and stopped when she came into view of my home. "Wow. Not expecting that."

I grinned. "Right? Wouldn't know it was back here, would you?"

She shook her head. "It's lovely. Looks...cozy."

"More space on the inside than you'd think. I studied a lot of different designs and layouts before I built it."

She halted, turned to look at me. "You built it?"

I nodded. "Yep. My cousin Lewis did an internship for an architect up in Anchorage. I drew up the design and had my cousin's boss look it over. I've got a shit-ton of cousins, so once I bought the raw materials, it only took a dozen of us a couple of weeks to put it up. Helped that one of my other cousins works for a home builder out of Juneau, so he made sure we didn't fuck anything up. Only things I paid to have professionally done were the plumbing and electric."

Liv grinned at me. "And, let me guess, you have cousins who got you discounts?"

I laughed. "I wish. But no. Out of pocket, full price, local union boys."

She eyed the home again: steeply pitched roof to

make room for the loft, dormer, doors on either end, which I call front and back but really are just left and right side of the house, in through the living space and out through the kitchen.

"Well. You did a marvelous job. If you weren't a tattoo artist already, I'd say you could have a career building these."

I couldn't help but feel a little pride. "Thanks. I've thought about that, actually. Still may do that, just for some variety from doing tats." I led her to the front door, meaning the left side. Opened the door for her, let her precede me inside.

Cassie was on my couch, a bowl of soup in her lap, wrapped up in one of my giant flannel blankets. She saw us come in, and seemed to perk up a little.

"Hi, Mom." Her eyes flitted to mine. "Hi, Ink."

"Feelin' better, huh?" I asked, taking a spot against the wall in the kitchen, where my bulk wouldn't be in the way of mother and daughter.

Cassie nodded, lifted the bowl of soup. "Yes, much better. This soup is amazing. You made it?"

I bit back a grin, anticipating the other half of this conversation. "Yep. Old family recipe."

She spooned a bite, and when she'd finished she glanced at me. "What kind of meat is it? Not beef, not pork, not chicken, or fish."

I waited, let her finish the last few bites before

answering. "It's, uh—like I said, old family recipe. An' when I say old, I mean *real* old." I grinned. "It's moose soup."

She blinked at me, and then stared down the empty bowl, going a little pale. "I'm sorry, what?"

"Moose. Moose meat. I did a thread piece on Fox last week, and he traded me a nice haunch of fresh moose."

She let out a sigh, and I could see her working through it. "Well. I knew it wasn't the usual suspects, so I can't say I'm shocked. And it *was* pretty delicious. Not as gamey as I would have assumed it would be."

"Well, it's fresh. I froze a good bit of it for later, but I've been makin' soup from it ever since I got it. Gotta use the right cuts for soup, and those parts don't freeze as well. It's lean, too. Healthy for you." I glanced at Liv. "Care for a bowl?"

She smiled, taking a seat next to Cassie on my couch. "Yes, please. I haven't had dinner yet, so if you have enough, I'd be delighted." She accepted a bowl from me, inhaling the steam. "This smells amazing."

"Moose soup was a staple around my house, growing up. At my house, or Juneau's, or go into any of my cousin's houses pretty much ten months outta the year and you'll find moose soup simmering on the stove. Can't tell you how many times I've poured some into a Thermos and taken it out hunting with me."

Liv tried a few bites, her face brightening. "So, you're a talented tattoo artist, you built this house, *and* you're a great cook?" She glanced at Cassie. "Probably the first time I actually approve of your friends, Cassandra."

Cassie stuck her tongue out. "You loved Amy and Britt. Can't pretend you didn't."

Liv shrugged. "I love you, and you loved them, so I accepted them. Not the same thing."

Cassie frowned. "Wait, what?"

"They were not the greatest influences on you, if you want the truth." Liv met her daughter's eyes. "Amy's home life was...troubled, at best, and I was never entirely comfortable with you spending time at her house. Britt was a sweet girl, but a little flighty. Between the two of them, you got into more trouble than I think you would have left to your own devices."

"Wow. I never knew."

"They weren't outright troublemakers, and you never spoke of any real issues at Amy's house, so I never saw enough reason to keep you from them."

Cassie frowned. "We rarely left Amy's room if we were there." She thought, eyes going up and to the left. "Now that I think about it, Amy was pretty cagey about her family. We tended to just stay in her room. If we wanted something, she'd get it for us." A glance at her mom. "What do you know about her family?"

A shrug from Liv. "Nothing concrete. But there were lots of rumors about her dad. The other moms would talk in the pickup lines and later on chat boards. The rumors were he drank a lot, and there were a few who suspected he hit her. But nothing ever concrete, like I said. Helen never seemed to me like an abused woman, and Bruce was never drunk when I was around him, so I couldn't stop you from going over there based on rumor and hearsay."

Cassie shook her head. "Weird to know what you weren't aware of, you know?" She glanced at me. "You built this place?"

I nodded. "Yep. Had a lot of help from my endless supply of cousins."

Liv was looking around. "Very simple and attractive layout. Good use of space. Lots of storage. In order to be more widely and commercially available, you'd probably need to include an eating nook or something."

I shrugged. "I eat at the coffee table."

"I know, and a lot of people would do the same. But I know from personal experience that most people want a dedicated eating area." She gestured at the end of the cabinets on the sink side of the space, where there was a few feet of empty space. "Build in a table there with a bench along the wall, picnic table style, and a bench on the other side. Wouldn't take up much room and would give you somewhere other than your couch nook to eat."

Cassie laughed. "Mom is an interior designer, so you're getting her professional opinion, free of charge, unasked for."

I nodded, thinking. "That's a good idea. I rarely have guests, so I didn't think it was necessary for me, but if I was gonna build one for someone else, I could do that." I laughed. "My cousin Juneau is the person I'm closest to, and even she rarely comes over here. You two are the first guests I've had in a long time."

"No girlfriend?" Liv asked.

I shrugged, looking away. "Nah."

"Sweet, multitalented guy like you, I'd think you'd have your pick."

I snorted. "You're thinkin' of Juneau's boyfriend and his family. Ain't nobody lined up for this mess," I said, slapping my belly.

"Mom!" Cassie snapped. "Don't be rude."

"I'm not being rude, I'm being complimentary," Liv answered, her voice calm and quiet, but hard.

"You're prying," Cassie insisted.

"It's fine. No harm, no foul." I ladled myself some soup, ate standing up.

Liv nudged Cassie with her shoulder. "So, are you up to going home today?"

Cassie nodded, not looking at her mother. "Sure. Just…don't push things, okay?"

"Push what?" Liv asked. "I don't push anything."

Cassie snorted. "Um, yeah, you do. You want to talk about things. You want me to tell you how I'm feeling every moment of every day. You want me to get back on my feet. You want me to process and cope and make healthy choices and…it's exhausting."

Liv looked down at her empty bowl. "I just want the best for you. You've been through a lot."

"And I just want to cope with it my way, okay?"

I kept quiet, knowing this conversation wasn't about me, and wasn't meant for me. I busied myself in the kitchen, not wanting to pry, but I'd admit to being a bit curious about Cassie's past since I knew almost nothing about her. I was trying to make myself invisible—pretty much impossible—but I was surprised at how open they were with one another. It was almost as if I wasn't there at all.

"I get that, Cass, but I'm worried your way of coping is to not cope at all." A pause. "Or to cope through overindulgence."

"Mom, god. Come on. I've been brutally strict about every aspect of my life, my whole life. You know how many Friday nights I stayed home and went to bed early instead of going to parties with my friends because I had dance in the morning? You know how much I missed out on? How often I sat and watched my friends have milkshakes and fries while I ate a salad or dry chicken breast? That was my childhood, my early teenage years, and my entire adulthood thus far. And it's fine. I chose it. I wanted it, I wanted dance and I willingly sacrificed all that to get there. But now dance is *gone*, Mom. It's gone. It's never coming back."

"You don't know that, Cass," Liv said. "Maybe—"

"I *do* know that. I have a hardware store's worth of metal in my right leg, Mom. It took *weeks* of PT just to be able to use it at *all*. Weeks after that, I still can't walk more than a couple blocks without it hurting. Shit, sometimes it hurts just sitting doing nothing, like right now. If I *ever* dance again, it'll be… months, at best. And that'll require a level of work I'm just not sure I'm up for. I worked so fucking hard to get where I was, and it was taken away from me in a matter of seconds. And now I have to start all over again? I don't know. I just…I don't know that it's worth it."

"You're a dancer, Cassandra. It's who you are."

"It *was*," Cassie whispered and then went silent for a long time. She got up and limped for the door. "I don't know who the hell I am now." She gave me a tight, small smile. "Thank you, Ink. For… everything."

I didn't smile back, because it wasn't what she needed. I just gazed at her steadily. "Be strong, little sparrow."

She swallowed hard, even as she pretended to laugh lightheartedly at me. "Weirdo."

She left, leaving Liv and me alone in the taut silence. "Sorry, Ink. Family stuff is messy."

I shrugged. "All good. Trust me, I know about messy family stuff."

She left then, too, and for the first time in four days, I was alone in my home.

It felt weirdly, uncomfortably empty.

At two in the morning, a couple of days later, I was at the laundromat, washing my bedding and the rest of my laundry. Sitting alone, sketchbook on my knees, I was working on a landscape I'd started. Or at least it had begun as a landscape. A mountain in the background, the channel, a pier. Then, somehow, the focus had shifted from the landscape to a wooden post in the foreground. With a small sparrow perched on it. Wings fluffed, about to take flight.

I specialized in animals, so sketching something like this was not a big surprise. But I'd never done much with sparrows. Not really a heavy hitter in the indigenous tattoo world, sparrows.

I heard the little bell over the doorway ding, but I didn't look up. Someone else coming in to wash clothes was none of my business, even in the middle of the night.

Except I felt a presence, and then someone sat down beside me. "That's an incredible drawing, Ink," I heard Cassie say. "I mean, really incredible." She huffed. "Thought for sure I'd be the only one doing laundry at this dumb hour."

I turned and offered her a smile in greeting. "Thanks."

She met my gaze. "A sparrow, huh?"

I shrugged, nodded. "Just doodling."

She frowned. "*That's* a doodle?"

I nodded. "To me it is, yeah. Just something I'm working on to pass the time."

She eyed the sparrow again. "It looks so real. Like, it could fly off at any moment."

"I sorta specialize in lifelike animal pieces." I flipped back a few pages, showed her the final charcoal drawing I'd done as a sample design for a client—a coiled cobra, hood flared, fangs bared. "That's a piece I did for a client. Final version on him was full color, and was even more lifelike."

She shivered. "Eew. Not a fan of snakes. But that's...I can't believe you can do that with nothing but pencils." She peered closer. "Even in black and white and gray, it looks...slimy. And...angry."

I laughed. "Yeah, he was a biker, and his gang nickname was King Cobra. So his tat had to be intimidating." I flipped back to my work in progress. "Nice guy, though. That cobra piece paid for a good chunk of my house, too. Full back piece, nearly thirty hours over half a dozen sessions."

"Thirty hours?" She sounded incredulous. "Of being tattooed?"

I laughed. "That's pretty common for a full-size, detailed piece. Those full sleeves you see, from shoulder all the way down?" I swept a finger down my own full sleeve of tattoos, albeit most of my sleeve work was done in the ancient threading style rather than full-color needle gun style. "Those can take even more, because sleeves are typically many different individual images all woven together, so each piece can take several hours."

She examined my arm. "Yours look different than the other tattoos I usually see."

I nodded, tracing the lines and angles and dots on the outside of my right bicep. "It's threaded."

"Meaning?"

"Certain cultures, like the Polynesians, and my people—the various Inuit tribes from here in Alaska, Canada, Siberia, Greenland, places like that, we sorta invented the idea of the tattoo. The word 'tattoo' itself actually comes from the Polynesian word 'tatau.'

They use small sharp sticks and an ink mixture and poke it into the skin. Like modern guns, except a lot slower and a lot more painful." I twisted to show her my ribcage under my left arm, where I had a stick-and-poke piece done in the traditional style. "That one was done that way. I traded a threading piece for a stick-and-poke piece." I tapped my arm again. "These are done in the Inuit way, with needle and thread and ink. Of course, if I'm doing it for a client, I use modern medical-grade needles, dissolvable thread, and tattoo-grade ink. But on me, I do it the ancient way, with whalebone needles and caribou sinew thread and soot."

She made a face. "Yikes. Does it hurt?"

I laughed. "To run a needle through your skin hundreds of times? Yeah. But after a while, enduring the pain of it becomes...I dunno. Meditative, I guess you could say." I glanced at her. "No tats for you, huh?"

She taps her earlobe. "Don't even have my ears pierced. Body modification isn't my thing."

"Was not piercing your ears an intentional decision?"

She bobbed her head side to side. "Not at first, and then yes, it was. Mom wouldn't do it when I was little, said I had to want it myself. And I just never wanted to. Then, when I was a teenager, it started to be a thing among my friends. But, I was different because I didn't have them pierced, and I liked that. And from then on, it became an intentional thing."

I smiled. "See, I look at you, and all I can think is that you have all this beautiful virgin skin for me to draw on."

She stared at me, into my eyes, hers wide and looking more blue than anything at the moment. She swallowed. "Yeah, I…" A pause, another swallow. A deep breath. And then she looked away and stood up. "I should put my clothes into the washer."

Despite her having stayed at my place for three-plus days, I hadn't really *looked* at her, other than her face and her eyes, until that moment. And when she stood up and went to the washer, dragging a black mesh bag of dirty laundry bigger than she was, my mouth went dry.

I couldn't look away.

Couldn't think. Breathe. Swallow.

All I could do was…look.

Legs. God, her legs. Long, long, long. She was five feet something, and from where I was sitting, most of that was leg. Bare, naked leg. She was wearing…I guess "shorts" is the word. Sort of. Booty shorts, dance shorts? I don't know the word. Tiny, barely there. Like, nothing but enough purple elastic material to stretch around each of her taut, hard, round tight buttocks, and that was it. Bare midriff. White tank top, cut off just below her breasts. As in, when she bent over to tug dirty clothes out of her bag and toss them into the washer, I got a brief, tantalizing glimpse of the underside of her breasts.

Her hair, long and platinum blonde, was loose and wild, in a tangled, shimmery sheaf down her back. God, good god, she was built.

She turned away after thumbing coins into the washer—visible abs, thick, strong, powerful thighs, toned arms, hard shoulders. Yet still soft in the right places. She tugged her thick mass of hair down over her shoulder, and her eyes met mine.

I forced air into my lungs, and managed to tear my eyes off of her body.

And you bet she noticed. Glanced down at herself, as if just realizing what she was wearing. "Laundry day, you know? Haven't really washed my clothes since leaving Paris and that was over two weeks ago." She did a little pose, popping a hip out, arm over her head, like *tada!* "So I ended up wearing these dance clothes."

I shook my head, but words took a moment before emerging. "I—um. I don't...mind."

"No?"

I shook my head again, slowly. "No."

"I wasn't imagining there would be anybody here

this late at night." She sat down again, rubbed her thigh where I saw scars knotting the flesh and muscle.

"There ain't, usually. Just me, mostly, which is why I'm here. Nice and quiet and peaceful."

She nodded. Glanced at me. "You ever wear a shirt?"

I shook my head. "Nah, not usually."

"What about in the winter?"

I rolled a shoulder. "If it's real cold, I might throw on a hoodie while I'm outside."

"Is it because of your tattoos?"

I snorted, a gently sarcastic laugh. "Nah. I just… I've never liked wearing anything on my body. It's a sensitivity thing. I get hot. I'm big, produce a lot of energy, a lotta heat. And I just…I don't like clothes, in general." I smirked at her. "But also, yes, it's sorta like free advertising, I guess. People ask about them, and I can tell them to visit my shop, if they're serious."

I felt my gaze wandering, trickling down from her eyes to her chest, to her abdomen, to her legs. Her thigh. The scars.

I felt the air between us tense. "Pretty gnarly, huh?" Her voice was small, cold, sharp.

I looked into her eyes, did my best to stay open, let her see that I wasn't intimidated or scared or grossed out by her scar, that I saw *her*. That I was attracted.

I kept my eyes on hers another moment, and she

was visibly fighting to keep her eyes on mine, to not look away.

I reached out, then. Just my index finger, and touched her scar. It ran from mid-thigh, twisting and gnarled, ropy and puckered, down past her knee. I traced it, feeling it. She flinched at my touch, and hissed. Murmured a demurral, then pulled away.

"Don't."

"Why?" I asked.

"It's...I—I'm not used to it. It's not...me. I don't know." She looked away from me, twisted her body so her leg was out of reach.

"Cass." I touched her shoulder. "Look at me."

She remained turned away a moment longer, and then slowly turned to face me, lifting her eyes to mine. "What." Almost petulant, but full of conflicted pain and confusion.

I took her hand in mine. My palm to the back of her hand. Placed her hand over her scar. "Touch it. It's you."

"I don't want it to be me!" she bit out.

"But it is."

She shot to her feet and moved a few steps away, arms crossed in front of her to hug herself. "You're not my fucking therapist."

I stood, moved up behind her. Not touching, but close enough I knew she felt me there. "No, I ain't."

"So why do you care if I accept my stupid scar?"

"Why shouldn't I care?" I hesitated. "You're my friend. I care."

She turned, looked up at me. "Friend?" She narrowed her eyes. "I felt you staring at me. Do you look at all your friends like that?"

"Friend is a broad term." I kept my eyes on hers. "Could be more to it."

A lift of her chin. "Ahhh. Now we come to it."

"Me takin' care of you when you got sick? That was me being a friend. Wasn't nothin' more to it. You can't stand there and act like there was." I held her gaze. "I've seen you lookin' at me too, Cassie. You wanna play that, we can play that."

She deflated a little. "I know." Looked up at me. "Friends is good." A sigh. "I've never seen anyone like you before. Never met anyone like you." She said all this with a carefully neutral expression on her features.

"Ain't too many folks like me."

"No, there aren't." She blinked at me, a barely there hint of a smile on her lips. "And I've been all over the place."

"Like?"

She shrugged. "I was lead dancer for a professional European troupe. We toured the world. I've danced in Moscow, St. Petersburg, Prague, Vienna,

Cologne, Madrid, Lisbon, and Paris—obviously, since I lived there. I toured Shanghai, Hong Kong, Beijing, Tokyo, Kyoto, Rio, Sao Paulo, Mexico City, and the usual places here in the States—Chicago, New York, San Francisco, LA, Detroit, Atlanta. That's off the top of my head, the big cities. Lots of smaller performances, smaller venues in between."

"Wow. You been all over the world, huh?"

She nodded. "Yeah, I have."

"What's it like out there?"

She laughed. "Big. Very, very big. Bigger than you can even imagine. And so, so wildly different, one place to another. It's hard to comprehend what a totally different culture is like until you see it first hand."

Silence. Oddly companionable.

She stood up again, paced away, limping gently. Stood with arms crossed, hugging herself once more. I remained where I was, sitting, waiting.

"I'm a mess right now, Ink." Her voice was quiet, soft. "I don't know which way is up, if you want the god's honest truth. Who I am, what I am, what I want, where I'm going. I don't know anything right now."

I kept my silence. She needed space to let it out, not advice, not sympathy, but the silence of a true listener, and not merely the space in which I waited for my turn to speak.

She went to the window and looked out at the dark street. Her shoulders hunched. She looked so small, so fragile, so delicate—I wanted to gather her in my arms and hold her and shield her from the world. Instead, I tried to reduce my presence, the visceral magnitude that is me. I let her fill the space.

"I had everything I wanted." Shaky voice, slow tremulous inhale. "I worked for it, worked my ass off. Danced until my feet bled. Danced until my legs literally gave out and I could barely crawl to bed. Ate clean. Didn't party. Went to the gym. Worked on technique. I'd spend literally hours perfecting a single turn, a single leap. My days could be spent practicing a single thirty-second sequence in a routine—over and over and over and over again, until I didn't just have it perfect, but could not physically forget it because I'd done it so fucking many times. You just cannot imagine the dedication, work, and sacrifice it requires to get where I was. Forget talent, sure, I have talent. *Had*, at least. But talent doesn't mean shit unless you work your ass off to be perfect."

Another long silence.

"I had Rick. I loved the *hell* out of that man. I'd have walked through fire for him. If he had asked me to give up dance and have his baby, I'd have done that too, and asking me to give up dance is akin to asking me to give up a leg." A bitter laugh. "So, I ended up losing dance *and* Rick. I *loved* him, so fucking much. Blindly, really. Maybe I should have seen it coming. The doctors say it was unpredictable the way his brain trauma presented. Some people lose motor skill, others lose memory, some lose cognitive function. Some just…change. He changed. Like flipping a light switch. Maybe what he lost was his ability to…pretend. Or filter through the desires of his id and the better sense of his superego. I don't know."

I had no idea what an id was, or a superego. I didn't say so, though. This wasn't a speech you interrupted.

"I don't understand it, even still. He just fell out of love with me. He woke up from a three-day coma and was no longer in love with me." A sigh, a pause. "In love. What a crock of shit. Do you really fall in love? Is it falling? Should it be falling? Or is it a choice? Something you do, you choose, something you *are*? Falling makes it sound like you have no choice over the matter. I mean, when I met Rick the first time, I just knew I was going to end up with him. Forever, I thought. I was all in. The sexual feelings, the romantic feelings, they were undeniable, and super powerful, but I was still able to look at the situation with something resembling objectivity and be like, 'yeah, I want this.' And I chose it. I chose *him*. Even though I knew he was rude sometimes. To me, to others. To anyone in a service industry role, he was a monumental jackass. That bugged me…a lot, actually. He was arrogant, and would savagely ridicule anyone who got in his way, anyone he thought was less than him. Which was just about everyone. But he was also funny, and an insanely talented dancer. And kind, in equal measure to his arrogance. He was entitled, and spoiled. Grew up with a silver spoon. His mother was one of those Upper East Side socialites, and his father was a French architect, so he lived part of the year in Manhattan and part of the year in Paris. Their Parisian condo literally had servants, like in full uniform, or what they called livery. Growing up, my family was always on the more well-to-do end of average, I thought, but then I met Rick and his family was just like…on a whole other level."

A long, thoughtful, reminiscent silence.

My eyes kept wandering over her form, her rounded shoulders, her spine and the muscles around it…and inevitably to her butt. And then she started speaking again, and I felt guilty for ogling her while she was pouring her heart out.

"I just feel so fucking lost, Ink. Dance was my anchor and my reason for being, and Rick was my wings, my reason to laugh and feel good. Now I don't have either one, and I…I don't know what the fuck to do." A sniffle. "I've never been so emotional in all my life. I didn't even know I *could* cry."

Finally, silence ensued, and it felt…finished. As if she'd run out of words. She turned, walked back to the row of shitty folding chairs set up in the middle of the laundromat. She sat down beside me—close enough that her thigh touched mine. She was staring at her scars.

"The scar itself doesn't bother me," she said, eventually. "It's what the scar means for me, for my life, that I don't know how to cope with."

I sorted through the many, many thoughts swirling in my head. I met her eyes, held them. "This is just my personal opinion. Obviously, I ain't you. I ain't in your shoes and I likely never will experience anything like what you're going through. But, I've been through plenty of hurt in my life. Lost things important to me—people, mainly. Been betrayed, been cut down. And I guess somethin' I learned is that sometimes in order to cope and process, you need to just give yourself time to…not. Not cope. Not process. Just feel it. Just let the hurt *hurt*. Just let yourself be fuckin' pissed off and angry and confused. Don't try to figure it all out all at once. You got to eventually, and you will. But right now, maybe this is your time to just feel what you feel and don't box it up, and don't label it and don't try to justify or make light of it." I touched her scar again, and she still flinched, but didn't pull away this time. "Just let yourself be a mess. Own it. It's okay."

She shook her head. "Mom makes me feel like I have to figure it out *right now*, like I need to therapy myself into a blissful state of happiness without Rick and without dance. It's confusing, and it makes me feel guilty for not being able to pull myself out of the funk."

"I don't know your mom at all, only met her the once. But if you want my impression—"

"I do."

"Well, I'd say she's just worried about you. Maybe she's pushing you to figure out how to be okay because she can't handle seeing you all depressed and fucked up and in a funk. She's your mama. She wants to see you happy. She loves you, and seeing you like this is probably hard for her."

Cassie sighed, nodding. "Yeah, you're probably right." A laugh. "Doesn't make it easier, though. Like, her pushing me to be better already makes me feel guilty, like I'm letting her down by being so fucked up."

"So tell her that."

"You've never tried to tell my mom that how she feels about something is wrong." Cassie laughed at that, an amused cackle.

"Doesn't change her mind easily, huh?" I smirked, knowing the answer was obvious.

"Yeah, no. Not in the slightest."

"Probably worth it, though, I think. I mean, you can't rush *your* process to your new normal, right? So, at the least, you gotta express yourself to her so she knows where you're coming from, even if she doesn't agree. But knowing she loves you, I think she'll come around to understanding where you're coming from."

She laughed again, her eyes searching my face. "You're good at this."

I frowned. "At what?"

"Relationship advice."

I snorted. "Well, it ain't because I'm some kinda expert. God knows I got my own set of problems with my parents."

She tilted her head. "Really? Like what?"

"Like, I don't really see them or talk to them much."

"That's kind of sad."

"Wasn't a falling out, or a blowout fight, or anything like that. We just...they don't get me. How I can live in the city. Why I feel so compelled to put all this ink on my skin, on my face. Plus, my dad is what you might call a functioning alcoholic and my mom..." I waved a hand. "Mom is just difficult. And they were just never...supportive, or very affectionate. When they figured they couldn't change me, couldn't stop me from doing what I was gonna do, they quit trying. And when they quit trying to change me and talk me out of art and tattoos, they just sorta quit on me in general. It was tough. It *is* tough. It's made it hard for me to connect with people."

She leaned against me, her shoulder on mine. "You connected with me pretty well."

I shook my head. "This is different."

She frowned, gazing up at me. "How so?" A pause. "You don't think we've connected?"

I hesitated. "No, we have. I know we have. We're friends. And that's more, and it's happened faster than anything else I've ever had in my life."

"I'm not following."

I swallowed hard. "Tricky to put into words."

"Try."

My turn to stand up, stretching my arms over my head and twisting my back until my spine popped. My turn to stare out the window rather than at those intense gray-green-brown-blue-everything eyes. "I don't go around sticking my head into people's business. Like, ever. Real deep down, I only really trust the best friend I've ever had in my entire life…my cousin Juneau. She's the only human I've ever really trusted, or genuinely liked, let alone loved. And she's my cousin. Like the sister I've never had. And even her, I don't let in very far. I mean, I trust her, but my shit is my shit. So I don't let others into my shit, and if I'm not gonna let others into my shit, I'm not gonna put myself into their shit. I just do my tattoos and go home. That's it. That's all it's ever been."

"What about girlfriends?"

I shook my head, fighting to find the right way to put this so I didn't sound lame and pathetic. "Been a couple girls here and there, but...nothing serious." I sighed, shook my head again. "That's a lie. There was one serious thing, but...that's a whole other ball of wax, and I don't really know how to even talk about it."

"So you don't really date?"

I shrugged. "Nope. Not really."

I wasn't looking at her, but I could feel her deciding whether to give voice to what was on her mind. I just waited. "So, maybe this is none of my business, and feel free to say so, but...what about sex?"

I shifted from foot to foot. Swallowed hard. Rolled a shoulder. "Like I said, there've been a few girls here and there."

"This is a weird conversation." Cassie laughed at this, a soft breathy sound that shot through my gut.

I was way too glad that she didn't push that line of conversation. "Yeah, it is."

She was suddenly there, behind me. Close enough that I could smell her: eucalyptus, tea tree, lavender. "I've never had anyone as deep into my shit as you are." The silence, though momentary, was profound and intense.

"I never set about to get up in your shit. I guess I just somehow ended up there."

"I'm okay with it," Cassie said.

I turned in place to look down at her. Platinum hair loose and wild and tangled, eyes burning like stars, her entire being blazing with chaotic, vibrant energy—she *burned*. Her cream-and-ivory silk skin beckoned my hands, called to me. Her body sang for my touch.

I didn't dare. Not with her. Not now. Maybe not ever—she was strong, yes. But she was fragile, barely keeping herself together, if at all. My hands, huge and rough, could wield a tattoo gun with delicate precision, could thread a needle. But to touch a person? A woman like her? Someone so small, so delicate? No. Tattoos didn't react. Didn't cause me to lose control. And I knew from painful experience that to lose control was to hurt.

I shoved my fisted hands into the pockets of my shorts, clenched hard, nails digging into my palms. Yet the way she was looking at me, silent, lips parted, eyes soft and searching.

I could kiss her.

Inches separated us. I could palm her cheek and kiss her. Those lips looked as if they tasted like cherries and wine. Her skin looked softer than plush and velvet and silk. She was wearing so little, tearing it all away would take a matter of moments.

I could hold her to myself and never let go, never tire of her.

I felt a surge of the desires I'd kept long buried. Desires so strong I barely knew how to deal with them under the best of circumstances, so powerful they scared me. Desires that led to a loss of control. And to lose control was to cause hurt.

I backed away from her, shuttering myself. Steeling myself against the siren song of her skin and her changeable eyes. The call of her lips and the pull of her curves.

I turned away, my entire inner being seething with a boiling mess of things I didn't understand and couldn't handle and refused to face—the same things I had refused to face for years.

"Ink?" My name—three letters on an upward inflection. A thousand unasked questions in that single syllable.

"I..."

The dryer with my laundry in it buzzed at that moment. Thank fuck. I yanked the clothes—mostly shorts and underwear along with my bedding—and shoved the whole mess into my bag, shouldered it, and headed for the door.

"Ink!" She reached the door first, touched my bicep, and her small hand on my arm set me alight, made me burn, melt, shake. "Where are you going?"

I had no idea what to say. I had no clue what I was feeling, or how to deal with it in my own head and body, much less how to communicate any of it to her. I couldn't help looking down into her eyes, though. "I don't know, Cass. I just…I'm—it's—"

I was almost never at a loss for what to say, but right then all words and all thoughts were tangled up in the driving, consuming, burning need to touch-taste-hold-devour this woman. It was sudden and unexpected and was igniting things I'd kept shoved way down deep in the farthest back corner of the junk drawer of my soul.

"I don't know how to do this with you right now, Cass. I just plain fuckin' don't."

"Do what?" But something layered like a web of spider silk through her words and the wild burn of her eyes told me she knew damn well what I was talking about.

I swallowed hard, felt myself chewing on my thoughts as I do when agitated or deep in thought. She was in front of me, blocking the door.

I let my bag hang off my shoulder, reached out and grabbed her around the waist—god, bare skin, hot and soft—and set her to one side. I should *not* have done that, though. Her skin, in that split second of contact, melted into my hand, dissolved into me, absorbed itself into my bloodstream and lit the furnace of need inside me to a snarling wildfire roar.

I pushed out the door and all but ran, my bare feet slapping on the pavement.

I ached for long hours after that.

FOUR

Cassie

I WATCHED HIS BROAD BACK RECEDE INTO THE SHADOWS. His ponytail swayed at his back, and the huge bag of laundry seemed like no more of a burden than if he'd been carrying a single pillow. Yet that bag had been larger than me and heavier.

God, he was strong.

He'd picked me up and literally physically set me aside, and I don't think it had required any effort whatsoever.

I stood at the door watching the sidewalk where he'd vanished for a long time, wondering.

Why had he left?

It had seemed, for a moment, as if he'd been about to kiss me.

His eyes had raked over my face, caught on my lips, stared at them. I'd felt his eyes on my body, and I couldn't bring myself to regret having dressed so skimpily. I wasn't overly modest anyway—as a dancer, I'd performed in this or something like it countless times. Practiced in it, sweated and been lifted and videotaped in outfits like this.

So why did it feel different with Ink? Why did I feel more naked? With anyone else I wouldn't think twice. I was comfortable in my dance shorts and midriff tank top, and often went without a bra late at night when I was not planning on being around people, or moving around that much. It wasn't a big deal, really. But with Ink, it just felt different. I felt exposed.

I felt…sensual.

And that was truly different. I am a physical person, a sexual person, a visceral person. But not a sensual one. Big difference. Ink made me feel intensely sensual, in that moment he was looking down at me like…

Like he wanted to devour me.

Has anyone looked at me like that, ever?

Did Rick ever look at me like that? Like if he didn't get to touch me and kiss me and do wild and dirty things with me he would just die.

Rick had looked at me like he owned me, like he

deserved me, like I was his. But not ever with such violent burning desperation, the way Ink just did.

And then Ink had just...walked away.

As if he couldn't wait to escape me.

The washer buzzed, and I went to switch my laundry over, still turning the last half an hour over in my head.

I was attracted to him, I realized. It seemed like a weird thing to have to realize, but there it was. He was drastically different than Rick—the polar opposite, in fact. In every way.

Yet I was more than just physically attracted to Ink. There was a lot to *him*. His presence was soothing and exciting at the same time. His size was intimidating and scary and thrilling and intense...and comforting. I had never in my life felt as safe as I did around Ink. Or as at risk, because he *sees* me. Knows me, despite not knowing a whole lot about me. I've told him things I've not really talked about even with Mom.

So, wait. Was I imagining him wanting me? Was I seeing something that's not there because I was lonely and sad and upset and lost and—

And fucking horny as hell.

God, *so* horny.

But was I using all that to see something that's not there?

I didn' think I was. I think he felt it—felt a connection, something hot and sizzling between us.

And then he walked away. Picked me up, set me aside, and walked away.

But there was a whole boiling shitload of conflict going on as he did so, which made me think he has some hang-ups of his own. He seemed so self-contained, so confident, so at ease in his skin and with who he was, which made it hard to imagine what he could be insecure about. I needed to know.

And, if I was going to be honest with myself, the look in his eyes, the burning desire that was so blatantly obvious…? It made me crazy. I wanted him to act on it. I wanted him to show me what it would feel like for him to let that loose. I mean, god what a feeling that must be. To have a man that powerful, that strong just…*take* me?

Yes, please.

Rick…I knew I had to stop thinking about him, but it was impossible not to compare them. Rick was my only truly serious relationship. I had a boyfriend in high school, my first kiss, my first trip to second base, and the boy to whom I'd given my virginity. We'd dated from sophomore year through me leaving for Julliard, and I'd known all the time that it would end upon graduation. He'd known it too, because he had his own plans—Stanford for a double major in computer science and business, and then intern at a dot-com in Silicon Valley for some experience, and then strike out to create his own startup dot-com, in the biotech field. Last I'd checked, William had done everything he'd planned on doing, and his startup was doing great. We'd been good together, William and me. It had been fun, exciting. We'd known all along it was a relationship with a finite term, and so we'd set out to extract the most amount of fun and enjoyment from our time together as possible.

As horny teenagers with busy parents, we'd had plenty of time and opportunity to explore and indulge our sexual curiosity, and that had been quite a wild time of learning myself and my body and my desires. And what I'd learned, more than anything, is that I just rev at a higher level than most. I think that's true of all of us Goodes. I know Lexie, more than any of us, has a libido that runs hot enough that she would probably call it an affliction. Charlie and I have talked at length about our struggles to find a partner who gets us, who satisfies us, who can keep up with us.

For my part, I've yet to find that. William came closest, I think. But that's only because I was a young adult, at best, a girl just finding herself and just beginning to understand my body and what I wanted, and how to ask for it. I would say I'm a pretty sexually liberated woman—I regularly and enthusiastically take care of myself, and when I'm with a man I have no qualms about asking for what I want and indicating what I like and don't. I just also know that most men don't have the stamina or patience to truly stay with me, to satisfy me to the point that I'd really truly feel well matched. I enjoy myself when I'm with a partner, no doubt about that—but I'm often left feeling like, once he's gone, that I need to find a few minutes to handle some un-finished business.

And I don't mean that as a complaint or insult or anything negative about the men I've been with. I'm just...I need more, want more, I'm ready for more sooner. I want things crazier, hotter, wilder. I'm not an exhibitionist, don't have any interest in being public about things. I just want a lot. And none of the men I've slept with so far have really met my deepest, strongest needs.

In a way, sexually speaking, Rick was honestly was my least satisfying partner. He was selfish. Well-endowed, had stamina, plenty of drive. But just didn't seem to think much about what I was feeling, especially once he was close to his own climax. If I wanted him to do something, and I asked, he would, and knew what he was doing, but...I don't know. I guess some part of me wanted him to put my needs first, at some point. To think about my desires as much as he thought about getting himself to his enjoyment. He took me, sexually, as his right, as his toy to get himself off. And unless I clearly expressed what I wanted, he wouldn't think about it.

God, now that I think about it objectively, Rick was an asshole.

And I stayed him with for…four years, nearly. I'd met him at Julliard, and we'd been hired at the troupe together, and the whole time, I don't think I'd ever once been totally and fully sexually satisfied. What about emotionally?

Nope.

He'd been aloof, hard to communicate with, selfish. Spent more time with friends from the company than with me.

A thought occurred to me, then.

A horrifying thought which, if true, would probably just flat out wreck me the rest of the way.

I scrambled for my phone so fast I dropped it, but thankfully I kept a rubber case on it because I was always dropping it. I didn't even think about what time it was, I just dialed.

It rang half a dozen times.

"Huh—hello?" A muzzy female voice. A pause. "Cass. It's…it's seven in the morning on a Saturday. What the hell?"

"Sorry, Charlie—if it makes you feel any better,

it's three a.m. here." I swallowed hard. "Do you think Rick is gay?"

A long, long, weird pause. "Cass. Babe. You dumb sweet bitch. Yes, he's gay."

"You're mean when you get woken up," I muttered. "You say that like it should be obvious."

She groaned, and I heard a faint click in the background as she turned on a light. "Cassie, sweetie, chicken dumpling, my lovey-dove."

Oh boy. The idiotic terms of endearment—that's when you knew Charlie was about to unload both barrels, usually something she had probably been harboring and keeping to herself until directly asked about. Like now.

"Rick is gayer than a gay pride festival." She sounded...almost like she was holding back laughter. "I thought you knew."

"No, I didn't fucking know!"

"Well how the hell am I supposed to know what you know? It didn't seem to me like he ever tried to hide it. He wears the tightest pants I've ever seen on a male who wasn't in tights on stage in a ballet. He's a fantastic dresser, and not just because his family is richer than god. He doesn't have the flamboyant lisp or anything—like, he doesn't talk like Jonathan from *Queer Eye*, but he's most definitely gay."

"We had sex at least once a week for four years."

"So maybe he's bi, or still figuring it out."

"You think he was…do you think he was sleeping with men while he was with me?"

A really difficult pause, then. "I…I don't know."

"Charlie."

"I don't! I don't know anything for sure. I suspect he was, yes." A sigh. "I never liked him. And not because he's gay…I couldn't care less about that. I just don't think he's a good person. He's a dick, an arrogant, selfish jackass, and he treated you like shit. I never understood why you were with him. You called me at least once a month complaining that he left you unsatisfied in bed. I thought that was…like, *duh*. I always assumed you knew he was either bi or curious or something. I mean, he's an incredible dancer, no doubt about that. And I'm not saying, like, that he can't be straight because he's a professional dancer. I just…he's just not straight. Not all the way, at least. And I really thought you knew, and I figured it wasn't my business. I told you straight up more than once that I didn't like him, and didn't like him for you, and that I thought you could do better. Again, I want to be clear, this is not because he's not straight. If you want to date a guy who's into dudes too, cool. Your business. I didn't like him as a person and didn't like him as your boyfriend because he's a piece of shit person and you deserved way better than him, whether he's into men, women, both, or kittens. I don't care. You just deserve a man who cares about you, who takes care of you, who puts you first. And he didn't do that."

I sniffled. "I'm gonna call him."

"Cassandra."

"Charlotte."

"Why? What are you going to get out of that?"

"It's over anyway, but I have to know." I wiped at my nose, swallowing hard. Hating the sting in my eyes. I shouldn't still be able to be hurt by Rick, yet there's the ache in my chest, a heaviness, an anger. At myself, and at him.

"Okay, but leave me on the line."

"You can't make a sound, though."

"I won't."

I added the call, hoping he hadn't changed his cell phone number. I looked at the screen, watching until it went from "calling" to counting the duration of the call. It rang, once, twice, three times.

"*Salut,* Cassie." That voice, not quite French-accented, and smooth as French chocolate. "What is it?"

"I...I need you to answer a question for me, Rick."

"I am going by Richard, now." He gave it a distinct French pronunciation—*REE-shar.*

"Great, good to know."

He sighed. "What is your question, *m'belle*?" A stammer. "I—Sorry. Old habits, you know."

He was suddenly really leaning into his French heritage. He'd always tried to balance it, to not sound too French or too American, but a suave balance of both. Not anymore.

"Are you gay?"

He laughed, a bark of amusement. "You know, that's a question I have been asking myself a lot lately."

"Rick, come on. It's three in the morning where I am, and I just need an answer. Were you sleeping with men while we were together?"

A tense pause. "To say 'sleeping with' is a very broad thing, *cherie*."

"Quit with the affectation, Rick. This is me, okay?"

A sigh, and he dropped the accent. "It's not an affectation, I'll have you know. I'm half French and I've lived more than half my life here. But whatever makes you feel better."

"What will make me feel better is to know you weren't messing around with guys while we were dating. Maybe you were confused or figuring it out—I could accept that. But if you were lying and deceiving me…" I sighed bitterly. "Whatever the case, just give me the straight truth."

"I was experimenting, yes."

"Meaning?"

"You really want to know what I was doing, play by play?" His voice was sharp, arrogant. "I'll tell you, but I don't think you want to know."

"If you'd just told me—"

"I was embarrassed, Cassie. And I really was attracted to you. I really did care for you. I wasn't lying about that. You weren't a beard or anything."

"Embarrassed? We lived and worked with… what, eight other gay men? You were *embarrassed*? They'd have accepted you in a heartbeat. The girls too. Everyone."

"It's complicated," he snapped.

"Then simplify it."

"You and me, we started out as friends. I wasn't sure what I was, then. I knew I had feelings for men, but I also really liked you. Things just sort of happened between us, and I wasn't sure how to bring it up with you after a while. What was I supposed to do, sit you down six months into our relationship and be like, 'hey, by the way, I know we're dating and all, but I think I may also like men?'"

"Yes, that would have worked just fine for me."

"You're delusional. You were in love with me. I didn't want to hurt you, and I wasn't sure if I was bi, or if I was lying to myself about being in love with you, or if I loved you emotionally but wasn't in love with you. It was confusing. I didn't know what I wanted."

"So you just kept dating me, but went off and screwed around with men on the side, without telling me?"

"I wasn't screwing around. I was figuring myself out."

"Well you should have had the decency to break up with me, or at least tell me what was going on. Not just let me keep thinking we were in love." I sniffled, working hard to hold back the real breakdown I knew was coming.

"I'm sorry I hurt you, Cassandra."

"Thanks." I wiped my eyes. "So is that why you dumped me after the accident?"

"It was a lot of things, really. The accident just... shook me up. I should have died, almost did. I should have permanent brain damage, like, be a vegetable. But I don't, I'm not. I'm alive. But I'm a mess. My emotions are all over the place. I don't know what I want. I don't know if I'm going to go back to dancing. I don't know what I want to do. I woke up from a coma, which I was in for three weeks. You know what it's like to lose three weeks of your life? I know, it could have been longer. I'm lucky to have woken up from it at all. And yes, it made me realize I'd been stringing you along, playing games with you, being unfair to you." A long silence. "I'm sorry I wasn't honest with you. I'm sorry I hurt you."

"I forgive you." I sighed.

"What brought this on? Why call me about this now, months later, at three in the morning?"

I groaned. "It's complicated."

"Simplify it." He laughed, a good-natured chuckle. "I do know you better than just about anyone, in some ways. I bet I can guess."

I laughed. "Okay, go for it."

"You're trying to get over everything. You're still healing because your leg is all fucked up, right? You can't dance, or not anytime soon. I broke up with you, and now you're obsessively going over everything in your head. And you were thinking through our relationship, wondering where you went wrong."

Wow. I mean, just wow. The arrogance in that statement was breathtaking.

"No, actually, *Richard*." I used his fancy new French pronunciation. "I was realizing how unsatisfied I was sexually the entire time I was with you. Like, trying to figure out why I was ever with you in the first place. You never made me come, you know that? Never. Not once. Most of the time, like ninety-nine point…like…five percent of the time we had sex, I waited until you were asleep, and then I finished myself off."

I sighed, then continued. "So no, I wasn't wondering where I went wrong, I was wondering what I missed, like, why was I so unsatisfied with you? I know I have a really powerful libido, but even taking that into consideration, our sex life was really kind of...pathetic. And I couldn't figure out why. Then, it hit me. You just weren't interested in me. You didn't want me. It wasn't *me*, like at all. *I* wasn't the problem. You just didn't want me. And listen, I know men have different tastes in women, okay? Like, I know some guys may not be into a girl who looks like me, short and thin, small boobs and butt, super athletic. But I'm *horny*. Like, all the fucking time. I was after you, *all...the...time.* Most guys I know would give their literal left nut to be with a girl like me, even if I'm not his preferred physical type. I also know, types aside, I'm pretty. So, your lack of interest, in all probability, wasn't because of anything to do with me, but with you. If it was you, then what possible reason could there be for you to not be sexually interested in a horny, attractive woman who was in love with you?"

"Cassie—"

"And the obvious answer is that you're just not into women at all. And once I realized that, it hit me like a ton of bricks. I missed all the signs the whole time. The fact that you were always going off and hanging out with the other guys. The other *gay* guys.

Clubbing together, shopping, everything. You did *everything* with those guys." I growled. "And then there was the fact that you could be backstage with all of us girls, and we'd have to do a quick change, and you wouldn't even look. Not once, let alone twice. At any of us."

"That doesn't make me an asshole."

"No, it doesn't. You just weren't interested. It all just started making sense. If you were really a straight guy in that situation, you would have looked, and then turned away. I've danced with straight men before, obviously, and they're professionals. But they're still aware that they're straight and it's not weird, not a thing, just a fact." I sighed. "But that's not you."

"So?"

"So, it just hit me all at once, and now I feel like a complete moron for not realizing it sooner." I let the silence grow. "So that's it. I just needed that confirmation. Thanks."

"It was that bad for you?"

I laughed. "You really care?"

"I mean, yeah? Sort of. I guess I thought it was pretty good between us."

"Of course you would, you selfish ballsack! You got off, every time. I did everything I could to make sure *you* always felt good, that you knew I *wanted* you, that I *appreciated* you, that I was attracted to you. I did things *for you*. So yeah, you wouldn't think it was bad, because I went out of my way to make it *good* for you."

He was stunned silent by that. "I…"

"There's nothing to say." I dragged my hand through my hair. "I was just an idiot, and wasted four years with you. And now I'm fucked up in the head and heart because of you. And you know what? I'm not accepting all the blame for it, Rick. I'm not. I should have seen it sooner, yeah. I should've known that sexual things aside, you just weren't thinking about me, didn't really care about me. But you were lying. And that's what fucking kills me. If you'd been honest, I probably would have been okay giving you space to figure things out. Instead, you played a game. You pretended. You lied. You cheated. And that puts the blame squarely on *you*." I sighed, bitter. "I just wish that helped me feel better about myself. But it doesn't, and that's not your problem. Not that it ever was, clearly."

"That's not fair, I was—"

I cut him off. "Rick, I don't give a shit. Just be honest."

"Easy for you to say—"

"I *am* honest. You want the honest truth? I'm a fucking mess. From the accident, from losing dance, from the way you dumped me, and now from realizing I was dating a fucking selfish piece of shit liar, that I wasted all that time and energy thinking I loved you, thinking you loved me. And I just wonder if I have any fucking clue what love is—you know? Like, I don't know, and I wonder now if I ever did." I growled. "But none of that is your problem." My dryer buzzed. "I have to go. Thank you for answering my question. Best of luck to you."

A pause, and Rick stammered a few times. Paused again. Started over. "I am sorry, Cassie. I'm sorry I wasn't honest, and I'm sorry I hurt you. I hope you find what you're looking for."

"You too, Rick."

I ended the call with Rick, and waited for Charlie to speak.

"Wow," she said, eventually. "That was…" A laugh. "That was awesome."

"It sucked."

"Yeah, of course. But now you know, you have the closure, and you can move on." A groan. "I just wish you'd waited, like, a couple more hours. I was going to actually sleep in today."

"You haven't slept in on a Saturday your whole life."

"I quit my job. I was going to try something new. Being a slacker sounds fun."

I laughed. "You couldn't be a slacker if you tried.

You'd overachieve being a slacker. You'd plan out your day, like, Saturday, sleep in till eleven—check. Eat like shit, check. Watch garbage TV for an hour, check. Half ass a walk on the treadmill in my rich boyfriend's swanky apartment building's fancy gym—check."

She sighed. "I broke up with Glen because he was sleeping with my boss, and the apartment was ours, not his, and I don't live there anymore because I quit my job and left Glen and I have no real friends because they're all Glen's friends, it turns out. So I'm living in a hotel in a kind of seedy part of Boston, and I've been drunk at eleven a.m. more times in the last month than I care to admit."

"Wow, Charlie, I had no idea."

"Yeah, well, you've been busy with your own life-altering crises."

"Glen, your super hot, super macho, super successful boyfriend…was sleeping with your boss? Your past middle-age, overweight, and just objectively not attractive boss? The one with a husband of twenty-five years, three kids, and two grandkids?"

"Yes. That boyfriend, and that boss."

"Wow. I…" I was at a loss. "I don't know what to say."

"Thus my current lifestyle of being a slacker, living off my savings, and day-drinking alone."

"Char-char—you're not that girl. You don't have

pity parties. You don't slack off. You don't even night drink, let alone day drink."

"Yeah, well. I guess I'm having a moment."

"Does Mom know?"

"Of course."

I started taking my clean clothes out of the dryer and folding them, putting the phone on speaker and setting it on top of the front-load dryer. "What are you going to do?"

"Hell if I know." An angry, bitter sigh. "Probably keep the pity party going another week or so, and then pull up my big girl panties and start my life over."

"Don't say panties, Charlotte. It's gross."

"Panties, panties, panties." She laughed, goading me. "Wait, I got a better one—*moist* panties."

I shuddered, faking a gagging sound. "Gross!"

She laughed. "I could barely say it, it's so gross." The humor faded. "I honestly don't know what to do."

"You talked to Mom, you said?"

A hesitation. "Yeah."

I laughed. "She told you what you should do, and you're just working up the courage to actually do it."

"Her advice was terrible."

I cackled. "Mom's advice is *never* terrible. We just don't like it because she wants us to do the hardest thing, and we don't like it, and we don't listen, and we regret it, but she never really says I told you so which only makes us feel worse because she *could* and *should* say it, but she's too good a person and won't. But she's always right, and we know it, we just don't like it."

"Pretty much," Charlie sighed.

"So? What was her advice?"

"Apparently Poppy is having a hard time with things, too. She wanted me to go spend time with Poppy, like we'd help each other figure out our lives or something."

I couldn't help a laugh. "You and Poppy—I don't want to say you hate each other, but you fight like cats and dogs over the dumbest shit. She annoys the hell out of you, and you piss her off."

"Exactly!"

I laughed again. "But she's right."

"Excuse me?" Charlie was incredulous.

"You should do it."

"Can I ask why you would betray me like this?"

"Charlotte, come on. It's not a betrayal. You and Poppy are both in the middle of shit, right? You have no life anymore, no job, no apartment, no boyfriend. I'm guessing Poppy realized she hates school and wants to just do art full time or something, because she just has no patience for rules or assignments, and doesn't have the guts to believe in herself enough to really try and be a full-time artist. And Mom is exactly right—this is the best, if not the only time you and she will ever have to spend real quality unhurried time together, figuring each other out, and learning to like each other."

"Would you do it?"

I considered. "You know, I would. I mean, shit, I'm living with Mom right now. Tells you where *I'm* at in life."

"Yikes. You're in Alaska?"

"Yeah."

"How is it?"

"Beautiful. Backward. Interesting."

"Backward. You snob."

"Fine. It's not backward, it's just different."

"You're just spoiled from living at Julliard and then Paris, and traveling all over the world staying in the best hotels." She left a long pause. "Who is he?"

"Who?"

She snorted. "Cassandra Danielle, I'm your older sister. I know you. There's a guy, and he's why you're having this crisis about Rick."

"It was bothering me."

"What's his name?"

"Why does there have to be someone?"

"Because if there wasn't, you wouldn't be arguing. You'd tell me there isn't anyone. You're dodging. Therefore, what the hell is his name?"

I sighed. Sisters. So annoying, especially when they know you better than you know yourself. "His name is Ink."

"What's his real name?"

"That *is* his real name."

"Really? That's kinda cool."

"He's a tattoo artist."

"And his name is Ink?" An appropriate amount of disbelief.

"Serendipitous, right?"

"To say the least." A pause. "What aren't you saying?"

"He's Inuit, six-foot-seven, and covered in tattoos from head to toe, never wears a shirt, and he calls me Little Sparrow."

A really long, really significant pause. "Wow."

"Yeah."

"Little Sparrow?"

"Apparently I'm delicate, but elegant, or something. I don't remember how he put it."

"Six-seven?"

"With a beard that hangs to his chest, a ponytail, and did I mention the tattoos on every inch of his skin?"

"And you *like* him?"

"I don't know!" I yelled. "Yes, I do. I do like him. I can't figure it out."

"You once told me tattoos were trashy, long hair

was effeminate, and beards were gross." She spoke over my protest. "And, I believe, you once said you hated being made to feel any smaller than you already were, so any man more than six inches taller than you was right off the list."

"Yes, Charlotte, I did say all that. He is literally everything I always thought I didn't like in a man."

"But?"

"But he's the nicest, warmest, most genuine, interesting, and unique person I've ever met. He's absolutely and utterly just himself. His tattoos are absolutely amazing, individual little works of art all connected and interwoven all over him. They're not trashy—they're an expression of who he is. And he's absolutely gargantuan, and I feel so absolutely incredibly tiny around him, I don't even know how to explain it, but it's...comforting."

"Are you attracted to him? Like, sexually?"

"I..." I paused, thinking. "Yeah."

"You had to think about it, Cass."

"I know. But that's just because I didn't even realize how much I liked him, or that I was even attracted to him. He's just so...different. I've never in my life met anyone like him. He doesn't judge, and he's so wise, and..."

Charlie was laughing. "Whoa, Cassie, babe. You *like* him, like him."

"Yes. I do. Who he is as a person is so…different, and so *much* that I've had to stop and think about how I feel about him physically. And that's complicated."

"Why is it complicated?"

"Because I think he's got some kind of hang-up."

"Everyone has hang-ups, Cass."

"But he's so confident, so comfortable in who he is. I can't figure out what he could be hung up about."

"So ask him. Get to know him and figure it out, and get past it with him."

"Sounds simple, but you don't know him. I'm not even sure how to start that conversation. He has this way of making me think about myself and making me face my own shit. But I don't think anyone ever really makes him face his shit. And that's why he's so complicated and internal. Because he's wise and insightful and seems to be so content in who he is that no one sees that he has his own insecurities."

"Like I said, everyone has insecurities. If they don't, they're narcissistic and arrogant."

"So what's your hang-up?"

"Oh my, I'm really complicated, Cass. Daddy issues up the wazoo." A yawn. "I'm going to go back to sleep. Go talk to your big fella, Cass."

"I will." I yawned, then. "Damn you, you gave me your yawn."

"Ha-ha."

"Go see Poppy."

"Shut up."

"You shut up. You didn't listen to Mom about Glen, and look how that turned out. Listen to her now, Charlie."

"God, you're as annoying as she is."

"I know. It's just because we love you."

"Love you too, Cass. Bye."

I tucked the phone back into my purse, and finished folding my clothes.

Talk to him.

Figure it out, with him.

With him.

Did I want that? I'd only known him a very short time, but he was stuck in my head. Of course, so was Rick, and dance. But Rick was done, now. I knew the truth, and while it hurt, I knew I was good to move on, for real this time. He was messed up, and selfish, and I'd been blind and probably a little desperate for attention. I mean, that was my inheritance from Dad. All of us girls had something, and mine was being desperate for attention. It's part of my love for dance—I love the state, the attention, the lights. I also just love dance, moving my body, being strong and graceful and powerful and elegant, I love the movement. But I also just love being seen on the stage. But the attention thing goes deeper. I need male attention because Daddy wasn't there enough. Cliché, much? Shit, I know it is. But it's true. And I was willing to blindly accept whatever Rick was offering because he was paying attention, sort of.

Ugh.

Am I falling into the same trap with Ink? Am I just attracted to him because he paid a little attention to me? Is he going to reveal some killer flaw, too? I mean, he's just too good to be true, otherwise.

No, it's not the same. Yes, he paid attention to me, but it was genuine. I'm still not sure what Rick's motivations were. Maybe he was just trying to figure out if he really did like girls, boys, or both, and really just didn't know how to face the confusion. I don't know, and I do have sympathy for what must have been difficult. I just think, regardless, he should've been honest with me, even if it meant breaking up with me. Not telling me what he was really going through, not having the courage to tell me the truth was lying, plain and simple, dammit.

What about Ink?

I groaned, bending over the dryer with my head in my hands.

I almost wished I'd fallen into the water. I'm too fucked up as a person to know how to navigate this. Like, I really, really don't know how to handle the fact that I'm catching feelings for Ink.

FIVE

Ink

I COULDN'T STOP THINKING ABOUT HER.

And it was a problem. A big problem.

My job requires focus, and the thoughts I was having were...distracting, at best.

My current client, fortunately, wanted a simple tat—a little butterfly on the nape of her neck. Small, but in vibrant color. A piece I could do almost in my sleep. I stayed focused as best as I could, because she'd come to me expecting a work of art, not something I'd done on autopilot.

I barely saw the client, though, except as a patch of skin and the way it called to me, spoke to me, told me what to do.

When I finished, she looked at the piece in the mirror, gushed about the colors and how realistic it looked, and paid me. I took a photo of it for my gallery book, and said my goodbyes.

It was a great piece, and I was proud I'd been able to do work of that quality with the crazy-ass thoughts I'd been having the last few days.

Thoughts of Cassie.

Thoughts of what she'd been wearing last time I saw her—those tiny skintight shorts. How they'd showcased exactly what her ass looked like, even though it was technically covered. The cut-off midriff shirt. The expanse of her skin, the hint of her breasts.

Her scent.

Her eyes.

The way, in those last few moments, that she'd looked up at me. As if realizing at the same time as me that we had more than just a mental and emotional connection. That I wanted her. I knew that had been obvious. I'd been fuckin' seconds from kissing her.

And she'd known it, too.

Had she been daring me to? Would she have let me? Would she have kissed me back?

I flipped the sign to closed—it was ten at night and I was done for the day.

No more clients until noon tomorrow.

I went home, started some eggs and tried to think about anything but Cassie.

Anything but her lips. Anything but her eyes—how wild and quicksilver they were, reflecting her mercurial moods in the changing colors.

Her skin was art. I usually looked at skin as a canvas, tried to picture what would go where. The few girls I'd been with, that's where my mind went. Oh, I appreciated them for what they looked like, but another deeper part was just appreciating their skin as a canvas for ink.

Cassie was different. Her skin was flawless. Cream and ivory, perfectly silk, not a blemish. It would almost be a shame to ruin her skin with ink, and that, to me, was a nearly blasphemous thing to say.

I couldn't improve on perfection, not with my best work.

I burned my eggs, thinking about her.

Need was building inside me. Need to see her, need to talk to her. Need to know if I'd imagined the moment between us, if I'd imagined her wanting me to kiss her.

Need to touch her skin, to know if it felt as soft and perfect as it looked.

I threw away my eggs and leaned back against the wall, groaning in frustration.

I'd kept a tight lid on my sexuality for a long time,

now. Years, in fact. It was just…simpler. Less painful. I knew it wasn't healthy, psychologically. I knew I had issues I should deal with, but it was just easier to focus on tattoos twelve hours a day. Easier to lock that part of myself down and pretend it didn't exist. It makes it easier, certainly, when a beautiful woman comes in requesting a tattoo somewhere sensitive. Makes it easier for me to remain neutral, to view the process as clinical. I've done plenty of pieces on breasts, thighs, buttocks, inner thighs, and even a couple around nether regions. Not a problem. Just a tattoo.

Years of doing this…no problem.

I've sort of thought of myself as a kind of ascetic, living a monkish life.

Then Cassie comes along, and wrecks all that in a matter of days. I haven't even seen her naked. Haven't touched her. Haven't kissed her.

But the old desires, so long buried, are coming back with a vengeance. Surfacing and doing so violently, demanding release…and with a drive due to the years of neglect.

"Fuck," I snarled.

I flopped down onto my couch and snagged a drawing pad and a pencil. Started sketching.

I got about ten minutes in and it became obvious that sketching wouldn't serve as a distraction either.

I was drawing Cassie.

But my imagination was having a fucking field day. My sketch, which at this point was little more than an outline, was obviously her. Facing me, nude, head turned aside, chin dropped, one hand up in the back of her hair, the other draped casually over the apex of her thighs.

God, I'm drawing her naked, now?

Something wrong with me, for sure.

I wasn't any kind of a regular exercise kind of guy, but I decided to try to work off the pent-up junk in my skull—I got down and did pushups until my arms and chest and shoulders burned. Squats until my thighs burned and turned to jelly. I faced away from my couch, stuck my feet onto the coffee table while propping my hands behind me on the edge of the couch, and lowered my weight slowly, pressed back up, again and again until I couldn't anymore.

Yet still, sweating and shaky and sore, the moment I sat and closed my eyes, I saw Cassie. Bare. Standing in the pose I'd drawn her in. Staring at me, into my eyes, her gaze sensual, chest heaving. Sweaty, from dancing maybe.

God, god, god.

Never going to happen.

But the way she looked at me at the laundromat...makes me wonder.

Gives me a hint of hope.

And that shit is dangerous.

I tried to banish the thoughts of Cassie from my head, but I couldn't.

See her bending over at the laundromat, midriff shirt gaping, letting her bare breasts sway as she moved. Her taut round butt spread apart.

Gahhhh.

I felt a temptation to do something I hadn't done in a long time.

No.

I fought myself.

No.

Don't do it. Don't think of her that way.

She's a friend. Just a friend.

I imagined that look in her eye.

She'd never look at me that way. Would never think of me that way.

I tried to meditate, to think of anything, of nothing. To breathe. To imagine myself in the woods, birds singing, wind blowing through tall pines. Standing at a waterfall, the crash and roar deafening, shaking the earth. Standing in the pool at the base of the waterfall.

Cassie would be there.

Standing near the fall—not under it, you'd get flattened. Just near it. Letting the spray wet her naked body. Her perfect cream skin would glisten. One thigh drawn up against her core, arm across her breasts, glancing at me with a laugh.

Ducking her head near the spray so her platinum hair goes wet and flat against her back. She'd drop her arm as I approach. Smile at me, laugh, eyes wild and bright. Reach for me.

Wrap her hand around me. Small, soft, quick hand. Sliding up and down, in no hurry.

I clenched my teeth, pretending my hand is hers.

Fuck.

I let my imagination take over and pictured her pressing her body against me, touching me, touching me in a way I hadn't been touched in a very long time.

You'd think after so long it would be quick, but it wasn't. Now that I'd allowed myself to think about Cassie like that, I couldn't stop. Didn't want to stop.

I realized, belatedly, that I hadn't thought about where the mess was going to go. It's not like I kept Kleenex next to the couch.

I stumbled awkwardly into the bathroom, leaned back against the door, snagging a handful of toilet paper off the roll. Killing the mood, sort of, but I was out of practice doing this, and I felt dirty enough as it was, like I was taking advantage of her somehow, like I was using her or insulting her.

But I couldn't stop, not now.

I felt myself shake, curling forward, reached my release and groaned through it, pouring into the wadded toilet paper.

Finished, I groaned, feeling dirty. Feeling… ashamed.

Which was also not healthy, I knew. But I'd used the mental image of a friend to jack off. Classy shit, right there.

I threw the mess in the toilet, flushed it, washed my hands.

Left the bathroom…

And found Cassie on my couch, the drawing pad in her hands, looking at the drawing I'd done of her.

I stopped dead in my tracks. "Um. Hey."

She looked up at me, and I couldn't read her expression. Was she mad? Disgusted? Curious?

I just couldn't tell.

"I, um." She set the pad on her knees. "I probably should've knocked."

I laughed. "I mean, it is kinda customary."

"What I mean to say is, I did knock. You didn't answer. I thought you were at the shop. I went around the back way instead of through the front door, in case you were doing a tattoo. I didn't want to disturb you. I…" She glanced at me, and if I didn't know better, I'd say *she* was nervous. "I'm sorry. I shouldn't have just shown up like this."

Yeah. Thirty seconds earlier, you'd've seen something you probably wouldn't be able to unsee.

"I—" I glanced at the drawing pad still balanced on her knees. "About that…"

Her eyes went to mine. Fixed on mine for a moment, then slowly slid down. Over my bare torso, which was probably still a little swollen from my futile efforts to alleviate the tension. Down further, to my shorts.

Which, I realized, were still slightly tented from my not quite fully subsided…issue.

She set it aside. "About what?"

"The, um. The drawing." I wanted to adjust, but didn't dare draw any more attention to it. "Of you."

Her eyes went back up to mine. "It's amazing."

I blinked. "I…" I swallowed, shuffled. "You…what?"

She touched the paper, delicately tracing a fingertip over the lines. "It's an incredible drawing."

I was not expecting that. "I…"

"What, Ink? Did you think I'd be mad you drew a nude of me?"

"I didn't set out to." I wasn't sure why I said that. The words just sort of tumbled out. "I was…I don't know. Out of sorts. I don't fuckin' know. I just started drawing, and that was what came out."

Her eyes flitted from the drawing, to my shorts,

to the bathroom. To my eyes. "You…is this how you see me, Ink?"

I moved closer. Struggled for words. "Couple different ways to take that question, Cass."

She stared up at me. Patted the couch beside her. "I don't bite, Ink. I'm not mad at you for drawing a nude of me."

Hesitantly, I settled on the couch next to her. "Glad you're not upset with me."

She remained sitting with her elbows on her knees, chin in her hand, head twisted to look at me over her shoulder—her hair was down, loose, staticky, tangled. She was wearing fire-engine red yoga pants, skin tight, and a tank top knotted up high just under her breasts, the knot at her diaphragm, leaving her belly bare, exposing shredded abs.

"Why would I be upset about that, Ink? It's a hell of a flattering drawing."

I shrugged. "I dunno."

"Don't you wimp out on me now, Ink. Why would I be upset?"

I sighed. "That I was…thinking about you like that. We're friends. I value your friendship. And I guess I was worried you'd be…I dunno. Grossed out by me…um. Thinking about you like that."

She didn't answer immediately. Just stared at me, chewing on the inside of her cheek, pensive and thoughtful. "Well, to be fair, one could argue that, as an artist, you have a bit of leeway or license or whatever to pursue your inspiration, and if I'm your inspiration, then it's art, and not…what could be considered lewd or inappropriate. Further, this drawing—" she tapped the pad still resting on her knees, "is not, in any sense, to me or objectively, lewd. It's just not. It's a classic nude pose, and a beautiful work of art in any objective sense."

"It's a quick sketch. Barely any detail to it."

She nodded. "I know. But still, I think that enhances it, in a way. It's…raw."

I smiled, a tight, curious tilt of one side of my mouth. "Thank you."

She looked down at the drawing yet again. "But, if I consider it from an angle of it being more than just art, or less than merely art…I don't know. It's very personal. Trying to look at personally? You've given me a sensuality, a look in my eyes that's…intimate. What's funny—funny interesting, not funny ha-ha—is that despite it being a nude, you've rendered my eyes with more detail than my body."

"I've seen your eyes," I said. "Had to guess and use my imagination for the rest."

She eyed me. "Your imagination, hmmm?"

I swallowed hard. We were in uncomfortable territory for me. "Yeah."

"Meaning, imagine me naked."

I exhaled sharply. "Yeah."

"And this is how you imagined me? Like this?"

I nodded. "I mean, it's how my pencil interpreted what was going on in my head."

Her quicksilver hazel eyes pierced mine. Drilled hot and fierce and intimate into me. "What was going on in your head, Ink?"

I shrugged. "A lot."

She glanced at the drawing. "Give me the story behind this moment," she said, tracing the lines on the paper.

"Cassie, come on."

"I'm curious. This feels...specific. Intimate. Sensual." She looked at me. "And I'm curious."

"What is it you want to hear, Cass?"

"The story." Her voice was pitched low, a murmur, smooth and melodic.

"The story of me drawing it, or the story within the sketch? The...context of the moment story."

"The context of the moment."

"Cass..."

"Why're you scared, Ink?"

If you knew, Cass...if only you knew. If only I was capable of talking about that. But I'm not.

I forced myself to speak, to push past the emotions and stand in my truth. I closed my eyes and let the story pour out—a fiction, an imagining. "There's a spot, north of here, way up in the bush, where it's totally wild. About twenty miles from the nearest road or trail. Only way to get there is hiking, off-trail, and to know exactly where you're going. It's a favorite spot of mine. I have a little cabin out there. There's a river, and I like to fly fish on it. Sit and draw. Just breathe. But if you hike upstream from my cabin a few miles, there's a little waterfall. Nothing spectacular. Just this spot where there's a hill and a quick drop, maybe ten or twenty feet at the most. But it's a beautiful spot, that waterfall. Like something out of a painting. Trees around it, a little pool of swirling water. The fall roaring all the time. Birds like to flutter around, singing. If you sit somewhere real quiet and still, you might see a deer coming to take a drink, if you're lucky. It's a hidden place, tucked in against a fold in the hills, surrounded by thick forest. Trees muffle the sound if you're more than a few feet away, and after the falls, the stream is pretty quiet and slow and gentle. So you just wouldn't know the waterfall is there unless you know where to look."

I paused. I knew she was wondering what this had to do with my sketch of her.

"The way I saw it, the way I'd finish that drawing, is you're in the pool, near the waterfall. You're standing there, the water is shallow near where the fall hits the pool, so it barely comes up to mid-thigh. Gets deeper before the river continues on, but right near the fall, it'd only be about thigh-deep for you. You'd just be standing there, looking at me. The spray would be slowly making your skin wet, making your hair damp."

I couldn't help it. I snatched the pad from her, flipped to a new page, and started over. Sketched her, just an outline at first, no details, just the lines and curves of her body, her hand in her hair and one across her privates, a hint of eye detail just because her eyes mesmerized and hypnotized me, and I could just draw them a million times and never capture all the thoughts and emotions and virulent, passionate, fiery personality in her gaze. I got lost in it, in drawing her. Forgot she was there, almost. Just drew. The waterfall, trees around, big tall pines and spruce and fir. The pool, swirling and eddying. Her, in the water up to mid-thigh. A muddied hint of her reflection. The perspective was that I, the viewer, was a couple of feet away from her, watching her enter the water.

"You'd be about to jump in," I said, muttering half to myself. "About to get your hair wet, and you're—you're looking at me. Waiting for me to come in, too. To swim with you. That's the look in your eyes."

Silence, a fraught space between words. A world of unspoken things between us.

"When I first asked you if you this is how you see me," she said, "your response was that there's more than one way to take that. What did you mean?"

"It's how I see you—could be positive or negative. I drew you how I see you—beautiful, sensual, and… elegant, and you were wondering if that's how I see you because you don't see yourself that way. Or it could be, is *this* how I see you, as just an object, a body to be objectified. As…as a sexual object."

"You put that last part, you seeing me sexually, as a negative?"

"Well. Seeing you sexually ain't the same thing as seeing you as a sexual object."

She nodded. "I see the difference." A pause. "So, which was it for you?"

I sighed. "Neither, and both."

She snorted a laugh. "Gonna have to explain that one."

"It was a compulsion. I had to draw. There wasn't any kind of thought-out intention to it. But the thoughts I *did* have, the reason I had to draw, was because I was having…um. Thoughts. About you."

"What kind of thoughts?" she whispered.

"Thoughts of wanting to see more of you." I swallowed hard. "In more than one sense. See more of you, as in I like spending time with you, talking to you. But more of you in a literal sense. I'm not

judging, but appreciating, and admitting my own issues when I say that what you were wearing at the
laundromat did a number on me. Made my brain
go haywire." I licked my lips. "Turned me on. And I
know, I realize very clearly that you weren't dressing
to be provocative. Or to turn anyone on. Just for comfort. I just…I'm attracted to you, big time, so I guess
it just doesn't take much."

Once again, she chewed on the inside of her
cheek, thinking. "Ink, I…" trailing off, she looked into
my eyes, a million thoughts obvious and at war in her
gaze. "I don't even know where to start."

"Wherever you want. Say whatever is true."

"Whatever is true, hmmm?" She bit her lower
lip. "What if whatever is true is…risky? Dangerous?"

"Dangerous how?" I asked.

"Dangerous as in it could open a can of worms
I'm not sure either of us are quite ready for."

"I think I already opened that can, Cass. That
drawing opened it."

She nodded. "Yeah." A weighted pause. "I'm flat-
tered by the drawing. That's one thing that's true. I
don't see it as objectifying me. I see it as a tasteful,
artistic, and flattering depiction of me." She looked
at me. "It's also obvious in the way you drew me that
you see me…in a way I'm not sure anyone has ever
seen me. That you're attracted to me."

"You damn well better see yourself that way."

She laughed. "I have a healthy self-esteem, don't worry. That's not it. I'm fit, I'm good-looking, I'm comfortable in my skin and I love who I am. I know I'm a lot to handle. I have a big personality. I can be loud. I can be opinionated. I have a lot of energy, and a lot of thoughts, and no filter. No patience for bull-shit. I'm a physical person. I'm touchy. Most people aren't comfortable with how physical I am, even just with my friends." She glanced at me, away, then back to me. "I'm intensely sexual. I know what I want, and I know what I like. I don't hold back in that arena any more than I do any other aspect of my life. And for most people, that's just too much—*I* am just always too much. But the way you see me, as evidenced in that drawing…it's *sensual*. I've never identified as sen-sual. Sexual, yes. Sensuality is different."

I felt my gut drop out. "Funny how you said that—that you're too much for most people." I worked my jaw, hunting for the words. "That's me, to a T. But now package too much personality, too many quirks, too much physicality, and put it all in a six-foot-seven, three-hundred-pound frame. And cover that frame with tattoos. And a big beard and long hair. Way, way too much for most people."

"Ink—"

"You know, the average height for an Inuit male,

across the entire tribal subspecies of my people, not just my particular tribe, but all Inuit—is five-four, for a male. Trending slightly higher in recent generations, but that's still the average. We are not a tall race, as a whole." I patted my chest with a fist. "Makes me a giant. Even for white people, I'm huge. But for my people? I'm a freak. I don't have giantism or anything. I'm just a huge person. Some sort of weird freak of genetics or something."

She nodded. Slid closer to me, so our thighs touched. Looked up at me. "I think you're perfect."

I laughed. "That's subjective, I think."

"Well yeah. But you know, when I told my sister about you, she was like *what?* You're not my type."

I laughed. "No shit, Cass. I'm not anyone's type."

She frowned at me. "Not what I meant." She leaned closer. "I've always gone for the tall, lean, shredded, clean-cut pretty boy type."

I snorted, and then burst into laughter. "Well that sure as shit is about as opposite of me as you can fuckin' get."

"I know." Her eyes bored into me, silenced my laughter. "Wasn't expecting it, but somehow, there it is."

"There what is?"

"Me. Being attracted to you."

"You are?" I blinked, stunned. "Why?"

"Just...you. Who you are. And it's not just your personality, like, making up for your looks or some bullshit like that. I am physically attracted to you even though you're the polar opposite of every guy I've ever dated, slept with, or been attracted to. Complete opposite. And maybe that's part of it. Those guys have mostly all treated me like shit. You treat me like..." She swallowed hard. "Like you really like who I am."

"Because I do."

She reached out, withdrew the drawing pad from my hands, the pencil, and set them on the coffee table. She held my hand, my huge paw in both of hers. "Why did you seem so surprised that I like you? That I'm attracted to you?"

"I don't know."

"Bullshit. You're a good-looking guy, Ink. You just are. I know not everyone likes tattoos and beards and all that, but you're just a handsome man." She smiled. "Just like not everyone likes tiny athletic girls with no boobs and no butt."

"You have boobs and a butt."

"Well, yes, I *have* them, but they're just small."

"Exactly perfect."

"Am I your type, Ink?"

I shook my head. "Don't have a type."

"You don't." She sounded disbelieving. "You've had girlfriends, yes?"

I bobbed my head to one side. "Sort of, but yes."

"And what did they look like?"

"One, my very first girlfriend, was Yu'Pik, like me. So short, dark hair, kinda curvy I guess." I sighed. "My first and only *serious* girlfriend, as in a real, lasting long-term relationship, was interracial. Her mom was Vietnamese, and her dad was African."

"I bet she's beautiful."

"She is."

She waited. "And?"

I shrugged. "And that's it."

"You've dated two girls your whole life?"

I nodded. "So I don't think that's enough to say I have a type."

"Well, you're still a guy. So when you go, 'hey, that girl is hot,' what do they usually look like?"

"Why does it matter?"

"It doesn't. I'm just curious."

How the hell was I supposed to tell her I'd been so hurt, so damaged by trauma, so viciously rejected and shamed that I turned off my sexuality?

I stood up. Paced away, stood facing the wall, hands braced wide on the wall… Fought for some kind of explanation that wouldn't leave me totally emotionally naked.

"Ink…what? What aren't you saying?"

I shook my head. "A fuckin' lot, Cass."

"So say it."

"It's a lot, and it's old, and I don't know how to fuckin' say it. Never told anyone about it."

She stood up and moved to slide between me and the wall, gazed up at me. "Secret pain."

I nodded. "Yeah. That shit sucks."

"So let's trade. I've got secret pain, you've got secret pain. Let's trade."

"Why?" I asked. "Why you wanna know?"

"Because I like you. I want to know more about you." She leaned her back to the wall, framed in by my arms and my body. Stared up at me, eyes wide and deep as the universe, drawing me in, closer and closer. "We can make a game of it. Secret for secret."

"I don't know."

"I'll start." She ran a hand through her hair, drew it over her shoulder. "Not a secret, since I talked to my sister about it, but I just found this out and it's as good a place to start as any. I just found out that my fiancé is gay, and was cheating on me with men during our entire relationship."

"Whoa."

"Yeah." A shrug. "Your turn."

"My parents couldn't afford to feed me when I was a kid. As a teenager, thirteen, fourteen, fifteen, I ate so much it was impossible for them to afford the amount of food I needed. I joined the football team just because the other parents would feed me. I was popular on the team because I was the star lineman on the offense and defense. I was big, but I could move. So the guys let me hang out with them so I'd stay on the team and help them win. It worked for me because the other guys' families could afford shit. I played all the way through high school just so I could eat."

"Wow. I can't imagine how much food a six-foot-seven teenager must eat."

"Well, I didn't reach my full height till I was like eighteen. I was six-four freshman year, six-six by senior year, and topped out at six-seven when I was nineteen. But yeah, you really don't even know how much food I'd eat. They'd order pizzas, like a dozen of them for the team, and I'd eat three by myself, and that was holding back to not be too greedy."

"Three large pizzas, just you?"

"Breakfast, lunch, dinner, snacks required a lot of food." I shrugged. "Of course, while I was active and athletic I was eating a lot and working out like crazy, but after I graduated and quit playing ball, I got fat as hell because I kept eating like that but stopped the intense exercise."

"You obviously figured that out."

I frowned. "Obviously?" I patted my stomach. "Ain't exactly rockin' an eight pack here." I poked her stomach, which was a clearly defined, even at rest, eight-pack, vascular and striated. "Not like this."

She looked at my stomach, explored my torso from chest to sides to waistband. "You're strong, Ink. Really, really strong. There are many, many different kinds of healthy, different kinds of bodies. Having ultra-low body fat percentage isn't the only kind of healthy and attractive there is."

"But that's your type. You said so."

She sighed. "Yeah, and maybe I was an idiot." She touched her own stomach. "This is the result of a lifetime of dedication and sacrifice. Hours and hours and hours of work, every day, to achieve and maintain this, because it's what I had to be. How I *had* to look to be lead dancer. Visually, as well as in terms of ability. It was functionally necessary to be like this." She frowned. "It's not necessary anymore, and I'm not sure how much longer I'm going to look like this. For one thing, I can't work out, and for two, I've been eating like shit. So you can say goodbye to this in the next few weeks."

She hesitated, and then reached out once more, this time running her hands up my chest to my shoulders, letting her hands rest there.

"So…" she said, as she looked up at me, as if perhaps to gauge the effect of her hands on my shoulders. "Body image."

"It wasn't really image, for me. It was…just the absence of food. The lack. Being too poor to literally afford to stay alive, just because I was so fuckin' giant. Made me feel like…like a burden."

Her face crumpled in pain. "Aww, god, Ink. That's awful."

"It was a fact. I was a burden to them." I felt my fists clench. "They're not bad people, my parents. They did the best they could. Loved me, in a parental sort of way. But they never understood me. I was never…what they expected. What they wanted. I mean, I liked being outside, hunting, hiking, fishing. But I wasn't…like them. They made ends meet all right, but when I started really skyrocketing in size around puberty, they couldn't afford me. I was a burden on 'em, and I knew it. I was on my own by fifteen, for all intents and purposes. Slept at their house, but I was fending for myself."

She sighed. "Wow, Ink. That's rough."

"But that's just background. That ain't a secret." I focused on her face rather than the feel of her hands— if I thought about that, I'd take her in my hands and this conversation would be over. "Only shit that's left to tell is the really heavy stuff."

"Same."

I closed my eyes. "Elizabeth Grace was from my neighborhood, my school. My family is…really traditional. Holding on to the old ways as much as possible. Hers was…not. She looked like me, but acted like them. And it was an us and them mentality, where I grew up. But she was pretty, and seemed to like me. We would hang out after school. Walk home together. Have lunch together. Do our homework in the library. Get a burger on the weekends. Wasn't much beyond that—we were just kids, fifteen, sixteen. Young. I just liked her. Liked that she talked to me, didn't seem to be scared of me." Glanced down at her. "You scared of me, Cass?"

She shook her head slowly. "No. I was a little intimidated by how big you are, at first, but not anymore."

"Right. Well back then, kids acted like I was an ogre or something. Like I'd eat 'em if they looked at me wrong. I already had tattoos then, you know. Not as many obviously, but I'd been marking myself my whole life, and I was working with Thomas by then and had some pieces I'd done on myself, and that he'd done on me. So there was that, too. Elizabeth Grace didn't seem to mind."

"You say her whole name all the time?"

I nodded. "Yep. That's how she introduced herself. Elizabeth Grace. Anyway." I fought the memories. "One time she invited me over. I wore a shirt to cover my ink. Tried to seem…smaller. Used my best manners. But her parents…"

"Didn't accept you."

I shook my head. "Nope. And she went along with it. She was only fifteen, so I got it then and I get it now. But she stopped talking to me entirely. Switched her classes so we didn't have any together. Somehow—don't know if it was her or someone else—but a rumor got started that I'd tried to force her." I swallowed hard. "My team knew I wouldn't do that, but the rest of the school believed it, and treated me like I was...I don't know. Like I was evil. Like I'd done it. The whole community believed it. Parents included. People whispered about me." I forced myself to release my fists. "We never even held hands. I was too chicken to try. Too scared that my giant fuckin' hands would like accidentally crush hers or something. I was a fuckin' virgin being accused of trying to force a girl to be with me. People whispered about it, the R-word. Can't even say it. Said I did that to her, and I'd never even had the courage to hold her damn hand."

"Jesus." Her eyes were so soft, so understanding, so filled with pain for me. "Anyone who took six seconds to get to know you would know you could never do anything like that."

"Yeah, well, I was six-five, two hundred and fifty pounds in tenth grade, with tattoos and facial hair. People were scared of me." I kept her eyes. Held them, tried to be open, to let her see how much hurt there was in that story. "Your turn."

"My dad is complicated. He lived with us, and he was around. He wasn't a drinker. Didn't hit us. None of that. From the outside, we would have seemed like an idyllic family. Mom, dad, five girls, nice house, plenty of everything. And in a lot of ways, it was. When we were young, Dad was great. Loved us. Took us out for things. Spent time with us. But as we got older, he just…changed. I still don't know why. I'm not sure even Mom does, but I know it affected her, too. It affected all of us. So it's hard for me to pinpoint what it was that left the psychological and emotional scars on me, but they're there and they're real. He stopped paying attention to us. To me. Was at work all the time. Didn't really talk to us when he was home. Seemed like…like he'd given up on life. When I needed my dad the most was when he just sort of vanished from our lives, even though he was physically around. So I just…I don't know. It put me into dance. Made me seek the approval and validation I craved in the audience. The judges. The coaches. The peers. If I could be the best dancer, they would love me. Getting into Julliard was me seeking that validation. Getting into the European dance troupe was validation. Making lead dancer was validation. Evening dating Rick was validation in a way because he was…

he represented…" she paused, eyes dropping. "I don't know. He was upper crust. Sophisticated. Aristocracy, basically, and I think on his dad's side his family does actually go way back to real French aristocracy sort of lineage. I thought it would make me the person people wanted."

I wanted to comfort her, to take away the pain. "You've put some thought into this, haven't you?"

She nodded, laughing quietly, sliding a hand through her hair. "Yeah, I guess so. When you're stuck in a hospital and then in PT, there's not much to really think about or do, so I tried to figure out some things about myself." She blinked up at me. "Your turn," she whispered.

"This game is gettin' awful deep, Cass."

"Yeah, I guess it is."

"What're you after?" I asked. "What is it you really want to know about me?"

She shrugged, but her eyes told me the shrug was more of a delay than an *I don't know.* She straightened, gazing up at me. "Are you attracted to me?"

I laughed. "What kinda question is that?" I reached up one hand, brushed the tip of just my middle finger across her temple, ever so gently, tucked her hair behind the delicate shell of her ear. "You know I am."

She touched a tattoo just above my hipbone—a

small piece showing a crow digging a worm out of the soil—and traced it, up my side. "No, I mean...I know you think I'm attractive. But...are you *attracted* to me, physically?"

I took a tendril of hair between my fingertips, wrapped it around my index finger. "Yeah."

"Meaning, more than just thinking I'm pretty. You want to...do things. With me."

I nodded. "Thought I'd made that clear."

She shook her head. "See, I'm a little confused by you."

My eyes followed the exposed line of her clavicle, to her breastbone, across to her other shoulder. Her skin was delicate and soft and warm. "Confused by what?"

"You're sending me mixed signals. Right now, you're *almost* touching me. I feel like you've *almost* kissed me. Like you want you. But you never do. And I'm just confused. Wondering...why you keep pulling back. Shutting down when things get heated physically."

"Cassie, I..." I sighed. "It's hard to explain."

She ran both hands up my chest. "Try? Please?"

I closed my eyes, feeling her hands on my skin and wanting so badly to feel that touch everywhere. Running south, exploring more of me. My fingertips, three of them, dared across her breastbone again, and this time I tested her by letting my fingers slip just a little further down, closer to her cleavage; I opened my eyes, watched her face and expression as I gloried in the satin of her skin as I dragged my fingertips over the swell of her breasts, one and then the other.

"When I say it's hard to explain, I don't mean complicated. I mean it's…hard as fuck to talk about."

"Would it help if I told you I'm attracted to you? That if you kissed me, I'd kiss you back?"

I met her eyes. "Cass…" I turned away. Had to. I raked my hand over my scalp, tore my hair free of the ponytail and shook it out—prepared to retie it, but Cassie's hands stopped me.

"I like it down," she said, moving around to stand in front of me once more. "Talk to me, Ink. You can trust me."

Fuck.

My brain was exploding. My body was on fire.

I was about to kiss her stupid. Pick her up and set her on the counter and kiss every inch of her body and not stop until I'd marked her. The primal, wild, demanding, testosterone-fueled sexuality I'd kept bottled up for so damned long was boiling up and about to spill out into an uncontrollable wildfire.

And that scared the shit out of me.

I couldn't hide that fear in my eyes; couldn't hide the fear of that need any more than I could hide the need itself raging through me—need for everything this woman had me hard as a rock, rigid inside my shorts, aching and burning and pulsing with need.

I pushed past her and stepped outside. I went around back, into the woods, barefoot. The air was cool on my overheated skin. Moonlight shone silver from a cloudless night sky washed by a countless million stars. I had a little spot, out here, a tiny clearing in the woods behind the shop and my house where I could lie down in the grass and watch the stars wheel overhead. I went there enough that I'd made a little path to it, lined with a few solar-powered tiki torch-like lamps. I sat down in the middle of the clearing and tried to clear my head.

She wanted me to kiss her?

She was attracted to me?

My brain couldn't quite fathom it. It didn't seem real, or possible, but there was no mistaking the look in her eyes, the body language which said in no uncertain terms *here I am, for you, touch me.*

I just couldn't believe it.

And I couldn't let myself have it. Have her.

Couldn't let that beast out of its cage. Look what happened last time, after all.

I forced that memory away before it took over. I knew that's what Cassie was angling at, but I just simply could not talk about it.

I felt her presence before I saw or heard her. Just knew she was here.

She sat down next to me, cross-legged in the tickling grass. Stared up at the moon. "Beautiful here, isn't it?"

I nodded. Tugged the right leg of my shorts up, showed her the tattoo covering most of my right thigh—a drawing of this spot. If you lay down on your back right around eleven, just before midnight, you'd see the moon pass over the clearing. The tattoo on my thigh was of the ring of trees overhead seen as you're lying down, with the full moon right overhead.

She looked at the tattoo, then up at the sky, where the full moon shone bright. "Wow. Just… wow." She looked at me, then. "This is your happy place, huh?"

"I dunno about happy place, but it's where I come when I need to find some clarity and some peace."

Her fingers traced the tattoo on my thigh, as if she could feel the ink. After a moment, her hand just rested on my thigh, and I did my best to ignore that sensation, the thrill of it, the ache of it, the desire raging inside me to feel her hand slide upward, upward, closer to my aching erection.

"Clarity and peace about what?" Her voice was

quiet, a whisper—suitably, to me; I am not a religious person, but I do have a spiritual sense of connection to nature, and this particular place has always felt sacred to me.

"Just…life. When things hurt, or are confusing."

"So why are you here now, Ink? What's confusing or painful for you?" Her eyes stayed on me, even though I was gazing up at the stars.

I sighed. "You. This. Me. Us."

"Why?"

"Because…" I groaned. Flopped to my back. "You ask hard-ass questions, Cass."

"I just…" She lay beside me, close, rolled to face me, eyes bright in the moonlit night. "You obviously want me, want *this*. But you keep pulling away from it, when I thought I was being pretty clear that I want it as much as you do."

I nodded. "It's not a matter of mixed signals from you. It's all me."

"Exactly. And that's what I want to understand."

"Why?"

A pause. "Because…" another hesitation. "Because I really like you. I don't know what that means, or what it is, or what it could be. I don't know what to do with it. I just know I want you." A choked sigh. "And I want to know you want me. I want—"

I turned to look at her. Saw moisture in her eyes. Pain in her features.

"I want to feel wanted. I want to be desired."

"Fuck, Cass. Ain't that obvious?"

She shook her head. "Seeing it in your eyes, that's one thing. Seeing it…" She rested a hand on my thigh, her meaning clear. "That's obvious. But seeing it isn't the same as *feeling* it."

"Fuck," I groaned. "Fine." I reached out an arm, and she lifted, scooted closer to me, tucking herself into the cradle of my arm, resting her head on my bicep. "Ain't a pretty story."

"Are they ever?"

I snorted, shrugged. "Nah, guess not."

She gazed at me. God, those eyes. So soft, so warm. Inviting me to trust her. "No judgment, Ink. No pity. Just…compassion and understanding, okay?"

I let out another long sigh. "Okay."

SIX

Cassie

H E WAS…CUDDLY. SEEMED LIKE A SILLY, CUTESY WORD for such a huge, strong, masculine man. But it was the only word that really fit. He had just enough padding over his muscles to be cushiony under my cheek, yet it was obvious as he wrapped a massively thick arm over my waist that the layer of fat was minimal and that he was enormously strong. A perfect combination, if you asked me. I wouldn't have thought so even a few weeks ago, but now it seemed like the most obvious thing in the world.

Cuddling with Rick never lasted long—for him because I realized now that he really didn't care about me all that much, and for me because he just wasn't comfortable to lay on, being all lean, compact, hard muscle and bone.

Lying here with my head on Ink's chest, and his bicep behind my neck, his hand on my waist just above my hip, I felt utterly safe, totally comfortable. I could fall asleep here like this. I wouldn't even need a blanket, because he just absolutely radiated heat.

Then, his voice began rumbling, a low murmur that rattled my bones with the deep, bass power of it; if a mountain had a voice, it would be his. "Elise Achebe. Moved here from New York. She was a swimsuit model, fashion photographer, tattoo blogger, and Suicide Girl." He paused, a long, cavernous silence. "Absolutely gorgeous. She came here to get away from everything, from the whole New York scene. She'd always had this cult following in the modeling and fashion industry, but then she created her own website and put up Suicide Girl-type photos of herself, and people just sort of lost their shit. Got judgmental and nasty. She lost some sponsors, got some hate mail and death threats, stalkers, just lots of ugly shit."

"By Suicide Girl, you mean...?" I had an idea, but wanted to clarify.

"Well, it's a specific thing. A movement, a community. They do pinup-type photography of themselves in varying degrees of explicitness, but it's all girls with tattoos and piercings and unusual hair color, stuff like that. She was a photographer for an agency that specialized in that type of thing, mainly for tattoo magazines and things like that. She was really out there, really bold and just liked to put it all out, wasn't ashamed of anything." He hesitated, glanced at me. "So, quick aside. How real you want this story?"

"The realest."

"Sure?"

"Yes, Ink, I'm sure. Don't hold anything back."

A sigh. "All right." A moment of silence as he picked up his train of thought. "She came to me for a tattoo. She'd heard of me, of my growing rep for traditional threading and stick-and-poke style tats, and she wanted one." He tapped his chest. "She wanted it, um. Here. On her chest. Super intricate design centered around each of her nipples and areolae. Several sessions, obviously private, and it required a lot of… uh, handling, I guess, of her boobs. I'm a professional tattoo artist, so I've done stuff in sensitive places before, but nothing even remotely that personal, before or since. Because even with a gun, it's different. Threadwork is…slower. More painful. Just…different, in a lot of ways."

"And one thing led to another?" I guessed.

He rumbled a wordless affirmative. "Not right away. She stuck around Ketchikan for a while, and we'd hang out now and then. She'd come by for a new piece, always threading, and it just became a thing." A long pause. "Emotionally, it became a thing, at least. She wanted more, and so did I. Meaning, the physical aspect. But after what had happened with Elizabeth Grace, I was sort of gun-shy when it came to women. Went out on a few daters, but nothing really…stuck. So, I was twenty, well established as a tattoo artist already and getting a rep for traditional work. And I was a virgin." He swallowed hard after the last word. Breathed into the silence, gathering what seemed to me like the courage to keep talking. "Told her as much, and she was just…I dunno. Weirded out, I guess. But a little excited, too, oddly. I mean, she was a little older, like four years or so. More experienced, obviously. Been on her own since she was seventeen, super independent, liberated and all that. Sexually, I mean. Like she just…I dunno. Not important to my part of the story."

"My sister Lexie is like that. Does what she wants, and if you try to slut-shame her for being bold about what she wants and how much she wants it, she'll tear you apart. So I get it. I'm not like that, or not nearly as much."

He nodded. "But a little bit?" he asked, glancing down at me.

I shrugged. "I'm pretty upfront about it, and I'm not concerned with what people think. The only person whose opinion ever matters to me is that of the person who I'm with, and even then, I'm not going to apologize for who I am or what I do with my body."

"Good. How it should be."

I peered at him. "You think so for real, or are you just saying that?"

He narrowed his eyes at me. "I never just say anything, Cass. I say it, I mean it."

"Okay." I met his eyes. "So if I told you that even though Rick was my only truly serious relationship, but I've had quite a bit of casual sex…"

He held my gaze, his eyes unwavering and honest. "What you do with your body is your business. Even if we were in a relationship, that would remain true. And what you did before you met me is part of you, part of your journey to being who you are. I like who you are. I ain't scared of, or threatened by, or jealous of what you've done before we met."

I melted, just a little bit more. "You really mean that?"

"Course," he rumbled. "Just plain old bein' a good person, is all. Ain't nobody gonna say boo to me if I was to have had a hundred or a thousand girlfriends or hookups or whatever. But when a girl does the same, somehow it's slutty. If it's slutty for a girl, it's slutty for a guy, plain and simple. And for either one—their body, their choice."

"You going to ask me the number?" I asked.

He shook his head. "You wanna tell me, I wanna know. It ain't important."

"So you're not a jealous person, then?"

He lifted his shoulder. "Not about the past, no. Not really into sharing or open relationships, though."

"Me either." I let the silence flow a minute, two. He seemed inclined to stay quiet, so I prompted him. "So. Elise?"

He growled. "We dated for three months before anything happened. Then, she started things. Started slow. Got me used to doing things to her, her to me." A heavy pause. "It was amazing. She was real nice, real gentle. Real patient."

"Good. Glad your first experience was nice."

He hummed. "Well. The lead up was nice. Just touching each other, I guess. Sexual, not sex. She spent a lot of time really teaching me to understand her, what she liked. How to know if she liked it. How to make her feel good. Told me that by taking the time to really help me understand her, and thus most women, and how to make her feel good, she was doing a service to whoever else I may end up with in the future."

My stomach flipped. "So. You're...uhh. Good at, like, foreplay?"

He rolled a shoulder. "Dunno what you want to

call it. Not really sure I want to go into graphic detail for your sake or mine, but she told me, and swore on her ancestors and her tattoos and her camera—all the things she held most sacred—that I was better than anyone she'd ever been with at making her... you know. Feel good. Get there, you know. Quick, or slow."

I swallowed, face heating, core tightening. "Wow. And you said she was pretty experienced?"

He nodded again. "Yeah. She knew what she was doing."

I licked my lips, pressed my thighs together. Swallowed hard. "Very interesting."

"What?" He must've caught the tightness in my voice, even in the whisper.

I shook my head. "Nothing."

"Don't nothin' me, Cass."

I stared up at him. "Fine, then. You want to know what I'm thinking?"

"Yeah, I do."

"I'm thinking that I'm really, really...*interested*... to experience for myself what you're...capable of." I pressed against him, so my breasts were crushed against his chest.

He gazed down at me. Eyes were deep and wild and inscrutable, and I felt him breathing hard, deep. "Best listen to the rest before you decide that."

"Did you rape her?"

He flinched as if struck. "What? Fuck no!"

"Did you beat her up?"

"No, Cassie, I did not." His voice was angry and tight.

"Did you intentionally physically, mentally, or emotionally abuse her or hurt her?"

"No." A pause. "She got hurt, but it was an accident." His voice was so tight it sounded close to snapping.

"Hurt how?" I shook my head. "Wait a minute, though. My point in asking is that is the only reason I'd be hesitant about anything with you...if you'd intentionally, out of malice or cruelty, hurt her."

"I didn't."

I snuggled closer. "Then no matter what happened, I'm not afraid of you. Or your past."

He sighed, deeply, painfully. "Like I said, you'd best hear me out."

"Okay, continue."

"We, uh. We messed around like that, what she called teaching me, for a while. Few weeks, a month or two maybe. I think finally her patience with waiting for actual sex wore out, and she decided it was time. But she told me she wanted to take a backseat from then on, in terms of who was in charge, was how she put it. In charge. Meaning, she didn't want to be...the aggressor, I guess. Starting things. She wanted me to do that."

I nodded. "I get that."

"Okay. Well. She said she wanted us to move to the next step. But when I was ready. And that when I was ready, I should lead the way." He sighed, swallowed hard. "I was nervous, I guess. I waited, thought about it. Made sure I was ready. I mean, I hadn't been, like, waiting for a specific reason, you know? Like, I wasn't saving myself for marriage. I just was...scared of getting hurt again. Rejected. Elise had made it pretty obvious she wasn't going to reject me, so I felt comfortable going for it."

A long, long pause.

"Obviously, we'd done plenty together, up to that point. So she knew...me. What I was like. What I looked like." He sounded...embarrassed, or something like it. "I ain't a small guy, not in any way. Okay? And she was well aware of this. Seemed to be pretty appreciative of it, if you know what I mean."

I bit my lip, laughed silently. "Yes, Ink, I can imagine." I threaded my fingers into his beard. "Nothing about you is small, so I can...well...imagine, that you're just as...big...in other ways." I buried my face in his chest. "I have to admit, I've thought about that."

He stared at me. "You have?"

I let my palm rest on his chest, and then drift to

his stomach. "I've thought about it quite a bit, lately especially." Swallowed my own nerves. "Thought about when I'm alone, and…worked up."

He let out a slow, controlled breath. "Dammit, Cass."

"What?" I asked, endeavoring to sound innocent, even as I laughed under my breath.

"Making it hard to think."

"Maybe you don't need to think."

He closed his eyes, breathing evenly, as if tightly controlling himself—his hand was gripping my waist, fingers dimpling my skin between shirt and pants. "Cass…you don't know what you're asking."

"Thus the story of Elise, I take it."

He nodded.

"You accidentally hurt her? Like, she wasn't ready for…um. All of you?"

He shrugged. "I…no. But there's more to it than that. Up until that point, she'd been encouraging me to just be open and honest with her about everything. What I was feeling, what I wanted, what I liked. To not hold back."

"Good advice."

"Thought so myself. Still do, but…what happened was a different story." He sighed. "No way to tell this without getting a little graphic."

"Doesn't bother me, Ink. Just the story."

"It was a few days after we talked about being ready to go all the way. Big deal for me, obviously not so much for her, but she said it was because she'd never been anyone's first before."

"I imagine being someone's first would be a pretty big deal."

"She seemed to think so." A pause, thoughts and memories obvious in his eyes.

"Tell me, Ink."

"We were at my place—a little loft over the shop—office space now, but it was where I lived then, before I built the tiny home out back. I started things, you know. Kissing and stuff. She knew what it was, and things just sort of progressed pretty normally. Remember, up until then, it'd just been hands and mouths between us. Exploration, experimentation. Kid stuff, to her, but all new to me." Thoughts, silences. "Worth pointing out, too, that I've always been way, way bigger than everyone else. Stronger. Even in football, I held back, except during games, and even in games I'd hold back. Scared of letting myself go, totally. Scared of hurting people."

I touched his cheek. "You're a gentle person, Ink. Just who you are."

"So holding back has been the defining feature of my life. Hold back physically, don't take up so much space. Don't be loud—don't draw any more attention to myself than my size and appearance already do. Getting bullied and made fun of and shunned like I was my whole life like I was will do that you. Teach you to be smaller, quieter. Less."

My heart cracked for him. "Oh god, Ink. That's totally wrong. You should be *you*, all the way. Be as *more* as you can be, and fuck whatever anyone else thinks."

"That ain't so easy when you're a kid."

I sighed. "No, indeed."

"So. Me, used to holding back. Her, telling me not to. Me, wanting to believe her. Wanting to be able to, just once, let go, even a little bit."

I felt the shape of what was coming, and it hurt to think of.

"She was into it. I was doin' everything she'd taught me to make her feel good. It was gettin'… rowdy. Not sure how else to put it. Aggressive. Not mean, not violent. Just…rowdy."

I grinned against his chest. "I know what you mean." I felt my cheeks heat. "That's how I like it best."

He growled. "Shit, shit, shit." A long hard tense fraught pause. "God, okay. So."

"What happened, Ink?"

"I lost control."

"That's what she wanted."

"Yeah." His voice was low, vibrating on nearly inaudible frequency. "She'd told me to let go, to not hold back. So that's what I did. I let go. I just...let go. Threw control and caution to the four winds."

"Good for you."

"No, it wasn't." He sounded...angry. "I was... with her. Holding her. Um...you know, on her hands and knees, facing away from me."

"Doggy style."

"Yeah." Pause. "Just...rough. Not trying to hurt her. She was makin' sounds like she liked it. Wasn't telling me to stop, wasn't...nothing. But then she pulled away, like scrambled away. I thought at first she was going for a different position. So I grabbed her. Picked her up, flipped her to her back. Before, she'd kinda liked it when I tossed her around a little. She had curves on her, so she liked feeling light, I guess." Another pause filled with harsh breath, halting, pained words falling out. "Took her like that, thinking it was what she wanted. Or, truthfully, not really thinking. Just feeling. Just...taking. She was...crying. Sobbing. Slapped me. Kicked me, hard. Scrambled to her knees, off the bed."

"Oh god."

"I'd really, really hurt her. Too rough. Too much."

"She never said anything? Never told you it hurt, never sounded like she was in pain?"

He shook his head. It may have been a trick of the moonlight, but it seemed like there were tears on his cheeks. "She was limping. Crying. She didn't say a word to me. Just dressed, wouldn't let me near her. Left. Never came back. Left all of her stuff—clothes, money, books. Everything but her purse and camera bag. Left. Never saw her again. Found a PO Box in her name, a few weeks later, and sent her stuff to her."

"Ink—"

"There ain't' no excuse for what I done." He swallowed. "I just lost control, and I hurt her."

"You didn't—you couldn't have known. She never told you to stop or to be a little more gentle. She told you to not hold back."

"She told me she knew I wouldn't hurt her, so don't worry."

"And then you hurt her, and she…" I shrugged. "Reacted unkindly."

"Reacted like anyone would being hurt by their sexual partner."

"No." I touched his jaw. "No, Ink. I've had partners get a little too rough before, and it's a matter of just asking him to be a little more gentle. And really, the guys who have done that were selfish assholes to begin with, and not thinking of me in the first place." I held his eyes, but he didn't want to look at me. "Ink, look at me. Listen. If a woman is excited, if she's

really enjoying it, if her body is ready, she can take…
well, a lot more than you might think."

"You weren't there—"

"Obviously not. But you want to know what I
think?"

He nodded. "Yeah, I do."

"I think she got scared. I think you're more than
she was expecting. Physically, and just who you are.
I think when you really let go, like she thought she
wanted, it was scary for her. She wasn't ready for
it. Didn't know what she was asking for. I think she
faked how bad she was hurt to make it your fault so
she wouldn't have to feel bad."

He tilted his head to one side. "Maybe."

"Think about it."

"I am." He nodded. "I was…loud. Wild. I mean,
I wasn't…uh. I wasn't, like, pounding super hard. You
know? Like, I wasn't so lost in things that I wasn't
aware of how much force I was using."

"You would never hurt anyone. Even letting go,
you wouldn't."

His eyes flicked to mine. "You think so?"

"I know so. Down to my bones."

"You barely know me."

"I know you better than you think." I swallowed.
"We may not have known each other a long time, Ink,
but the time we've spent together has been…intense.

Personal. Real. Quality counts for as much as length of time, if you ask me."

"I hurt her, Cass. No way around it."

I shook my head. "I think she twisted things to hurt you because she was scared. And then she ghosted because she was ashamed."

"Cass—"

"No. I don't buy it."

"I'm telling you the truth."

I moved up so my face was closer to his. "I know you are, Ink. I'm not questioning *you*, I'm questioning her." I rested my head on his chest. "So after she left, you…what?"

He sighed. Stared up at the sky again. "Shut down. I was so upset, so angry at myself, so ashamed, so…rejected, in a way, that I just…shut down. Put the part of me that had anything to do with women, with sex, dating, all of it, put it all in a box, locked it up inside me, and never opened it again."

"Oh, Ink." My cracked heart broke for him. "Ever since?"

He nodded. "Couldn't handle the thought of hurting anyone else. And the way she left, it was rejection. Worse than Elizabeth Grace. Compounded on it. She had told me she wanted everything I had to give, and all I ended up doing was hurting her so bad she left most of her belongings behind. How do you come back from that? After everything else I had been through in life, that was the last straw. I shut it down. Focused on tats."

"You never dated again? Never did anything with anyone again?"

He shook his head.

"It's been years, Ink."

He nodded. "Yeah."

I waited, but he didn't seem inclined to fill the silence. "Maybe it's none of my business, but when you say you shut down everything to do with sex, does that include…things on your own?" Why was I tiptoeing around it? "Meaning, you stopped masturbating, too?"

He just nodded. "Everything. Just shut it down. Cut it out of my life." He glanced down at me. "And then I met you."

I bit my lip. "And something about me woke it up, huh?"

He let out a slow breath. "Yeah. Hell if I know what." A laugh. "No, I do. It's that I've never been as attracted to anyone the way I am to you. Physically, but also just who you are. I dunno."

"But you're still…"

"Keeping that part of my life shut down is automatic now. Habit. Ingrained. And the fear and the self-hate that comes with it, it's as strong as it's ever been." His brow furrowed. "You're strong, Cass. But you're tiny."

"And you're even more afraid of hurting me, because I'm short."

"Not just short." He wrapped his hands around my waist. "I can touch my thumbs and middle fingers around your waist."

"You have the biggest hands I've ever seen, by several orders of magnitude." I put my hands on his, keeping them in place on my waist. "But yes, I'm a small person."

"I know you're strong. I can see exactly how strong you are. Physically, sure, but mentally, and emotionally, too. You're strong. I'm not at all doubting you."

"You just don't trust yourself."

He shook his head. "Not at fuckin' all, babe…"

He hadn't engaged in any kind of sexual or romantic activity of any kind, for *years*.

Fear of rejection cuts deep; memory of rejection cuts deeper yet. And clearly, the fear of being hurt is as powerful as rejection, but the memory of having hurt someone is more powerful than just about anything.

I wanted to take it away. Make him feel better. Restore his ability to trust, both himself and others.

To trust me.

To trust himself with me.

Where do I even start?

He was looking at me sideways. "I know that look."

I snorted. "What look?"

He tapped the tip of my nose. "The one you got on right now, Little Sparrow. It's a look that says you wanna try and fix me."

I just smiled at him. "I don't think 'fix you' is the right way to put it. You're not broken."

He frowned. "Feels like I am." He lifted up to lean on one elbow, gazing down at me. "Here I am, got a gorgeous, talented, smart, sexy woman interested in me, wanting me. Can't bring myself to do shit all about it, even though I feel like I'm fuckin' dyin' for wanting you. I just don't know how to get past my fuckin' damage. How to let go of the…the vise grip my shit has on me. I want to, Cass. So fuckin' bad, I want to let go and just be with you. But I don't know how."

"I don't want to push you into anything you're not ready for, either." I sat up, and shifted to sit on his lap, wrapping my legs around his waist, resting my arms on his shoulders, toying with his long fall of thick black hair. "But I guess I just wonder if…" I trailed off, not sure how to say it.

He tilted his head to one side; he brushed an index finger through my hair, over my temple and behind my ear, then down my jawline to my chin. "Wonder what, Cass?"

"If maybe you and me could…sort of ease

into things, somehow." I dragged my fingers down through his beard. Tugged on it. "As I see it, your hold up is two different but related things. One, you've been rejected so harshly and in so many different ways, you don't trust me to not hurt you and reject you—deep down, you're afraid of that happening. Part of you worries it's inevitable, that I'm just going to do that, somehow, at some point."

"Cass, I don't—"

I touched his lips. "I'm not offended by it. Your life has forced you to put that up as a defense. I get it. I have issues like that myself. This thing with you is a lot, and it scares me. I don't know what the fuck I'm doing with you any more than you do. I just know I like who you are, I'm attracted to you physically, and I want you. I want how I believe you can make me feel—physically, at least, if nothing else."

"You got more balls than I do, then."

I shook my head. "No. I'm afraid of getting hurt. But I'm already hurt, Ink. Rick hurt me, bad. The accident fucked me up. My dad fucked me up. Life fucked me up. But I'm more afraid of getting stuck than I am getting hurt. I'd rather go through life hurt and broken than stuck in place forever because I'm too scared to move forward."

He winced, brow lowering. "Shit, Cass. That's pretty fuckin' harsh."

I covered my mouth, aghast. "God, Ink, no—I'm sorry. I'm so sorry. I didn't mean that as anything about you. I swear I didn't. I was just talking about me. That's been my philosophy my whole life. Guys have hurt me before, and I just refuse to let it shackle me to the past, to the hurt. I guess I liken it to dance, to performing. I've twisted my ankle in rehearsal and I just refused to sit out the performance. I performed an entire week-end's worth of shows with a badly twisted ankle and broken pinky toe, because I just fucking *refuse* to sit out, to let pain stop me. I won't do. Not on the stage, and not in life." I stroked his beard, from cheekbone to chin, down through the long silky mass. "I didn't mean it as a criticism of you, I promise I didn't."

"But that's what I've done, ain't it? Let it stop me. Let it hold me back. Let it keep me down. Been stuck."

"You've been through things I can't imagine, Ink. Don't judge yourself."

"Kinda hard not to." He sighed. "You're somethin' else, you know that?"

I just laughed. "So I've been told." I toyed with his beard some more. "So, being afraid of rejection, that's the first part. The second part that's got you all knotted up and locked down, as I see it, is that you don't trust yourself. You said so. You're afraid you'll lose control again and hurt me."

He nodded. "Terrified of it." He closed his eyes,

pain written on his face in every line. "You shoulda seen her face, Cass. Pain. Fear. Not just fear, outright terror. Like I was…like I was a monster. Like I'd… done somethin' horrible to her. I don't know how to even wrap my head around it. What makes it hurt so bad is that I thought, until I saw her face, that it was good. For her. For us. I thought—I thought she wanted me, all of me. But when I let that out, all it did was fuckin' wreck her. And that wrecked me."

I settled closer, burrowing against him. Feeling his waist wedge my thighs open, feeling his powerful body against mine, over and around me. I ached to be touched—but instead, I buried my face against his neck. "What if we just…what if I just did this…?"

I kissed his neck. His throat. His cheekbone.

"What does that feel like, Ink?" I whispered.

His eyes were closed, screwed up tight. "Like heaven itself is kissing me with the lips of an angel." He swallowed hard. "Makes my heart pound so hard it hurts. Makes my stomach do flips."

His hands rested on my waist. I put my hands on top of his, pushed them down, so he was cupping my hips.

"Don't think, okay?" I kissed his cheekbone again, and he gasped at the touch of my lips. "Just feel."

"Tryin'."

I slid off of his lap, settled in the grass beside him, sitting on my feet. Pressed a hand to his chest, and he complied by lying on his back, stretched out. He looked at me, wondering, curious, hesitant.

"I'm just going to…do whatever I want, okay?" I rested a hand on his chest. "For me. Because I want to do it. I don't want, need, or expect anything from you. Since the moment we met I've been curious about this, about you. Wanted to know what it would feel like to touch and kiss and do things with a man built like you. So this is for me, okay? All you have to do is lay there and let me have what I want."

"Cass…"

"I mean it."

"Think I don't see what you're doing?"

"What am I doing?" I asked.

He tucked his hands under his head, elbows flared out. "Showing me that you want me. That I can trust in the fact that you want me."

"Is it working?" I asked, grinning.

A shrug. "Dunno yet."

"Then let's find out, shall we?"

He sighed. "I'll try."

"That's all I'm asking. Just try. Just let me touch you. Because I want to." I smiled at him. "Do you believe I want to?"

"Yeah, I believe that." A pause. "What I don't

think I believe is that you don't want anything in return."

I laughed. "Of course I do. But only what you want to do, when you want to do it. For now, this is what I want."

"This, being what?"

I shrugged. "I don't know. I haven't decided yet."

I rested a hand on his chest. Roamed the broad expanse of his chest, tracing the myriad tattoos. Bent over him, touched my lips to his skin. Flicked my tongue against his flesh, over a tattoo of a salmon. Let my hands explore his waist and stomach, and my lips descend in tripping kisses from chest to belly.

I glanced at him—his eyes were closed, but his face was twisted in an expression that seemed equal parts rapture and distress.

Resting my face on his diaphragm, I touched one leg. Just above the knee. Tugged the leg of his shorts up, baring his thigh. So many tattoos, mostly animals, nature scenes, or abstract lines, glyphs, and runic shapes. All tangled and jumbled and woven together into a tapestry on his skin. I ran my hands over his thigh, feeling the muscles at rest there. Rumpled the leg of the shorts up around his upper thigh, on both sides, tracing and touching each thigh, the tattoos, and the muscles.

Then I let my fingers walk up to his belly. A

sunburst was done in wavy lines radiating out from his belly button, a piece that was clearly older than most of the others, done in either thread or poke-and-stick, which I wasn't sure. The wavy lines of the sun merged with other curves and angles and dots and lines, all disappearing under the waistband of his shorts. I was curious, if nothing else, how extensive the tattoos were, between thighs and belly button. I looked up at Ink again, gauging him; brows furrowed, jaw clenched. Breathing hard. Utterly still.

"Try to relax," I murmured.

He drew in a deep breath, his enormous chest filling and then his belly going taut. He held the breath. Let it out slowly, and some of the tension bled out of his features.

At least until I tucked three fingers under the waist of his shorts and drew them downward. The tension returned then, with interest. But yet, his belly drew in, and his butt lifted, letting me tug the shorts down past his buttocks.

He was bare underneath.

Not exactly slack, but not aroused yet, either.

And fucking *enormous*. Even at rest.

I bit my lip, hard. Ohhh god. Oh god.

So big.

Curled in a comma shape against his belly and hip. Lighter in shade than the rest of him. A close-trimmed thatch of curly black hair around it. Tattoos, runic and tribal, around the pubic area, down each thigh—his manhood was unmarked, however.

"Everyone's question is if I have tats on my dick." He laughed. "I like tats, but not that much. Hell no."

I just huffed a small laugh, and traced the designs on his thigh and lower belly. His laugh faded quickly. I glanced at him again—eyes open, now. Watching me. I let my fingers dance around his belly button, thigh, back around, in a circuit. Avoiding what I wanted to touch. My finger ached to wrap around him, to feel him engorge under my touch. God, so beautiful. I wanted him. Wanted to climb onto him and see how much of him I could take, feel him split me open and drive me to screaming orgasm. It would take no time, even without any foreplay. I was so worked up right now, that a single touch to my center would make me come apart.

God I wanted to fuck him so badly.

But I held this all back, kept it relegated to the back of my head.

I wondered if he could see it on my face, if he could read me that well. I knew it showed. I wasn't very good at hiding my emotions—as a dancer and performer I was trained to let my emotions show, to emote. And as a person, I just couldn't hide my emotions—they boiled too strong, too close to the surface.

Palm gliding over his thigh, up to his belly, I paused in my avoidant circuit, hand coming to rest just below his belly button. Preparing to touch him.

His eyes flicked open, and his hand rested on mine, stopping me. "Gotta tell you something, Cass. Gotta admit it."

I met his eyes. "Okay?"

"I…that drawing of you." A long hesitation. "The story I told, of you in the waterfall…I've got that image in my head. Can't get it out. I've been thinking about you for days, can't get you off of my mind. Drew that sketch of you naked, and…I just couldn't stop myself from thinking about you. Picturing you naked. In that waterfall. Looking at me. Wanting me. Touching me." His eyes met mine. "I was in the bathroom when you came over."

"Yeah?" I had a feeling I knew where he was going with this. Had suspected as much.

"I was…touching myself. Thinking about you." He closed his eyes. Seemed embarrassed. Upset about it. "Couldn't help myself. Felt dirty for it. Like I was using you."

I slid upward, toward his face. Bent over him. Gazed down at him. "Look at me, Ink."

His eyes opened. "Thought you oughta know."

"You jacked off, thinking about me, naked, touching you?"

He nodded. Pained. Upset, still. "First time I done that in...years. Since before Elise."

"Want to know what I think about that?"

He nodded again. "Yeah, I do. The honest truth of it."

I put my lips near his ear. "Good." I pulled back, smiled at him, a helplessly aroused, sensual smile. "I'm glad you did that."

He frowned. "You...what?"

"If that's using me, then Ink, I want you to use me like that." I touched my lips to his cheekbone again, kissed him wet and slow. Moved my lips to his, hesitating. Whispered. "Want to know something else, Ink?"

"What?" he murmured back.

"I thought about you, too. Tried to picture you, naked. Touching me. Tried to imagine you naked, hard for me. Pictured my hands wrapped around you..." I let my hand drift south to his belly. "Pictured myself touching you. Making you feel good. Pictured myself naked and on my back, with your face between my thighs."

He groaned as I inched my hand lower. "Jesus, Cass."

"Would you do that, Ink?"

"Do what? Put my face between your thighs? Eat you out?" He groaned again, a long, tortured sound. "Until you begged me to stop."

"I wouldn't. Not ever. I'd never want you to stop."

"Then I wouldn't."

"But what really turned me on, Ink, what really made me touch myself and make myself come so hard, was thinking about touching you." I watched his face as I reached for him. "Just…like…this."

I curled my fingers around his cock, and he let out a long low growl. Hardening in my hand, he grew and grew, to improbable proportions. The tip extended past his belly button. Thick as my wrist, straight and lying flat against his belly. His arousal was shockingly huge. My mouth watered, my core ached.

"Fuck, oh fuck," he breathed. Eyes flicked open to watch me. "You lyin', Cass?"

I just held him. "Lying? About what?"

"Touching yourself, thinking about me."

"No. Not at all." I stroked him slowly. "I masturbate every day, Ink. Sometimes more than once. It's been a long, long time since I've been with anyone, and I'm so horny I could explode from it." I bit my lip, watching his huge erection slide through my tiny hand. "I made myself come so hard I saw double, thinking about you, about touching you. Making you feel good." I stroked, and stroked, slowly, relishing the feel every satin-soft and hard as iron inch. "I have needs, Ink. Crazy, intense, insatiable needs."

He was breathing hard. "Needs." As if making sense, full sentences, was now beyond him.

"Yes." I used both hands, then, and with both fists wrapped around him at the root, his erection still stood several inches up out of the top of my upper fist, and my fingers only just barely closed around him. "You want to know something about me?"

"Yeah," he muttered. "Tell me."

"No one has ever been able to keep up with me. I finish, and I want more. And more. I just always want more. I want it more intense, more of it, faster, harder, rougher. And no matter how much or how good it is, I want more. I just always want more." I looked at him, met his eyes. "It's been frustrating, my whole life. Makes me feel like there's something wrong with me, that I just can't get enough."

He didn't seem to know what to do with that information. "Before—all that shit happened, you know. When it was just messing around. I felt that way. Like, no matter how good things were, how good it felt, how frequently we did things, like I would just never be satisfied."

"You still feel that way?" I asked.

He shrugged, shook his head. "Dunno. Haven't let myself feel anything for a long time."

I rubbed my thumb over the tip of him. "What about right now?"

He didn't answer immediately, as if he had to catch his breath, organize his thoughts into something like coherency. "It's been so fuckin' long I don't…you, what you're doing. It feels like the first time, all over again."

"Is that a good thing, a bad thing, or just a thing?"

"I dunno. It feels so good, though. I don't want it to ever stop. I don't—I don't want you to ever stop."

"What else do you want?" I asked.

One hand gliding his length, root to tip, in a smooth slow rhythm, unhurried, I used my other hand to cup his heavy sac, massaging. Filling my hand with their soft, delicate weight.

"I want…" He lifted his hips. Feeling the surge of need, I assumed. Rising, filling him. I wanted to draw it out as long as possible, but I also wanted to see him let go, watch him explode, know I brought him the first true pleasure he'd felt in who knew how long. "I don't fuckin' know, Cass. Just you."

I saw a million things on his face. "I see you, Ink. I see you feeling more than you're saying." I met his eyes. "Say it all. Tell me what you want. Tell me you want it. Ask me for it." I grinned, a sultry smile of desire. "Or better yet, show me. Take it."

"Scared to want too much," he bit out.

"Scared that you'll want something I won't want to give?"

He nodded.

"Won't happen." I nipped at his earlobe. "Try me."

"Shit, Cass."

I laughed. "Well, there's one thing I'd say won't ask for." I giggled, squeezing him. "I won't put this thing in my ass. But anything else…?"

He rumbled, and I wasn't sure if it was a laugh or something else.

"Won't ask for that. Wouldn't anyway."

He looked down at my hand, still wrapped around his immense, straining erection. At my face. His eyes flicked down to my chest. To the knot in my shirt.

He reached up, hesitantly. Unknotted the hem of the shirt with one hand. Gauged my reaction—I let go of him and lifted my arms over my head, and he drew the shirt off. I sat next to him in the grass, dressed now in yoga pants and a sports bra. He was naked, his shorts down around his ankles. He kicked them off and toed them aside. Sat up. Faced me. Even sitting, he still towered over me. His palm touched my cheek, and he brushed my cheekbone with a thumb. Ran that same thumb over my lips, the pad rough and broad. I met his eyes, and the fierce hunger I saw blazing there, just for a moment. It stunned me with its raw ferocity.

But, all too soon, habit had him shuttering it.

I took his face in both hands. Leaned close. "Don't hide that from me, Ink. Don't. That's what I want."

He furrowed his brow. "Hard to let it out."

I smiled. "I'm patient. Just know that I want it. I want to see it. Feel it. Experience it."

"Trying."

With another hesitant glance at my eyes, he grazed his fingertips over my ribs, up my spine. Caught against the strap of my sports bra, I just waited. He tugged it up, ran his fingers around the strap to the front, and pulled up. My breasts lifted, caught in the tight garment, and then bounced free, and his eyes fixed on them.

"Want to know something?" I whispered.

He, with effort, moved his eyes to mine. "What?"

"Never done anything like this outside."

"Me either." He looked again at my breasts, and then at my eyes. "God*damn*, you're beautiful, Cassandra."

My heart swelled—I wish I knew how to communicate how badly I needed to hear that. Needed to feel that. "You look at me like you've never seen a naked woman before."

He shrugged. "Looking at you, it feels like I never have." He moved closer, and his lips touched mine.

It was a delicate, questing dance of lips soaring against lips, tongues finding each other, a delving from first kiss to lost in bliss. I whimpered at his kiss, because, god, his lips were soft, strong. He kissed as if he'd never kissed before, as if I would stop wanting to kiss him if he allowed me a single moment to even think of anything but his kiss.

I drowned in his mouth, kissed him until I was dizzy and gasped for breath, and then we touched lips and tasted tongues, and his eyes found mine, a brief moment, and then another small kiss, another. Short, soft, wet, inaccurate, lips missing, tongues not quite finding each other, the kiss all the more intense moment by moment. A dozen tiny kisses, each one a rifle bullet straight to my heart. Straight to my core, where I ached to be touched, ached for his fingers, his tongue, his arousal.

I whimpered into the kiss and pressed my chest against his, leaned into him, felt his body against mine as a massive, immovable wall of muscle and man. He curled his hand around the back of my head and kissed me harder, and I knotted my fingers in his hair, gasping against his lips as his kiss sent me into a paroxysm of need. I clutched at his erection, found it waiting for me as hard as a rock, and tall and thick and straight. I plunged my fist around him. Let go of his hair and used both hands. Pressed against his chest and he lay back. I went with him, leaned over him, one hand now braced on his chest to support my weight, the other now greedily stroking him.

I kissed him, and kissed him. Now it was my turn to kiss his fierce gentle mouth as if I might die if I didn't kiss him again, and again, and harder, and more intensely. I kissed him with all the ferocity I felt in my soul and in my body, and I caressed his erection with unhurried rhythm, slowly, making sure he felt and remembered forever each individual stroke of my fingers around him.

His hand settled on my thigh, just below my butt. I pressed my core against his hip, angled against him. Urging. Giving him tacit permission to touch me more. His hand, huge and powerful, was utterly gentle as he cupped my ass, one side only, for a moment. Squeezed. Gathered the other side in his hand, massaged. Explored each taut round globe, moaning and murmuring—whether from my fist slowly plunging up and down his erection or at the feel of my ass, I wasn't sure, and didn't care, because that moan, those murmurs, wordless and distinctly rapturous, was like a drug. I needed more. The rumble of his voice, the bass vibrations against my chest, the tense need in each sound...

More, god. More.

His hand slid up my bare back, traced the S of

my spine. Gathered the falling sheaf of my hair and tossed it over the other side. Out of the way. His touch slid over my waist, my side. I stopped breathing as he paused, and then cupped my breast. I ached at this tender touch. Whimpered as his rough paw brushed delicately over my nipple, bringing it erect.

"My nipples are very, very sensitive," I whispered. "Like, crazy sensitive."

He looked at me, curious. Aroused beyond all ability to even think clearly. Ever so gently, his eyes on mine, he pinched my nipple between thumb and forefinger, twisting, flicking. "That so?"

I gasped, eyes squeezing shut as lightning seared through me, falling over to lay beside him, one thigh over his. "Ohhh god. Super, super, crazy sensitive. I've even had a breast orgasm, a couple times. Well, once, that was a real all the way orgasm. Couple other times it was just a heightening of a regular one." A whimper, a moan. "Gave it to myself, though."

He watched as I writhed under his touch. "Damn."

I'd stopped stroking him, so lost was I in the wild electricity of his fingers on my breast. I wanted more, of him, of me. I guided his other hand to my breasts, and sighed in pure bliss as he toyed with me, as if he seemed to just *know* exactly how I liked to be touched. My core was pressed against his thigh and hip, and I

writhed against him. Felt him filling my hands, both
of them, as I resumed my slow caresses of his huge
arousal.

He was groaning, and his hips were lifting. I
forced my eyes to open, watched him. He was lost in
this as much as I was—more. Eyes closed, head tipped
back, spine arched, hips flexing. Even my breasts were
momentarily forgotten as I began increasing the speed
of my caress.

Not too much, not too fast. I wanted this to last.
Wanted him to remember. To have this seared into
his memory. I wasn't a jealous or possessive person,
but with him, for some reason, I wanted nothing
more than for this experience to scorch away all other
memories. I wanted him to have no one in his mind,
in his memory but me, no touch but mine rising in his
mind whenever he was alone.

I rolled against him, crushing my tits against his
ribs and taking his lips. He groaned, and his hands
caught me, pressed gently but implacably against my
nape, taking the kiss deeper. I felt him moan, felt the
buzz and rumble of it, tasted his tongue and swallowed his groan. Kissed him deeper, demanding more
from him. Wanting everything from him.

Stroked him, caressed him. Kissing and kissing, I
put all my desire for him into the slow sensual grinding of my hands down his length, twisting on the way

up, pausing at the top to flutter and twist and rub my thumb over the weeping tip. He lost the kiss, head flopping back.

"Ohhh god, Cass—oh god, Cass." His voice was low, rough. "What the hell are you doin' to me?"

There was no reason to answer that. Nothing to say to it. I just kissed his throat in response, under his chin where his beard line was. The hollow between his neck and shoulder. Stroking and caressing, as slowly as ever. Feeling him rising, feeling him swell in my hands, feeling his hips begin to pump. Kissed lower, his chest. His belly.

His hipbone.

"Cassie, ohhh god," he whispered, every syllable piano-wire taut.

I pressed my lips to his ear. "Give it to me, Ink. Let me feel you come." I went slow, slowing down as his hips began to flex rhythmically. "Show me how it feels for you. Let me hear you."

"So—so fuckin'—" He lost the train of his thoughts. Started over. "So fuckin' good, Cass. God, I've never felt this way before. God, Cassie—please, don't stop. Don't stop."

I laughed. "Why the hell would I stop? I want you to come. Let me feel it, Ink. All of it." I cupped his balls, stroked him root to tip, twisting at the top and gliding down, paused at the top and pulsed my fist around the plump round head quickly, until he tilted his hips up hard, and then I plunged down again, beginning the cycle over.

He curled his body upward, straining forward. "Ohhh shit, Cass. I'm—ahhh god, oh shit…I'm gonna come."

I watched eagerly, everything inside me begging for me to climb on him, to take this huge magnificent incredible organ inside me and ride it until I couldn't come any more. Or, to take as much of him into my mouth as I could manage, and taste all the cum that was about to spurt out of him, swallow it all and milk for more. I wanted to make him lose his mind. I wanted be all he could ever think about. I wanted him to lose control so beautifully that he just had to take me, to have more of me. The urge to come the only thing he could even imagine was all-consuming. I wanted more than anything to just be *his*, and the sudden ferocity of that need scared me stupid.

So I did none of the things I really wanted to do.

I don't think I'd given a handjob since high school, but it was just the only thing possible. Anything else would be going too far, too soon, for him and for me.

But I was absolutely ravenous for him. For his release. For his wildness. For his raw unfiltered masculine climax.

He growled, an ursine snarl of exertion, flexing

into my hand. Wanting more. Needing me to give him more, to take him there.

Ink flopped back to the grass, pressing his heels into the dirt and pushing his hips up. Groaning, long and low and feral. I kept going, slowly, twisting downward and fluttering upward. Never the same thing twice, until I felt him pulse and twitch, heard his breath catch and his voice break.

"Cass..." a broken whisper, my name chanted. "Cass, Cass, Cassie, god, Cassie..."

"Yes, Ink, for you. Just for you. All for you." Faster, then, feeling him reach the utter edge. "Give me all of you, Ink. Right now. Come for me. Come all over my hands. I want to feel it. I want it. I want you, Ink. I want you. I want *you*." I really had no clue what I was saying, or why, just that I knew he needed my voice, needed to hear me. How I knew I couldn't have said, but I knew.

He shouted, a hoarse, guttural, wordless cry as he came. At the moment of his release, his eyes snapped open and met mine, and I didn't look away, held his gaze as he came all over his stomach and my hands, spurting again and again as I continued stroking him until he had nothing else to give.

Our eyes locked, a sticky mess all over him and me both, he just stared. Seeming amazed.

I ached, oh how I ached.

I had told him I expected nothing in return, and I meant it. But god, how I hoped. I had never needed an orgasm so badly in all my life.

After a long silent moment, he climbed slowly to his feet, gathered his shorts and my shirt and bra, and extended a hand to me. Tugged me to my feet. Didn't let go, but walked with me through the woods back toward his home. Naked in the woods, bathed in moonlight and cool air—my nipples stood achingly hard, diamond points, the cool air swirling over them. He moved with silent grace despite his size, leading me to the kitchen door, which was bathed in shadows. Led me inside. Tossed our clothing on the floor.

Used a wad of paper towel to clean himself with while I washed my hands.

Standing in silence, he just stared at me. Thinking.

"What, Ink? Say whatever it is you're thinking." I resisted the urge to cover my breasts with my arms, instead standing bold, bare. Wondering what he was thinking. How he felt about what had just happened.

"I know you said you didn't want anything in return—"

"Ink, you don't—"

He palmed the small of my back, tugged me up against him, his slack manhood pressed against my belly, residual stickiness tacky against my skin. I didn't mind that—only wondered if maybe it meant we'd get to take a shower together. He stared down at me.

"I really hope you were tellin' the truth when you said there wasn't anything I could want that you wouldn't give."

"I was. God's honest truth. I want it all. More than you can imagine." My voice quavered, my own need getting the better of me, my legs shaking, knees pressed together, ache low in my belly growing as his hand descended to cup my backside.

"Still scared shitless of wanting too much," he whispered. "Of just being too much."

"I'm not scared, Ink."

"Maybe you should be," he murmured. "Not sure you understand what you just started."

My grin was darkly amused, wildly aroused. "Show me what you mean, Ink. I dare you."

SEVEN

Ink

HER EYES WERE WILD. ALIVE WITH NEED. I DON'T THINK I've ever seen anyone so manic with sexual ferocity in my life.

I shouldn't have been able to feel a thing, not after the way she'd just milked every last drop of seed out of me, especially after having gone once already by myself. But I had her half-naked in my hands, beautiful small pert firm breasts with those hypersensitive nipples pointed slightly upward, as if begging for my mouth. She'd given me a gift of such precious beauty that I doubted I could ever communicate its worth to her—somehow, what she'd just done had shown me that she was for real. That she truly did want *me*. That she wasn't afraid. That I could let go, a little bit, at least, and that I wouldn't hurt her. I wasn't "healed," if there even was such a thing. I was still scared of hurting her, and an insidious little voice way down deep was still whispering poisonous thoughts—*she'll turn on you when you least expect it; she doesn't REALLY want you; she'll find a way to blame something on you, just wait, you'll see; she has no idea what she's asking for, thinking she can handle you; you're going to hurt her, it's what you do; she doesn't really want you, she doesn't really want you...*

Her eyes told me a different story. Her blazing hazel eyes were greener than ever, green with a wildfire of fervent sexual arousal. Those eyes begged me to make her feel good. To show her how much I wanted her. How good she'd made me feel. I wanted to show her. To make her whimper, to see her arch that slender whipcord back with the sensual serpentine S of her spine, to watch her press those lush little tits to the sky and come apart for me. I wanted to devour her until she was a puddle of screams.

The raging power of my need to *own* her terrified me with its intensity. I couldn't let her see that, couldn't. It was too much, too deep, too wild, too big.

But the look in her eyes defied that fear.

Her eyes pleaded with me, begged with abject need for me to show her every bit of that berserk, frenzied desire, that testosterone-mad, rampaging alpha-dominant ownership.

"Ink?" Hesitancy in her voice. Wondering. A quiet question, a nudge.

Test her, a little?

She was standing pressed against me, breasts heaving with uncertain breaths, eyes wide, hands curled against my diaphragm like tender sparrows, fingers fluttering. She wore nothing but those tight red yoga pants. But I wanted her totally naked.

I wanted her screaming.

The crushing madness of my need to make her climax had me shuddering from the effort it took to hold back from just yanking her off her feet and holding her slit up against my mouth right here, right now, standing up.

She weighed so little I could hold her one-handed and use the other to slide a finger inside her.

I held absolutely still, or I'd do exactly that.

Her quivering thighs and wide eyes dared me to.

"What are you thinking, Ink?"

I shook my head. "Bad things."

The wicked curve of her lips told me more than anything she could say. The flex of her hips against me said more yet. "Promise?"

I just laughed, but it didn't quite reach my eyes, I knew. Another long moment passed, silence between us.

The need to see her naked and shaking was too strong. I fought it, fought the need to roughly yank those crimson tights off her and violently devour her. Good god, I'd forgotten how crazy I could get—this was why I'd shut down. I couldn't handle this. Couldn't manage the intensity of it. Couldn't resist how ferociously and ravenously I *needed*, once my libido was pumping.

And holy shit, was it pumping. The way her hands had wrapped around me? So slow. So tenderly. *Affectionate*—that's the only word for how she'd fondled me, caressed me. As if to have me in her hands was the single greatest joy she'd ever felt, as if touching me brought her as much pleasure as it did me. The way she'd watched me explode—with proud, eager arousal. My climax was *her* pleasure.

"Cass," I said, biting the words out. "I don't know what to do with myself—with *you*."

"Whatever you want." Humor dancing in her eyes she said, "*Show* me."

Humor, but she was dead serious. I knew she meant it.

I hoped to god I wouldn't regret what I was about to do.

"Fuck it," I breathed. "I hope you know what you're doing, cutting me loose like this."

My hand spread over her ass, covering it. I

pressed her against me. Delved my fingers down, under, between her buttocks and through her thighs. She whimpered, sagged, her thighs opening. Pressed my fingers against her core—even through her pants and underwear, it was obvious from a single touch that she was soaked with arousal. She let her forehead bump against my chest, gasped once, deeply, held the breath with a low whine, and then, when I gently began pressing and exploring and delving around her sensitive center over the fabric of her yoga pants, she sank her teeth into my skin and bit down gently, groaning.

"Shit, Cass—you're right there, ain't you?"

She just nodded, shaking all over. "So fucking close."

I had to see. Had to taste. Had to lick away her orgasms, one after the other, until she begged me to stop.

God, I was crazy with it. For her. I'd held this down inside me for so long, and now that it was out, it was more manic and delirious and frenzied than ever. Reminding me why I'd shut it down in the first place—the power of it was scary, and every instinct I had told me if I showed her the full force of it she'd run, ghost me so fast I'd get dizzy.

But the look in her eyes—I kept coming back to her eyes, because they told me the truth, a truth I couldn't believe, a truth my instincts rebelled against. The truth in her eyes was that she wanted all I had and more.

I just didn't dare believe her.

But now, god, now she'd broken the bonds. Set loose the monster inside me, and I couldn't hold on any longer.

Couldn't.

I cupped her ass in one hand and lifted her. Pinned her against me, kissed her mouth. My lips trembled with the effort of restraint—all of me shook. I wanted so much, so badly, but I dared not let go all the way. I had to be careful.

She wrapped her arms around my neck and eagerly devoured my kiss, knotting her fingers in my hair and hooking her legs around my waist, keeping herself aloft. I walked her forward, into the house. I wanted her in my bed, but I wouldn't make it that far.

I set her on the kitchen counter, still kissing her mouth, tangling my tongue with hers. Hooked my fingers in the elastic of her red yoga pants, inside the waistband of her underwear, and tugged both down. She let out a high breath of shock as I yanked them off, peeling them inside out, her black thong tangled up with red pants, and tossed both aside. Knelt on the floor in front of her and buried my face between her thighs—she smelled potently of female arousal, and

I got drunk on it, on her scent. Lapped at her, tasted her. Sweet, a little tart, a little musky. A taste all her own, and utterly drugging. I was dizzy with the scent of her, the flavor of her private center, laid open and bare for me, displayed all for me.

She caught at my hair and shrieked in surprise at the sudden onslaught of my tongue and lips. "Ohhh— oh god, oh god, oh god, Ink, oh fuck, *fuck* you're good at that, ohhhh my god, Ink! Yes, god, please—just like that. Just like that, Ink. Don't stop. Don't you fucking dare slow down." She spoke through it, dirty words pouring out of her, an unexpected and arousing stream of encouragement. "Ohhh yeah, oh shit. Shit! You like how I taste, Ink? Oh fuck, you do, don't you? God, yes, more, more! Faster, right there, faster! Oh fuck, your tongue is amazing!"

She shook, her thighs quaking against my face, abs tightening as she thrashed against my mouth, feet pressed against my shoulders, hands reaching down between her legs to grip my hair and pull me hard against her. I tasted her essence flowing against my tongue, lapped it up. Felt her coiling. Slipped a finger inside her and drew it out, curling it just so. She went *wild*, then, screaming wordlessly, and I plunged that finger back in and lapped at her and alternated plunging it in and curling it where I knew she liked it best, my tongue circling and spearing and licking.

She came apart, her screams loud and unrestrained, arching against me. Her voice, raised in climax, screamed one syllable that did more to erase the past than anything else—my name. "Ink! Ink! Oh fuck, Ink! God yes, god yes, oh god *Ink!*"

When she finished coming, shaking and limp, I gathered her in my arms and carried her up my ladder to my bed and set her down. She shook, trembled, gasping. Disoriented.

When she seemed to regain her senses, she looked around. "We're in bed."

I just nodded. "Yeah."

"Holy shit, that was wild." She bit her lip, gazing up at me. "You are truly incredible, Ink."

I shook my head. "Not me, you." I wasn't anywhere near sated. I needed more. "Not done with you yet, Cass."

She frowned, sitting up.. "But you just—"

I sucked her entire breast into my mouth, licking her nipple until she whimpered. Clutched at me. I slid my hands under her tight little ass and lifted her, settling her thighs over my shoulder and down my back, supporting her weight in my hands.

"Whoa-holy-shit, Ink—wait, what…?" She didn't get another word out before I had her against my mouth all over again.

I held her there, balanced precariously, and she

braced herself against the ceiling as I began devouring her all over again. Slowly, this time. No hands, no fingers. Just my tongue and my lips. Kissing. Flicking. Licking. Tonguing in fat lazy slurps against her delicate center. She sighed and sighed, the first few minutes, just slow pleased gusts of languorous enjoyment. Then, as her delight built into burgeoning need, she began pushing her slit against my mouth, grinding into my tongue. She was nothing at all to hold up like this. But I wanted all of her need, so I lay back, never disengaging, so we landed against my nest of pillows with her sitting over my mouth, shins and feet tucked under her thighs, hands braced wide on the wall above my head, and she just let go, gave in with complete abandon. Writhed on me, staring down at where my mouth met her core, watching me as I drowned myself in her.

"Oh god, Ink, holy shit, holy shit, oh god." One hand buried in my hair, she pulled me against her, roughly, grinding herself against my mouth. "I'm almost there, Ink. So close, so fucking close. Keep doing it just like that, oh fuck, that thing with your tongue—fuck, yeah, *that*, do that and don't fucking stop!"

I loved how she told me what she wanted, what she liked. It made me crazy. Made me want to spend every moment of a thousand years learning how to make her feel like this, just like this, wild and cut loose into a frenzied sexual mania, writhing on me, eyes wide and teeth gnawing on the left corner of her lower lip, breasts heaving and bouncing, crying my name and begging for more and more and more.

When she came again, it was with a scream that left my ears ringing, left her taste seared onto my tongue. It was a wordless scream, hoarse. She folded forward with the power of it, shaking all over, quivering uncontrollably, gasping for breath—half sobbing.

She rolled away, off of me, onto her back, moving bonelessly, with effort. "Holy. Fucking. Shit." Her voice was hoarse.

I just looked at her—all five feet three inches and hundred-some pounds of gloriously, decadently, perfectly beautiful naked woman, in my bed, taut abs still tightening and distending with ragged breaths, thighs shaking with aftershocks. Breasts falling to either side. Hair a mess of blonde explosion on my pillow. Eyes closed, mouth agape as she came back to earth and regained her breath. Sweat dotted her perfect skin, dripped down her delicate temple, slid between her breasts and into the hollow of her belly.

"Good god, you're fuckin' perfect," I breathed, unaware the words were aloud.

Her head snapped to the side, eyes laser-focused on mine. "Don't fuck with me, Ink."

Unexpected. I reared back a little. "Ain't. Didn't even mean to say that out loud. Thought I was thinkin' it, but it just came out."

She turned her head away from me, eyes watering. "Sorry. I just…"

Tucked my hands under my head and gave her space to consider whatever it was she was chewing on.

"I don't know why I'm so emotional right now," she muttered. "I'm sorry."

I shook my head, grunted a negative. "Don't apologize."

"You just gave me the two best orgasms of my entire damn life, and I'm snapping at you," she murmured. "Not like me. Don't know what's come over me."

"Sure you do," I said. "Just don't know how, or don't want to say it."

She rolled to her side, facing me, frowning. "Like you said what you were thinking and feeling out there?"

"I honestly don't know what the fuck to think or feel, Cass. Legit, I'm lost."

"So you can be lost, but I can't?"

I gazed into her eyes. Saw a tumult of emotions, mixed and coruscating, high and low and wild and tempered. "I see you, Cass. You know what you're

feelin', but it's deep and it's a fuckin' lot, and powerful, and you're scared. I am too, I get it. Not asking
you to say any of it."

"And I think you're very much in the same place,
Ink." She pillowed her head on her folded arm. "But I
won't push if you won't."

I felt my gut churning with my own hurricane of
butterflies and violent, confusing, intense emotions I
just didn't know how to process, how to even feel all
the way, much less express. I wanted to try, though.
To at least find a way to let her know how much what
she'd done meant to me.

"Cassandra, I…" I closed my eyes, fighting for
the right words. Losing them as fast as they flitted
through my disordered brain. "What you done for
me, out there. The way you touched me. The way
you…talked to me. Looked at me." I met her eyes.
"You don't even know what you did for me."

"You accused me of trying to fix you," she murmured. "I don't want to fix you. You're not broken. I
just want…I don't know. I want things with you, but
it scares the almighty fuck out of me, how much I
want, what I want, how bad I want it. I wasn't trying to fix you, or heal you. I just wanted to…to give
you something good, something you can remember
that'll replace…" she fluttered a hand vaguely, "everything that came before. The bad stuff, at least. Not

trying to take away or…tape over…the good memories, you know?"

I laughed. "What good memories? It's all bad shit. I mean, there was some stuff that was nice while it lasted, with Elise, but what happened afterward just sort of…ruined those memories for me. Don't think on 'em."

"I just wanted to…try to help you unlock yourself a little, Ink." She touched my beard, splayed out on the pillow, mixed in with her hair and my own, black on blonde. "I don't think it's healthy to have your sexuality locked up, shut down. You deserve to be open. To be free. You're amazing, Ink. An amazing person. Gorgeous. Kind. Talented." A pause, her cheeks pinking a little. "Really, really talented."

"It's all you, Cass. You make it easy. Making you scream is the easiest thing in the damn world. You're so fuckin' responsive, so easy to read. You make me feel like…like a god. Like I can't do anything wrong."

"No, Ink. You don't know, you just don't. I'm sensitive, I know. But I'm not easy to read, and it's easy to get me close, but not so easy to make me come as hard as you did, and more than once to boot. And I mean, shit, the second time was even better than the first. You just…" She bit her lip, shrugged, a movement that had a delicious effect on her breasts. "You just *know*. You played my body like a fucking violin."

Silence. There was so much unspoken. So much in her eyes, so much under the surface, and I was just as turbulent within.

Neither of us seemed to know how to bring any of it all the way up and out, though.

"Can I ask you something, Ink?" Quiet, not hesitant, just…quiet. Reserved. "And have a one-hundred percent honest answer."

I nodded. "Do my best."

"Were you still holding back?" Her eyes, this close, were so complex, so multihued, multilayered. Half a dozen shades of brown, shades of green, shades of blue. And as complex as the hues were, even more complex were the emotions I saw there.

Worse yet was the kaleidoscope of emotions in me. I didn't want to answer. But I did. I nodded. Swallowed hard. "Yeah. I was."

She nodded. "How?"

I shrugged. "Just…tempered things, I guess." Went for a risky bit of truth. "I want you and want things with you in a crazy, crazy, wild fuckin' way, and it scares me. Scared I'll scare you."

"You won't, Ink."

"How do you know? How can I know?" I shrugged, shook my head. "If I hurt you, I'd—I don't know. If I scared you—I don't think I could handle seeing you look scared of me. I can't go through that again."

"You won't scare me, Ink. You won't."

I shook my head. "Wish I could just believe that. Not that I don't believe you—I do. I know you believe it."

"But you don't."

"No, I can't. I just fuckin' *can't*, Cassie. I simply can't fuckin' afford to. What you did, who you *are*—getting me to let myself feel anything at all is a win, don't you fuckin' see that? Getting me to see you as a sexual being, giving in to being attracted to you. Giving in to thinking about you—jerking off to thinking about you...that's a fuckin' *big* goddamn deal, Cass. This? What we just did? What I let you do? What I let myself do *to* you? *So* fuckin' huge, for me. You don't even know. So yeah, I still held back. But it ain't all just gonna go away all at once. It's a lot of years of painful shit all callused over, babe. Can't fix it overnight."

"I'm not trying to fix it."

I sighed, rubbed my forehead. "But you are. You are. That's okay. I get it. I appreciate it. You just gotta be patient."

She laughed, an amused bark. "Yeah, not so good at that."

Silence.

I lay on my back, she on hers—we were side by side, my hands folded over my stomach, hers curled together over her diaphragm, just under and between her lovely little breasts, fingers tangled and curled and twined together. God, those pink nipples, pert taut firm little nipples. I wanted them in my mouth again.

She caught me staring, and a slight smile crossed her lips. "What? You see something you like?"

"You know I do," I said, rolling toward her.

She bit her lip, watching me, not moving. "You… you don't mind that they're small?"

"Mind?" I wedged my body against hers, leaning partially over top of her.

I palmed one breast as I kissed her shoulder, her breastbone. Slid my tongue around the underside of one breast, my thumb flicking her other nipple. She moaned, gasped. Head tipped back, eyes closed. I suckled her entire breast into my mouth, and then let it out and circled her nipple with my tongue, tweaking and twisting the other between my finger and thumb. Her moans became louder, and her hips lifted. I leaned across her, using my mouth on the other breast now, and flicking and tweaking with my fingers the one I'd mouthing moments ago. Sucked, tweaked. Twisted, licked. Cassie moaned, murmured, whimpered. Her hips began flexing, and I gave her a rhythm—pinch, twist, lick, flick, flick, pinch, twist, a complicated rhythm.

She rose to the occasion, spine arching and

her voice calling wordless encouragement to me, as I switched mouth and fingers from one side to the other until she was mad with it, hips driving, seeking.

Finally, when she was crazed and gasping and moaning, I palmed both breasts and pinched her nipples hard, so hard she screamed, and at the moment of the pinch and the moment of her scream, I devoured her clit, sucking it into my mouth and twiddling it with my tongue and thrashing it side to side, and Cassie's scream broke, shattered, became ragged and breathless and she was arched off the bed, spine bowed up, all of her weight on her neck and heels, thrusting herself against my mouth, seeking the heat and pressure and movement I was giving her as fast as I could move my head and tongue.

Until I ached, until the delicate, complex flavor of her arousal was seared into my taste buds and her essence was smeared on my mouth and cheeks, until she went limp, gasping, panting, utterly spent and stunned.

"Fucking hell, Ink. I have never, ever, ever..." a pause to suck in oxygen, calm her pulse, "EVER in my life come as hard as you make me come."

I grinned, moving up her and kissing her belly and then her ribcage and then her breasts again, until she cackled and pushed me away.

"Too sensitive, too sensitive! I need a second. Jesus." She pushed me away from her nipples, but yanked me by my beard up to her mouth, used her palm to wipe away her essence, and then pulled me in for a kiss. "God, all I can taste is my own pussy."

I laughed. "Me too. And I'm more than okay with that."

She laughed with me, kissed me again. The kiss deepened, and then she rolled into me, pressing me onto my back. She broke the kiss, still gripping my beard under my chin in one hand, the other cupping my cheek. Kissed me once more, a swift peck on the lips. And then she grinned, wickedly.

Shifted down my body.

"Cass, wait." I caught at her. "Don't. Not that."

She transferred my blindly groping hands to her hair. Kissed her way down my belly. "I want to."

"It's…I'm—too much."

"I'll be the judge of that." She hesitated as she settled between my thighs, grinning up at me. "What if I want to taste you as much as you like to taste me?"

I groaned, because I ached. Hard as a rock again, ready again. More ready for her than I'd ever been in my life. Wanting her. I wanted her. I didn't want to come in her mouth, I wanted to be buried inside her.

I needed it.

Nothing mattered to me except the need to

feel her sweet tight hot sex clamped around me, her breathing raw in my ear, whimpering my name.

I felt it, saw it. Saw it happening. Needed it.

"Cass, I need—"

She cut me off by taking me into her mouth. I lost the ability to speak. To breathe. To think. To exist outside the sensation of her warm wet mouth sucking hard around me, plowing downward. Taking me. Accepting me deeper. I felt her breasts sliding against my quads. I groaned, aching, throbbing.

"Fuck, oh fuck, Cass." I heard my voice, but it sounded alien. From someone besides me. It sounded hoarse, raw and ragged and weak and whispery and destroyed.

Sweet unholy blissful hell.

Her mouth, god her mouth.

It was too good.

Too much like heaven. Too much like a perfect home for my cock that I never wanted to leave, ever. Could it just go on forever?

How was she breathing? She hadn't stopped. She was just plunging her mouth down on me, swallowing around me, sliding her lips up and swirling her tongue all over me, and her hands were everywhere, cupping my balls and squeezing and massaging, a finger sliding along the tenderest underside, then clasping around my base as she spent a moment with her lips wrapped around the head and sucking and licking and bobbing hungrily, eagerly, almost desperately.

"God, Cass...Cassie, oh god—why?"

She just hummed, what sounded like an affirmative, and slid back down my length until she was swallowing around me again and her hands were doing incredible things, pumping at the base and cupping my sac and fondling and driving me absolutely insane.

How long?

I couldn't fathom time. Couldn't count seconds or minutes. I was just utterly lost in her, in the glory of her mouth.

And she never stopped, never slowed.

I ached. Throbbed.

My pulse pounded in my ears, drowning out everything, and my hips flexed and heat soared inside me and pressure mounted behind my belly and inside me and through me but it never stopped and she didn't slow down and I wanted it to last forever.

Then, after a moment, she pulled free, gasping. Staring at me with wonder and awe and something like frustration. "Fucking hell, Ink. How long can you last?"

The moment she took her mouth off of me, I was done. It was over.

Madness took me.

I growled something, a curse perhaps, or

something without words. Just a sound of feral sexual insanity. Need gone berserk.

I reached down, picked her up, threw her onto the mattress. She bounced once, on her side, and then I gathered her to me. Up on my knees, aching and pounding with the need to be *home*, to be inside this woman who was fucking *mine*. Mine for the taking.

God, the need was making me see double, red.

All I knew was Cassie. Round ass taut and spread apart. Skin slick and smooth and warm. I palmed her ass in one hand, wrapped my other arm around her hips, across her belly, and yanked her to me. Grabbed myself with one hand, fingered her opening with the other. She gasped, reached back, took me from my hand and guided me where I belonged.

"Ink, fuck, fuck, fuck, Ink, ohhh god—there you are, oh god, you're fucking *huge,* Jesus…" A ragged whimper as she began accepting me inside.

I watched myself bury into her. Slowly. She was whimpering, a low long moan of ecstasy.

"Cass…god, tell me it's okay. Tell me it feels good. Tell me it's okay."

She just cried. Sobbed. "Holy*shit*you're*huge*— it's okay, it's okay, Ink, more than okay, it's beautiful. It's beautiful, god it's beautiful."

She was watching us join, head turned to one side and angled to watch down the length of her body as I drove in slowly; her head and shoulders were on the mattress, ass high, thighs pressed against her belly. Feet crossed over each other, toes curling. She was shaking all over. Trembling. Even her voice was shaky.

"You're beautiful, Cassandra, so fuckin' beautiful. So perfect. God you feel…" I choked on sentiment, gagged on it. "Home. Fucking home."

It took an eternity to slide all the way into her hot slick sex. She clenched around me—so tight it nearly hurt, and then she squeezed, did something with muscles I didn't know she had and clamped even harder around me as my thighs and hips seated home, pressed against the gorgeous firm squish of her ass.

All the way.

She had all of me. I didn't know that was possible. Yet there was the evidence, wrapped around me like a vise of hot wet silk.

"Cass, god, how are you taking all of me? How is it possible?"

She sagged forward, and then reached out with both hands and grasped and scrabbled desperately at the sheets, blankets, mattress, fingers flexing and curling spasmodically. Shaking all over, she suddenly pushed back against me, and sucked in a breath which told me she'd been holding it, not breathing for quite a long time.

"FUCK!" She surged forward, and I stuttered

through her spasming channel. "Move, Ink! Move. Just fucking—*god*, you fill me like I've never been filled." Another ragged gasp. "You fit me perfectly, Ink. No one's ever fit me like you. I thought I was…I thought I was too big, inside. Small outside, tiny body…oh god, oh god, you feel so good."

A pause, and she kept talking, through our joining. Conversational even as she shuddered, shaking like a leaf in a long wind as I drew back, pulling out most of the way.

"I thought I was too big, thought my—my pussy was too big. What a joke, right? Like, thanks, God. Give me tiny legs, tiny arms, tiny hands, tiny feet, tiny tits, tiny ass, and a huge gaping pussy no cock has ever filled."

I pushed in, with exquisite care, slow, gentle, and now I was the one shaking with the effort to be what she needed—slow, careful, gentle, soft. "Cass, you're perfect. I didn't think anyone *could* take me."

She met me, thrust for thrust. Impossibly wanting more. Surging forward as I pulled out and sinking back into me as I pushed in. Whimpering all the while, shaking, fingers clawing at my bed.

Slow, so slow. Agonizingly slow. It was torture to move at all, because all I wanted, down to my molecules, was to ram into her, pound home, go savage with the caveman need to dominate and take and claim and use and show her that she was mine and I was hers.

I could not. Dare not. Would not.

She began to spasm, whole-body shivers, folding inward, torso contracting into itself to pull me out, and then her spine torqued in, down, and her ass slammed backward—taking me in. I had that sweet delicate round perfect ass of hers in my hands and I was palming and squeezing and gripping as I fought with every fiber of my being to hold on, to hold back, to not tear her apart, as my loss of control surely would.

Was already more than half-mad.

Snarling.

Growling.

Pushing in as my hips met her ass cheeks and pushed deeper, and she cried out, cried my name, reached back to grasp at her buttock and pull it aside, and somehow I went deeper yet, as if she was truly just endless and able to take more and more and more, and want it all.

I felt a ravaging madness boiling in my veins.

Knew it was nearly time.

And I had no clue how I would hold back through my orgasm. I had to, though. Had to.

She was lost, then. Spasming thrusts, slamming into me, crying without compunction, and then she clenched around me so hard I thought I was going to explode inside her from the force of her clenching heat, and she screamed, long and loud and hoarse, and pushed back against me so hard I felt like I was about to explode through the front of her.

"Cass, ohh god oh fuck oh god oh fuck—" My voice was a ragged whisper as I struggled with the last dregs of my restraint to keep from letting loose, from ripping her open with my animal need.

She pushed back, sobbing. "Ink, oh my god, Ink, ohmyfuckinggod, Ink…"

"Cass, I'm—I'm—I have to come. I have to."

She surged forward, but this time it wasn't to push back into me—it was panic. "You can't! Ink, you can't! God, no, no, you can't. You can't!"

I yanked myself back at the last second, roaring out loud as I fought to control myself, rolling away, gasping as if I'd just sprinted a hundred yards full-out. "Fuck, fuck, fuck, fuck!"

My eyes were closed, squeezed shut. Fighting to keep it back. To hold on.

Straining, all over. Every muscle tensed.

And then…

Utter softness, wet soft heaven all around my aching, straining erection.

And I lost it all, in a single instant.

The moment she sank her mouth onto me, I lost

it. I couldn't even warn her. It was automatic, beyond my capacity to control. She gulped, shocked, and then recovered, and her hands gripped around me and stroked me hard and fast, both hands blurring on my sex-slick shaft, and I pulsed and my whole body shook, clenching, spasming.

I couldn't even breathe. My lungs were empty. My heart pounding fit to explode. I couldn't even thrust, because she was doing it all for me, but then I had to—*had* to. Pushed up, once, and she didn't pull away. No, she took that, too, measuring her movements to accommodate my helpless thrust.

She had my balls in her hand, massaging them sweetly, gently, lovingly, pressing a finger under them and I came even harder, came again, and she swallowed it all.

Finally, she let me go.

I flopped with a loud slap against my belly, and she lifted my arm, settled herself into the shelter of my arms. Nuzzled against me. I groped blindly, found a blanket, and tugged it over us.

EIGHT

Cassie

SUNLIGHT STREAMED IN THROUGH THE WINDOWS. I WOKE slowly. Became aware, gradually, of myself and my surroundings…and last night.

I was sore, down there. Beautifully, incredibly, perfectly achy.

My mouth tasted like…well, like him.

I didn't mind that either, although I wanted a toothbrush in the worst way.

My whole body was sore, and I realized it was because I'd come four times, each time harder than the last, and the least incredible of those four orgasms was a million times better than the best orgasm anyone—including I myself—had ever given me.

I was still in his arms. We hadn't moved the whole night.

And I didn't want to.

Which scared the living blazes out of me.

Because this feeling, this not wanting to leave the safety of his arms came with…a depth of other feelings that I could not handle having.

"You're panicking," I heard a deep, low, sleep-raspy voice say.

"Yeah," I whispered.

"Don't." He tightened his grip on me.

"Yeah," I whispered again, this time laughing sarcastically. "Let me just will myself to stop having a panic attack."

He rolled to his back, taking me with him, so I was lying entirely on top of him. And…it was surprisingly comfortable. He cupped my head in his hand, pressing my ear to his chest. "Just listen to my heartbeat and tune everything else out."

I curled up into a ball on his huge body, which was an odd combination of hard and soft—hard with deep, powerful muscles, but just a little soft, too. So perfect. A perfection I hadn't known I'd always craved, this particular, specific sensation of hard and soft all together. Soft embrace, gentle and sweet, but beneath it was a well of unutterable power. Vibrantly masculine strength—masculine without being at all macho. Just confident. Male.

I thought of him last night—shaking as he slid into me. Just…shaking, like I'd never felt anyone tremble before. And I knew, with total surety, that he'd been shaking with the effort of holding back. I'd been so delirious with the sheer breathless wondering shock of the way he felt inside me to do anything about it last night, or to even fully understand it. But now, as I lay here with a sore sex, knowing that he'd been in complete control, holding back… what seemed to me like *everything*, I knew I wanted—*needed*—to know what it would be like to feel him lose that edge of control.

He hadn't hurt me.

If anything, I'd wanted more. Even then, drowning in the incredible out-of-this-world feel of him inside me, more than I'd ever even guessed was possible, fitting in me as if whatever artist had created this world had created Ink and created me and created us to fit together like two pieces of a puzzle—even then, I'd wanted more. Wanted to feel him move. To be gone for me, as I was gone for him.

The one thing that hurt in a not so nice way was my leg.

It hurt like a bitch. Throbbed with soul-shearing agony.

The muscle, the bone, the screws and plates. Everything. It just *hurt*. Reminding me that I'd been slacking on my mobility exercises. Slacking on my whole post-PT rehab routine. If I wanted to be able to walk without a limp, to run, to even think about dancing again, I had to work on it.

And I hadn't been.

But I couldn't.

What was the point? There was no point. *I*, as a person, had no point.

Ink's heartbeat was all that kept me from shattering into tears on the spot—*duh-DUM*—*duh-DUM*—*duh-DUM*. Solid, steady, reassuring.

Damn him, though, he knew.

"Cass."

I shook my head, clenching around him, clawing into him, every muscle paralyzed as I attempted to shut down and hold back the breakdown.

"Let go, babe. It's okay."

I shook my head again, swallowing compulsively against the hot lump in my throat, trying to swallow the burn and sting in my eyes.

He rolled to one side, bringing us to our sides, and he curled up around me. And somehow, I was wrapped in a warm solid sheltering cocoon of Ink. He was everywhere. His heartbeat was loud all around me. His heat was like a kiln on full blast, like standing over an open oven. His power was all around me, a visceral presence.

And he just…held me.

I curled tighter, tighter. Into a woodlouse ball.

"It's okay, Cass," he murmured. "It's okay."

I wondered if he knew I'd never really grieved for everything I'd lost?

How could he know that? I'd held it together until Mom showed up, and then when I'd seen how delicately she was holding herself together against some mysterious tension of her own, yet was there for me, worrying with frantic desperation about me, as only a mother can, I just…kept holding it together. We got here, and she was clearly deliriously happy to be with Lucas, who sometimes grated on my nerves and annoyed the shit out of me, but Mom was blissed into nonsensical incoherency when she was with him and I just couldn't anchor her down with my sob-sob bullshit pity party.

But I wasn't okay.

I'd never really cried.

Not for the trauma of the accident itself. Not for the vicious pain I'd been in afterward. Not for the realization that I'd never dance professionally again. Not for the way Rick had treated me, in the weeks after the accident. Not for the way he'd dumped me, so coldly, so callously, so indifferently. Not for what I'd discovered about him recently. Not for any of it.

I'd never cried about any of it.

I wasn't a crier. I'd cried for a couple of hours after Dad died, and then I'd pulled it together to be the steady one in the family, the emotional rock my mom and sisters needed. I'd never truly grieved that, either.

Shit.

I'd never really dealt with any of it, had I?

But it all came out.

Naked, in the bed of a man I'd known a matter of...days? A week? A couple of weeks? I couldn't remember. As a matter of fact, it was hard to think back to when I *didn't* know him, which was even weirder.

I bawled.

Just...broke, totally.

He stayed curled around me, breathing evenly, deeply, slowly. Arms resting on my bare back, not scratching or patting or rubbing. Just there, as I sobbed and sobbed and sobbed, until I was hoarse and snotty and drained of everything.

He reached somewhere, blindly, snagged a Kleenex—I heard the soft sound of the Kleenex leaving the box, and then he pressed it into my hand. Tucked it down between my hands and face. It was an odd, cute gesture and I almost laughed.

Almost.

I cleaned my nose, and kept the Kleenex clenched in my fist. He never said a word. Just held me through it all. Didn't ask any questions. Didn't tell me it would all be okay. He just…held me.

And that, out of everything that had happened since I showed up here last night, was the scariest thing of all. Because it was so deeply, particularly, exactly what I needed, and he just fucking *knew*.

I felt him slow. Release. Heard him snore.

Still holding me, still curled around me, his body between the whole world and me.

I turned, wriggled, twisted, and, accepted my place in this warm strange frightening little world—the little spoon. Accepted my place…

And hated both how right it felt, and how much I loved it and craved it, and hated how scared I was of feeling this way, hated that I was too afraid to do anything but be utterly paralyzed with fear.

———— ✦ ————

When I woke again, I knew it was several hours later, judging by how stiff I was, and how disoriented, and by how much my soreness had receded.

I became aware, gradually, of Ink, still behind me, great chest at my back rising and falling with giant huffing breaths. Hot on my spine. Reassuringly steady.

He was hard, his cock standing ramrod stiff, and tucked between my buttocks.

I giggled, but under my breath. Ohhh my.

Flushed.

How easy would it be to just…slide him inside me?

Take him where I wanted him—deep. And how I wanted him—hard.

The urge to do exactly that was overpowering.

And that more than anything made me remember last night—how close he'd been to pouring all that hot wet cum inside me.

I'd wanted it.

But prudence had won—and he'd managed to control himself. I wasn't sure anyone else could have, not with how close he'd been.

Finishing him the way I had—that'd been instinct. A need to give him the release he deserved, after all those mind-altering, drug-like, body-shattering orgasms.

He even tasted different. Better. *More.*

I would take him that away again in a heartbeat.

Considered it, right then.

But he stirred.

And I panicked. Couldn't breathe for the sudden panic.

He'd want to *talk*. And if he talked, he'd get things out of me that I didn't want to talk about.

I felt so conflicted at that moment. I wanted him

desperately, hungrily, needily inside me, but I didn't want to talk about the tears, the grief, the upset.

Thinking back on the past twelve hours I knew a few things for sure:

World? Rocked.

Pussy? Shattered.

Orgasms? Unforgettable.

Heart?

Ruined.

Fuck.

Fuck!

I wriggled out of his arms, carefully, silently. His breathing didn't change. He didn't move.

I stole down out of the loft. Found my clothes, strewn everywhere. Yanked my thong out of the tangled mess of my leggings, righted both, stuffed one leg and then the other into my underwear, tripped with them halfway on, because my leg was giving me hell.

"Fuck it," I whispered, and kicked the stupid thong off, sat down bare ass on the floor and put my leggings on sitting down like a little girl. Shrugged the shirt on hastily, braless, and shoved my thong and bra into my purse. Which was a tiny little clutch only big enough for a credit card wallet and phone, so needless to say the undergarments didn't really fit.

With one last glance up at the loft, my heart aching, I let myself out.

I wasn't even sure why I was running, only that it was an instinctual, gut-deep urge. I knew it was wrong. I knew I would regret it. I knew I was hurting Ink.

But the panic and the confusion and the aching emptiness left in the wake of finally crying out all my residual shit, coupled with the need for Ink, the clinging clenching wringing gutting churning blossoming swelling heart-bursting EVERYTHINGNESS—all the hurricane-wild confusion of feelings I had for and because of and about Ink… was just too much.

So, like a foolish, self-sabotaging, tail-between-the-still-very-sore legs puppy, I ran away.

NINE

Ink

I'D KNOWN THE MOMENT SHE WOKE UP THE SECOND TIME. The instant her breathing changed, I'd woken up. I kept my breathing even, and hadn't moved. Hadn't even opened my eyes. She'd frozen, lying stock-still, not even breathing.

My erection had been painful, more painful than any hard-on I'd ever had in my life, and it had been stuffed between her butt cheeks. For a moment, she'd feathered back against me, and I'd thought for a heady, dizzy moment that she would slide me inside her.

But she hadn't.

She'd wriggled away.

My heart had dropped out of my chest, stupidly

disappointed. I mean, if she hadn't let me come inside her in the heat of a mutual orgasm, she wasn't going to in the light of day, having just woken up, and completely lucid.

Clearly, she wasn't on birth control, which was a little odd to me, but none of my business, clearly.

I had been meaning to ask about it when we woke up. I'd been intending to make coffee and eggs for us, and talk on my porch, wrapped up in blankets.

Maybe go out for condoms.

I hadn't expected her to *run*.

When she was off the ladder, I'd silently angled over to peer down, one eye open, watching. She'd fallen over, and then just sat down, visibly struggling, frustrated. In pain—her leg was bothering her.

She got dressed, sort of.

Then she stood there, at my door, hand on the latch. Struggling.

Shoulders heaving.

Conflicted—the war of emotions written in every line, angle, and curve of her lithe, athletic body. Run, stay, run, stay.

She ran.

And it fucking hurt.

I mean, I got it, to a degree, why she chose to run. But it fucking cut me open like a razor blade slicing open the tender inner skin of my wrist.

God. I could see how conflicted she was. Shit, the way she'd cried last night had been gut-wrenching to hear. She'd cried for so long, and for so many things. Cried herself hoarse, and empty. Cried herself to sleep. The pain in her leg was part of it—but I wasn't sure how it fit in.

Dance, and the absence of it?

Lack of purpose, perhaps. She'd been a dancer her whole life, it had been her singular goal. To dance.

Now it was gone. She'd said so, and had made it clear she had no clue what the fuck she was going to do with her life.

So there was that.

Then there was us—the Cassie and Ink combo.

Such a beautiful thing, her and me.

The way we'd been together last night had been utterly glorious. We'd understood each other perfectly, without needing to be told.

She had fit around me as if the earth mother and sky father had formed us to be one, always.

God, the feel of her, bare around me, gasping, panting, needing, it was burned into my memory.

I still had a hard-on of utterly agonizing magnitude.

Despite my emotional turmoil, I let myself think of Cassie. She'd given me permission to do this, so I gave myself permission. Thought of her, last night.

On her knees in front of me, ass lifted as I buried into her. Writhing, mewling as I pierced her, penetrating deep.

In my imagination, though, she begged me for more. Begged me to let go. To fuck her harder.

But I couldn't even imagine that, and it somehow morphed into her mouth around me, like she'd done last night after I'd wrenched myself away from her. Unexpected, and incredible. Sudden wet hot suction around me, and I'd just lost it.

Thinking about this I came all over myself, gasping, the hard-on taken care of, but the need and the emotional ravaging no better. Worse, really.

I used Kleenex on the worst of the mess, clambered down the ladder and took a long shower. Thinking, wondering.

Should I let her go? Give her time to think? Go after her?

If I went after her, my need to talk things through would take over. I'd drag her truths out of her, and if Cassie hated anything, it was to have the things she'd kept buried dragged out of her. I think she was equal parts relieved and almost resentful for the way she'd broken down in my arms.

She'd needed it, but now that it was out, there was no putting it back.

Just like with me, and my sexuality.

It was loose, now.

There was no putting it back into the cage.

If I saw Cassie, I was worried I'd go feral. Become a caveman. Drag her back to my cave and fuck her senseless.

It wasn't like me, this wild ravenous, possessive need. It was…almost abstract, a thing other than me. I'd cultivated this persona of untouchable reserve. Complete calm. Wisdom. Composure. Artistic expression, and being in touch emotionality. This other part, cut loose by Cassandra Goode, was all animal. Primal sexual drive. Mad need. Possessive male dominance.

It scared me.

Absolutely terrified me, if I was being honest. What was I supposed to do with it? How did I express it? I couldn't let it loose. I couldn't give in to it. Cassie wasn't mine. She clearly didn't want to be, judging by the way she'd left. Secretly, sneaking out.

I'd seen the conflict, but she'd still left rather than face me, rather than face what we'd done last night.

What we'd created, together.

Namely: us.

That sense of us had been conceived last night— I'd pulled out before coming, true. But it was a thing no less real and physical for all that. Us.

And she'd run away from that.

And, for once, I wasn't content to let that stand.

I wasn't going to just let it slide. Accept it. Tolerate it.

I deserved more. Even if it was her telling me she didn't want me, didn't want us, couldn't handle us, that I was too much for her, that what we'd done was a mistake never to be repeated, I deserved her giving me that face to face.

But, I'd give her three days to figure that out herself. Three days to decide what to do, on her own. To find me, to talk to me.

———

The first day was hell. I had a full schedule, so that mitigated things, a bit. But it wasn't enough to keep me from dwelling on Cassie. So, for the next day, I called the first half a dozen names on my wait list and filled in gaps, so I was booked back-to-back for twelve hours straight, with a single thirty-minute break for lunch.

It wasn't enough.

I did the same for day three, and it took every ounce of control I had to not tear Ketchikan apart looking for Cassie.

Finally, well after midnight on the third day, I flopped onto my bed and resolved to go look for her the next morning.

TEN

Cassie

"CASSANDRA DANIELLE GOODE. GET YOUR ASS OUT of that bed this instant. This has gone on long enough, young lady." Mom was *pissed*. "I don't know what happened, but I've allowed you three full days to wallow in whatever misery you're in. I get it. I've been there, sweetheart." Softer, now. Gentle.

I just grumbled under my breath and turned away from her. Faced the wall. The bed dipped as Mom sat beside me, and her hand brushed through my hair.

"Talk to me, honey. What's going on? It's not like you to lay in bed for three days."

I ignored her.

"Cass." Firmer. "Stop this. Stop being petulant. Put on your big girl panties and *deal* with it."

"I'm not going to fit into my big girl panties in another week, Mom," I groaned.

She just laughed. "Is that what all this is about? You got on the scale and it was a few pounds up?"

"A few pounds? Mom." I finally sat up and turned to face her. "Try ten. *TEN*! I weigh one-fifteen, Mom."

She just cackled. "Oh, the horror! What will you do?"

I glared at her. "What the hell, Mom?"

She touched my cheek. "Even with the ten extra pounds, Cass, you still have lower body fat than ninety percent of the rest of the female population on the planet."

I wriggled. "You're missing the point."

She stared at me, *into* me, seeing me. As only a momma can. "Cassie-lassie." She gathered me in her arms, held her to me. "Talk to me, baby. Talk to Momma."

This was like sitting on Ink's floor to put on my pants. Crying in a ball, surrounded by him.

And now, Mom?

Was I a child all over again?

"I messed up, Mom."

"How?"

"Ink." I swallowed.

"You messed up with Ink?" She stilled. "You're not—"

"NO!" A little too loudly, because that *had* almost happened. "No, Mom. I'm not pregnant."

"Thank god for that," she breathed.

I pulled away to eye her. "What does that mean?"

She shrugged, unapologetic. "It means you are in absolutely no shape, mentally, physically, emotionally, spiritually, or financially, to be having a baby." A pause. "For that matter, neither am I, if you must know."

I laughed. "Yeah, you know what—you're right about that."

"So, then, what?"

I shrugged. "It's just…a lot, Mom."

"I can't decipher that, Cass. You're going to have to elaborate."

I groaned. "I need a shower."

She moved aside so I could climb off the bed— still dressed in the red yoga pants and tank top.

Mom sat on my bed while I got in the shower, and then she sat on the toilet lid. "So."

I sighed. I shampooed, washed, lathered in conditioner.

Finally, I spoke over the shower noise. "I don't *know*, Mom. I don't know. He's a lot. He and I… we had…we have…it's…" I groaned again, rinsing conditioner out of my hair. "It's just a lot. And I don't know what to do. And I ran away because he scares me shitless, but not because of the way he thinks. I ran, and now he's going to be hurt and angry because he has serious abandonment and rejection issues, and I played right into them in the worst possible way. But I'm scared. Emotionally. Of him. Of...possibility. Of—of everything being around him means for me. Mostly, that he knows I'm not—that I haven't..."

"That you're a train wreck of unresolved issues?" Mom suggested.

I laughed. "Wow, Mom. Thanks." I laughed again, wryly. "But...yeah, I guess that's accurate."

She was silent as I rinsed off one more time, and then shut the water off. Mom handed me a towel from around the back of the shower curtain, and I toweled off and wrapped it around me. Tucked it in place, and stepped out, around Mom. Brushed my teeth. Brushed my hair.

Mom watched, thoughtful.

Heedless of Mom still being in the room, I dropped the towel to get dressed—the six of us, Mom, my sisters, and I were not concerned with family modesty around each other, and we frequently changed in front of each other as the situation required. So this wasn't an unusual or weird thing, for us.

When I turned to fish underwear out of my

drawer, though, she gasped. "Cassandra! You…you're bruised like crazy."

I blinked, turning to glance at her, baffled. "I…what?"

She made a face, one I, for one, couldn't quite read. "On your fanny."

I laughed. "Fanny? Mom, come on. Join the twenty-first century, geez."

I turned in circles, trying to see my butt, but of course I couldn't, so I went back into the bathroom and craned my head to see my buttocks in the mirror.

Fingerprints.

Where Ink had gripped me, held me in place.

Where he'd held on to me for dear life, while desperately, with every ounce of his strength, holding back. I'd felt that restraint, as if that fine line of control had been all that separated me from being run over by a runaway freight train.

Buttocks, hips—I glanced down, and found fingerprints on my hipbones, around front, where he'd gripped me there, too. All over my hips and ass.

I giggled. Blushed.

What to tell Mom, though?

I left the bathroom, chewing on answers. She just waved a hand at me. "I'm an adult, Cassandra, and so are you. But I don't need to know *anything*. Not about that."

I bit my lip, holding back laughter. Hysterical laughter—not hysterical in the *OMG that comedian is hysterical* sense, but in the literal, archaic, original sense of the word. Close to madness, inappropriate laughter, *I can't control what I'm feeling anymore* kind of hysteria.

She looked at me, and was fighting laughter of her own. "Well, I only need to know one thing."

"What's that?"

"That you're okay with those bruises. That you bear them willingly."

I *liked* them. I liked knowing he'd marked me. They twinged a little, but only enough to remind me that they were there, and how I got them. I wanted more of them.

But I couldn't say that to Mom. Shit, I wasn't sure I could say that to Ink.

Because there was so much else tangled up in it.

Finally, I just sighed. "Yeah, I...yes." Another sigh. "Yes, I'm okay with them. More than okay."

She just smiled. "Okay, then. That's all I need to know about *that*." A silence, as I dressed.

Jeans, tight and stretchy, ripped at the knees— putting them on hurt my bad leg. Everything hurt my leg, and I know Mom saw that, too. She didn't miss a thing, dammit.

"You're not doing your mobility stretches."

I sighed, a sound more growl than sigh. *"Don't,* Mom."

"Or exercising."

"No shit! Why do you think I'm gaining weight?"

"Cassie, you have to take care of—"

"What's the fucking point?" I snapped. "There *is* no point. And that's the point."

"Cass."

I hooked a bra on with the clasp at my belly, twisted it around, and shrugged into the straps, adjusting my tatas into the cups, and then pulled on a T-shirt.

"Where are you going, Cass?" She frowned at me. "It's past midnight."

I paused, glancing at the clock. "Then why the hell did you wake me up?"

She sighed. "Because you've been in bed for three days straight. I've come and gone over the past three days, and I've not seen you leave the bed even once. It was time."

I nodded. "Well, you're right. It's time."

"For what?"

"For me to do what I have to do."

Mom tilted her head. "Which is what, honey?"

I sighed, rubbing my bad leg. "Fuck if I know, Mom," I said. "Fuck if I know. But something. He deserves it."

"So do you, honey," she said, her voice quiet. "You deserve it."

I pulled my hair back into a ponytail, grabbed my purse—which still had my bra and thong in it. I tossed them into the hamper, stuffed my feet into a pair of ballet flats, and glanced back at Mom.

"Thank you, Mom."

She shook her head. "You're my daughter. I love you. I want you to be happy, or barring that, at least okay. And right now, babe, you're not okay." She stood, wrapped me in a tight mom-hug. "And that's okay. We'll figure it out. I'm always here, and I'm always on your side, sweetheart."

"Even when I fuck up?"

She pulled back, palms on my cheeks. "*Especially* then, darling."

I sniffed back a tear. "Dammit, Mom. Quit being saccharine."

She just laughed, and popped me on the butt. "There's the Cassie I know."

I laughed and paused to kiss her on the cheek. "You're a good mommy."

"Go figure yourself out, kiddo."

I smiled, and wondered if she could see that I was scared stupid. "Yeah, I guess we'll see, huh?"

I walked over to Ink's, in the dark, alone. It was a couple of miles, but it was good. Exercise for my leg, time to think. Fresh air, after three days in bed, like a loser. Wallowing. Hating myself. Missing Ink. Refusing to think about how much I missed him and how badly I'd fucked up by panicking and running like I had.

I still wasn't entirely sure, even now, that I had the courage to walk into his house and talk to him after leaving like I had. I didn't know what I would say. Or even what I wanted.

All I knew was, Mom didn't raise me to be the kind of woman who would run out on a man in the middle of the night after earth-shaking sex, after said man had held me as I bawled my eyes out in a re-al-deal nervous breakdown, ugly crying in a full-body dry heaving sort of way. After said man had made it very clear he was not someone to walk out on, so if I wanted what we'd done, I couldn't walk out.

And I'd walked out.

I found myself at his door, looking in through the glass storm door at the darkened interior. Hesitating. He must be asleep.

But I was here, and I wasn't going back, not now. I couldn't.

It was hard to breathe.

I quietly opened the door, and shut it behind me. I listened and heard the soft steady huff of a sleeping Ink. Why was I here? What was I going to do?

Wake him and be like, hey, I'm sorry I ran like a scared little girl?

I saw his phone on the counter, and an idea struck me. Dumb, and silly, but I couldn't stop myself once the idea was in my head.

Ink didn't bother with a passcode, I knew. He only had a handful of numbers in his contacts, no email, didn't text, rarely took pictures.

I went into his bathroom, closed the door, turned on the light, and spent the next several minutes doing something I never anticipated I would do, ever.

I took…salacious photos of myself.

Started with me, clothed.

Then with my shirt off. Then with my shirt on and my pants off. Then just in my bra and underwear. Different poses, some awkward AF and which I immediately deleted, others that took a few tries to get right and which ended up…good.

Then I took my bra off and took more of myself topless, in just a pair of light gray high cut briefs.

I took those off, and took even more of me totally nude. When I had taken what I felt like was enough, I put all my clothes back on, and then went through and selected all the photos and put them in a hidden album.

I wondered if he'd find it. Probably not. Would probably need a hint or two.

I wasn't sure why I'd done that. Just that I wanted to, so I did. Because the man needed to get his sexuality back, and the taste of it that I'd gotten was... so impossibly good I knew I'd be haunted the rest of my life by it. If nothing else ever happened between us, I knew, beyond a shadow of a doubt, that what I'd had with Ink that night was far and away the best thing that had ever happened to me, and probably ever would happen.

And I'd had to make him pull out.

I should have stopped for condoms so I could wake him in a sexy way.

But I was scared of that, too. Terrified. It would be too good.

I'd never want anything else.

I already didn't.

I couldn't fathom touching another man, or letting another man touch me. Not after Ink.

I put his phone back where I'd found it, summoned my courage, and climbed up the ladder. Ink was still asleep. He looked...innocent. Huge, powerful, sexy.

Troubled.

A small frown furrowed his brow, even in sleep.

I'd put that there.

I sat a couple of feet away, just looking at him. Wired, not tired at all, wondering what the hell I was doing here, and what I would do if he woke up, what I would say.

I just looked at him.

At his tattoos—a deer walking through mist, head turned, eyes bright. An owl swooping among trees, round yellow eyes. An elk with the sun framed between its huge antlers. A bear. Wolf tracks, abstract and blending in with runes and lines and dots. Lost in the jumble, a little bumblebee, fat and cute. Ants in a line, disappearing into an anthill.

I wanted to kiss them all, taste them all. Trace and touch and mark them all as mine.

The power behind that word—*mine*...it shocked me. Mine.

He wasn't.

And I wasn't his.

I'd never belonged to anyone. I'd never felt like I belonged anywhere, except on stage, lost in the dance. The troupe, Europe, my apartment in Paris with Rick, back home on the East Coast. Here in Alaska...

I've never belonged.

But I wanted to.

I wanted to belong to someone.

I wanted to *be* someone's.

Not just someone's.

HIS.

My eyes watered.

Stung.

This couldn't be. *Couldn't* be.

How did this happen?

How the hell was I falling for this guy? And why?

He stirred, and I froze. I felt his breathing change. Felt the air solidify.

"Cass." That deep, quiet, smooth, powerful voice.

"Ink." I swallowed hard. Tried to breathe. "I…I'm sorry. I'm sorry I left the way I did."

"You're here, now."

"Yeah."

"Why'd you come back?"

"Because you…you deserve better than for me to run away like a scared little girl."

"And why'd you run?"

"It was…a lot. You and me, that night."

He sighed. "Yeah, it was."

"It's still a lot," I muttered.

He nodded. "Yeah. It is."

"Not sure what else to say."

"The whole honest truth, babe." He was still lying as he'd been when asleep—on his side, head on his crooked arm. Hair loose and splayed everywhere behind and around him.

"I don't even know what that is."

"Why you ran. Start there. Start small."

"I don't fucking know."

"You do."

I hated the anger that rose up—why did he have to push? Why couldn't he just let me have my stupid lie?

I blinked. Gave up trying not to cry, and put the effort toward not sobbing, instead. Just, sort of quietly letting tears trickle down. Keeping the anger buried. It was my anger, but not at him. It was irrational, and I knew it.

But it came out anyway.

"If you know so damned much about me, then you tell me why I ran." Good god, I sounded petulant.

Didn't take it back, though, because he was pushing deep into my psyche, and I didn't want my demons exorcised. I didn't want my layers of shit unearthed.

"Because you're scared."

I felt the tears flow harder. "I'm not scared of you, Ink."

"Didn't say that." He sat up, but didn't move any closer to me. Just stared at me in the darkness. "Of yourself. Of feelings. You've kept yourself closed off your whole life. Something to do with your dad. And I think sex is confusing for you because you want to use it as a substitute for emotions, but you're too emotional for that, and not very good at keeping your equilibrium. So you shut down. Pretend to be all stoic. And something about us threatens all that. So you're scared."

"And I think you're scared too. I think you know damn well that I can handle everything you've got, and more, but you're still scared of rejection. It's not about hurting me. It's about me hurting you. I hurt you by leaving, and that's what I'm sorry for. I was scared, you're right. I'm still scared. But I'm here."

"Yeah, you are. That's something, and I see it." He sighed. "I think you used me, in a way."

I flinched. "What?" I swallowed hard. "What the fuck does that mean?"

"You have shit you haven't dealt with. Your dad. Your future. I don't know. Mainly who you are and what you want, now that you don't have professional dance anymore. You're too scarred and scared to face that, and you don't know how or where to start. So you latched onto me, and this, and us, as a distraction. As a way of putting off having to face yourself. And when shit got super fuckin' real between us that night, it scared the shit out of you because us bein' real with each other made it harder for you to keep pretending you're okay not dealing with the fact that you got no fuckin' clue who you are now, and what the hell you're gonna do with your life, because you put all your eggs in the one basket."

I felt the anger as a protective shell, keeping his

truth bombs out. It wasn't working for shit, but damn if I wasn't going to keep trying.

"Yeah? Well…I think you're…you're scared me. I think you want things with me that scare you shitless. So you held back, not out of fear of me or hurting me, but because the things you want and how bad you want them scares you. But you've been hurt and you don't trust me to be there and to accept who you are, what you are, what you want."

"Yeah, I'm fucking scared!" he yelled, a shocking loudness in the small space, more shocking yet because it was coming from him. "No one has ever wanted me! My own parents couldn't fuckin' handle me! My school, my team, the woman I fuckin' loved, nobody can fuckin' handle me. And yeah, I want shit with you that I don't know how to fuckin' deal with. It's too damn much, Cass." He seemed to swell, to take up more space than he usually did. Became bigger, louder, *more*. "You wanna know *my* truth, Little Sparrow?"

I was not afraid of him. Despite his size, despite the increase in his massive presence, despite the way he prowled toward me, I was not afraid. I was excited. Thrilled. "Yes, Ink. I do."

"My truth is, I held back with you because I was scared I'd rip you in fuckin' two. I wanted to fuck you so hard you'd just…break into pieces. I wanted to fuck you so damned hard you'd feel it in every god-damn bone in your body." His voice was a feral threatening snarl that shivered into my center. "I wanted to fuck you in every position there is, a hundred times. I wanted to fuck your mouth and fuck your pussy. I wanted to watch you go down on me until you choked on my cum."

I shook all over at his words.

"I want to hold both of your hands in one of mine and pin you down so you can't get away and fuck you until you scream." His eyes *burned*. "I want it so bad I'm fuckin' crazy with it. I wake up hard as a damned rock needing to fuck you so bad. I want you till I'm...till I'm fuckin' crazy. And that scares me shitless. How bad I want you. The *things* I want. The way I want them. I'm not a violent person. Not a demanding or aggressive person. But you? You make me something else, woman. You *do* things to me just by bein' you."

"Holy shit, Ink."

"And you know what scares me even more?"

"What?" I whispered.

"When I say I want to *fuck* you," he hissed the word, drew it out, emphasized every letter, every sound, "I mean make *love*. In the deepest, truest, rawest sense of the phrase."

"Ink..."

"*That's* what scares me, Little Sparrow."

"What if I told you I'm just as scared?" I slid closer to him. "That I'm just as scared because I want that same thing, those same things, just as much?"

"I believe you," he whispered.

Silence. Tense, tight, boiling with unspoken ideas and thoughts and words and emotions.

"So, now what?" I asked.

"Now you tell me what your future looks like."

Totally unexpected. So unexpected I blinked in the darkness, mouth flapping open and closed. "I—I—what?"

"What do you want, Cassandra?" He took my hand. Held it. Squeezed hard. "Not about me, or us. For you. What do *you* want? Who are you? Who are you, now? What are you going to do?"

"What does that…" I swallowed a hot thick burning lump in my throat, only to have it lodge in my chest. "What does that have to do with us?"

"Fuckin' *everything*, Cass. Everything."

"I don't understand."

"Think about it, boo." He traced the pad of a fingertip over my knee, on the skin that showed through the rip in my jeans.

"I am, but I don't understand what me figuring out my life has to do with you and me wanting each other."

"I ain't a hump-and-dumper, Cass. I don't do temporary. Don't do casual. Don't do hookups."

"I…I mean, I have, but that's not what I want with you." I hurt. God, this hurt, so fucking bad. "I want…more. What, I don't know. But more."

"Me too. I want everything."

"Okay, so I don't get the issue." I blinked back tears. "You want to be with me, I want to be with you. So maybe I still have some shit to work out. I will. I *am*."

"You are?"

"Yeah." Uncomfortable.

"So you ain't just usin' me to avoid working out your issues?"

"No."

"Don't fuckin' lie to me, babe." His voice was a growl. "Don't lie to *yourself*."

"Why are you being so mean?" I snapped, yanking my hand away and scrambling away from him. "Why do you fucking care what I do with my goddamn life?"

"Because I want our lives to be one life. And you can't offer yourself and your life if you're still lost and refusing to face your shit."

"It's hard!" I yelled. "You have no fucking idea how hard it is. I lost *everything*. I had to sell and donate half of my life and belongings because I couldn't afford to ship it home from Paris. I lost my career, my passion. My fucking *mobility*. My fiancé, and everything I thought I knew about him and our relationship. I—lost—*everything*—in that goddamn car wreck. So yeah, I'm still a bit of a mess. Still figuring it out. But that doesn't mean I don't have anything to offer you."

"That's not what I meant." He frowned, puzzling through his thoughts.

"It's what you said." I was fighting another sob-fest.

"I know. But you're missing my point. It's not about what I'm getting from you. It's what I want for you. For the us that could be."

"Okay, Yoda. Whatthefuckever."

"Don't, Cass. You're avoiding yourself. You're scared to face it. That's okay. I'm here. I'll help. And if you need time, I'll be there waiting when you figure it out." His voice was soft and quiet and tender. "I'm not pushing you away. I'm not rejecting you. I'm just saying we can't have a real relationship until you face your own shit."

"And what about you?" I snarled. "You have your own share of demons, don't you? What about the fact that you didn't even jack off for what, almost ten years? Because one woman messed you up? One woman hurt you? You took that all on yourself and shut down totally. You think that's healthy? You think one night of messing around has fixed all that? You think I'm the only one that has shit to face?"

"There's a difference, Cassie. Yeah, I have shit to handle. Yeah, it affects you and us—but that requires us working together. Me learning to trust you, and learning to trust myself. To open up. It will happen, but it'll take time. I'm willing to do it. I'm admitting I have a hard time being open. I admit I hold back a lot, don't express shit very well when it comes to physical stuff. I admit I'm afraid of letting go. You're right. It's at least in part because I'm afraid of *me*, not you. I know you don't want to hurt me. Even when you left, I knew it was not about me, it was about you. I watched you leave, you know. I watched you struggle. I got it then, and I get it now. Yeah, Cass, I'm fucking afraid of intimacy. I'm afraid of vulnerability. I'm afraid of letting go. But I'm admitting that, and I'm committing to you, right here, right now, that I can and will actively work toward total trust and vulnerability with you, emotionally and physically. Because I believe you and me have a real shot at a relationship like my cousin has, like all her in-laws have. I see all fuckin twelve of 'em, Lucas included, havin' these deep meaningful fulfilling fuckin' romances…and I *want* that shit."

His eyes bored into mine.

"I want that shit for myself. And I want that shit with *you*." He was utterly still, and that stillness, the quiet intensity in his deep voice made his words hit me all the harder, like a comet smashing into earth. "I want that shit with you, and I am willin' to do whatever the fuck it takes to be the man you deserve. To be *good*. For you, for us. So I can fulfill you. I'll *do* that shit, Cass."

Tears, fucking tears. Lump in my throat. Ache in my chest. Can't breathe. Can't swallow. Can't make my limbs or fingers or brain or mouth or anything work. Just paralyzed.

"I don't believe in falling in love, Cassandra." A pause, fraught and significant. "I ain't fallen in love with you."

Another pause. I tried to digest what he was saying. "Ink…" a broken whisper.

"I believe love grows. It's *built*. It ain't a fuckin' accident. What is it my cousin's teenage kids say all the time? I caught feelings for you. *That* was an accident. I didn't mean for that shit to happen. Feelings come and go, though. I coulda stayed shut down, coulda taken the progress you helped me make and walked. I got offers from tattoo parlors all over the world. I could move to Tahiti and do tattoos full-time. Anywhere. I don't gotta be here." A shake of his head. "But I *am* here. I'm with *you*. I'm facin' my shit and saying the hard things, the hard fuckin' truths, scared out of my mind you won't get it, you won't agree. Because I choose—I *choose*—to build a love with you. To grow a love with you."

"Fucking hell, Ink." The world was blurred through a screen of tears.

"All that bein' said, babe." Big rough fingers brushed my tears away. "What do *you* want?"

I shook my head. "I don't fucking *know!*"

"I ain't askin' you to have all the answers now, Cass. I'm just asking you to be willing to actually *look.*"

My leg ached. Throbbed. Burned.

So did my heart.

I felt anger. Unreasoning anger, unrealistic, irrational. At him. At myself. At life. At god or fate, or luck. At Rick. At the lorry driver who ran the light. At him. At Ink. Because he was saying shit that scared me into the kind of irrational fear that became anger.

I was ready for hot sex, with feelings.

I was okay having caught some feelings for this man.

That's fine.

But love?

I wasn't ready for *love*. It's too soon for love. Because love requires commitment. Honesty. Vulnerability…

God, all the shit he said.

I was not ready for that.

I wanted to be.

I wanted him.

If I was going to have that, I wanted it with him.

But I was too scared. Too paralyzed by fear of…

See, I can't go there. My head shuts down. What am I so afraid of? I can't even face that.

So, instead of handling it like a grown-up, like a mature woman, I watched myself act like an idiot child. Like a hormonal teenager.

Lashing out. At Ink. The one who least deserved it.

"Go to hell, Ink."

I heard the words. And I immediately realized the stupidity in them, the unfairness in them. I heard the bitterness in my own voice. Heard the irrational panic, felt it, knew beyond a shadow of a doubt that he saw it and heard it, too.

He understood exactly what was going on with me.

He probably knew this is how I'd react.

Damned insightful motherfucker.

He knew.

And he still had the balls to speak his truth.

Instead of taking a moment—a rational, quiet moment—my sad, confused broken heart had taken over, and I was unable to stop myself from acting the way I was acting. And, believe me, I tried. I tried to tell myself to turn around and say sorry and kiss him and tell him I'd figure it out. I wanted to promise him that I would do what I needed to do, because I wanted to grow a love with him, too.

But I didn't do any of that.

I just couldn't.

My brain knew better. My body sure as hell knew better.

But my heart? No way.

My heart told me to get off the bed, go down the ladder, and out the door.

ELEVEN

Ink

I WATCHED HER LEAVE, AGAIN, AND MY HEART BROKE.

Not for me.

For her.

I'd known, deep down, that she wasn't going to take my honesty well, yet I still said what was in my heart.

I'm upset and hurt.

I'm hurting for me.

Because that—*that* was rejection.

I slid out of bed, knowing I couldn't sleep anymore.

I had to get out of this place for a bit.

I wasn't sure where I was going. My feet wanted

to take me to where I knew she was, but I couldn't do that. She had to figure herself out. I couldn't do it for her. I knew I was right. I knew she was avoiding figuring herself out, and if I let her use me as a distraction, she never would. And it would fester. And, eventually, she'd resent me.

I knew, deep in my heart, that I had to put the truth out there, and accept the consequences.

And consequences can really suck.

A few minutes later I found myself at the door of the apartment building where Juneau and Remington lived. I knew it was late but I pressed the buzzer anyway.

A pause.

"It's one thirty in the goddamn morning." I heard Remington's sleepy, irritated growl. "Who the fuck is it and what the fuck do you want?"

"Sorry, Rem," I murmured. "It's Ink. I—"

"Shit, sorry brother," he cut in the moment he heard my voice. "Come on up."

The door buzzed and I padded up the stairs to the third floor, and saw Juneau standing in their open apartment door, waiting for me. She was dressed in a short black silk robe. Barely covering anything. But she was my cousin, and I wasn't bothered by it in the slightest.

I leaned down to hug her. "June Bug."

She breathed me in, rubbed my back. "Ink." She pulled back, grabbed my hand, and led me inside. She closed the door and pushed me toward the couch. "What's wrong?"

Rem was leaning a shoulder against the hallway wall, watching, wearing nothing but a pair of boxers—all muscle and tattoos, a ripped IG model / trainer physique covered in gorgeous ink. "Sorry about the shitty welcome, Ink. Don't like getting woke up."

I waved at him, dismissing his apology. "I wouldn't be here like this but I'm just…"

Juneau was bustling in the kitchen. Pulling something out of the fridge, stuffing it into the microwave, beeping it into humming life, waiting—when it dinged, she brought me a glass container full of my aunt's incredible elk stew. "Here. Talk and eat."

I laughed. "You know me too well, June Bug." I took a few bites, savoring the flavors. "Thanks, cuz."

A few more bites.

Juneau sighed. "It's Lucas's girlfriend's daughter, isn't it?"

I nodded. "Yeah. Cassie."

Juneau sat beside me, tugging futilely at the hem of her stupid little robe. "Did she hurt you?"

I laughed, bitterly. "It's complicated."

"If she hurt you, I'll kill her. You know I'm not a violent person, but you've been through enough."

I reached up behind me and grabbed the knitted throw blanket off the back of the couch and spread it over Juneau's lap. "I must've interrupted somethin'," I muttered, "you dressed like that."

She ducked her head, but was grinning like a fox leaving an unguarded henhouse. "You didn't interrupt anything."

"Nah," Remington said. Then chuckled. "We were between rounds."

Juneau threw a pillow at him. "Remington Badd! Don't be gross."

I just laughed. "You're in love. It ain't gross. You're my cousin, so I don't need details, but it don't bother me. Just glad I didn't interrupt you in the middle of something."

Another laugh from Rem. "Don't worry, bub. I wouldn't have stopped."

Juneau watched me eat. "What's going on, Ink?"

"It's kind of a long story, and I hate bothering you guys with it."

Remington sat on the arm of the couch, rested a hand on Juneau's nape. "Nah, bro. Tell us."

I looked from one to the other. "It's…a lot."

Juneau rubbed my shoulder. "Ink, you've been there for me my whole life. It's largely because of you that I'm living my dream of being a tattoo artist. You challenged me and encouraged me and pushed me and provoked me and counseled me, and then Rem came along and he was the last catalyst I needed to live my truth." She leaned against me, her head on my bicep. "My point is that now it's my turn to be there for you."

I nodded. "Okay, well...I guess you probably need the whole story."

So, I started at the beginning, telling her the things I think she'd long suspected and guessed at. Then I told her about Cassie, how things had developed, leaving out the details they didn't need and which I wasn't about to share, cousin or no cousin.

Juneau and Remington listened attentively, asking questions here and there. Finally, when I was done, Remington got up and paced the living room a few times. Then sat down again, picking at a hangnail and not looking at me.

"Ink, I gotta be real with you, bro."

"Always," I said.

"I think what you told her was true, and right. But I think she just needed you to give her space and time to figure it out on her own. I think maybe you were a bit...harsh."

I sighed. "June Bug?"

She tilted her head to one side. "I don't know. It sounds like she *is* avoiding things. But I guess what Rem is saying is that maybe you guys could have figured out the way forward without having to drop the hammer."

I hung my head. "Shit. So what the hell do I do now?"

"Don't get me wrong, Ink, you're right about everything you said to her, and I bet one day she'll thank you for your honesty. But she just had her whole life turned the fuck upside down, and she had already taken off once before, so maybe you coulda been a little more understanding about that." Rem shrugged. "What do *you* want to do now?"

"Go find her and…fix things."

"Except you can't, can you?" Juneau smiled at me, not quite sadly. "And that's the point. I think you need to give her time. In the meantime, make it clear to her that you care about her and you're here, waiting for her. No rush, no pressure, no expectations."

"I thought I'd done that."

Remington snorted. "Yeah, well, that kinda thing sorta bears repeating, in situations like this. She's probably hurt and pissed off, and maybe isn't remembering the good shit you said."

I ran my fingers through my beard. "I'm no good at this."

"Who is?" Juneau asked. "I'm sure as hell not."

"No one is *good* at this," Rem said. "You just muddle through it best you can and hope to hell the person you're diggin' on don't break your fuckin' heart to pieces in the process."

I looked from him to her. "So that's what you're doing? Muddling through?"

Juneau smiled at me. "After a while, you learn to trust. Not just the person, but the relationship. It's still scary." She glanced at Remington. "He could still decide he wants someone skinnier, taller, blonder. He could decide he's bored with me. He could decide a lot of things. He could just get drunk and bang somebody. I could tell him I'm pregnant and he could panic and run. All of that is possible. But I choose to trust him. Rem has shown me that he loves me. That he wants me, and only me. That this thing between us is beautiful and real and lasting."

Remington tugged on her hair. "Babe, I know you were sayin' all that shit for emphasis, but...don't. I don't want anybody skinnier or taller or blonder. I couldn't get bored of you if I spent a million years with you. And even drunk, I would never want anyone but you." He frowned. "You're not pregnant...are you? If you are, I'm not panicking."

She just laughed. "No, babe, I'm not pregnant. But if you do what you did a little while ago, I will be."

"We used a condom," he protested. "Mostly."

She just laughed and patted his cheek. "Yes,

darling. But it's the other side of *mostly* where you get unexpected babies." She tugged on his beard. "But babe, if I got pregnant, I wouldn't be mad. I'm not ready to actively try, but if it happens, I'll be happy."

He sighed. "Me too. Not looking for it, but wouldn't freak out." He laughed. "Well, maybe I'd freak out a little. But I wouldn't run."

I just watched this back and forth between them. "So."

They glanced at me, and Juneau smirked. "Sorry, cousin."

I laughed. "Why don't I let you two get back to sort of, not really, but kind of, maybe, possibly making babies. I got some thinkin' to do."

Remington wasn't super quick to argue.

Juneau frowned at me. "You can sleep here on the couch, if you want."

I shook my head. "Nah, I'm okay. Just puzzling on this. Thanks for listening."

I got up, put my bowl in the sink, hugged Juneau and did the manly half-handshake-half-hug thing with Remington. I left their apartment, and let my feet carry me.

It was no big surprise that I ended up at Liv's condo complex. Not sure why. It was near three in the morning. She was asleep. Her mom was asleep. I wasn't about to wake them up.

Yet my feet carried me to the correct building. To the steps. I sat on the steps outside the door, staring at the stars, wondering at myself, my life. Wondering if I'd done the right thing, or the wrong thing, or the right thing in the wrong way.

At some point, I fell asleep.

I was woken by a door smacking me in the head. "OhmygoshI'msorry," I heard a familiar voice say, as I rubbed my head. "Oh, Ink. It's you." I blinked blearily up at Liv Goode, Cassie's mom.

"Yeah, it's me."

She knelt and poked my head with motherly concern. "Are you okay? I wasn't expecting anyone to be there."

"Nah, I'm fine. I didn't mean to fall asleep here. I was just…" I wasn't sure what to say, so I didn't finish.

She moved to sit on the step next to me. "Cassie came home pretty upset."

I growled. "My fault. I was misguided. Meant the right thing, but didn't go about it the right way."

She looked me over. "You're half-naked. Aren't you cold?"

I chuckled. "Nah, ma'am. I don't get cold. I

don't like clothes all that much, so this is about as dressed as I tend to get."

She blinked at me. "You're not even wearing shoes."

"Nah."

"You walked here?"

I nodded. "Sure. Don't got a workin' car."

"Barefoot?"

I brought my foot up to show the bottom of my foot, which was thickly callused. "I could step on a fu—on a nail, and not really feel it. Been barefoot my whole life." I laughed. "Matter of fact, I own a pair of winter boots for when the snow is real deep, and a pair of flip-flops, and a pair of hiking boots for hunting and shit—stuff, I mean. Sorry."

She just patted my shoulder. "I'm dating Lucas Badd. If you think curse words bother me, then you've clearly never met a Badd."

I snickered. "Yeah, they're a potty mouth crew. I ain't much better."

"I raised my daughters to be ladies, but I'm afraid it hasn't entirely taken for some of them." She sniffed, but it was meant in jest, I could tell.

"Ain't met none of the others, but Cassie is all lady. Salty language don't make her not a lady. Sometimes a curse word just fits."

She sighed. "Yes, and being in a relationship

with a man with a mouth like Lucas's has not done wonderful things for my own desire to avoid strong language."

I laughed. "I bet." I looked at Liv. "I didn't mean to hurt her."

Liv snorted. "She wasn't hurt so much as angry. 'How dare he' and 'who does he think he is?' That kind of thing." She patted my shoulder again. "But she's thinking, now, so perhaps it was what she needed to get her really putting effort into working out what she wants for herself."

"I just…I care about her. And I felt like she was… using me, I guess, as a way of avoiding it. And I didn't want that for her."

Liv nodded. "I understand. And, like I said, as much as she didn't like it, it did work, in that it has her really thinking about things." She lifted an eyebrow. "Some advice from her mother?"

"Please," I said.

"Give her time. Once her temper is up, it's slow coming down, and she's not always very quick to listen to reason, or be rational when she's angry. But once she comes down and has gotten her anger out, she works things through in her head. So just…give her time." She tilted her head, eying me. "You care about her?"

I nodded. "Yes, ma'am."

"You love her?"

I sighed. "Don't know that I've ever really been in love. So I ain't sure I can…wrap it up in those terms. What I told her is, I don't believe in falling in love. I believe in intentionally growing love. So I can say I want to be with her, to grow a relationship with her. And that's why I wanted to see her not use me as an avoidance mechanism—'cause if she's doing that, any relationship we have wouldn't be…what it could be or should be. Because she wouldn't be who she could be. I don't know how to put it any better than that."

She nodded. "Well, I understand your meaning perfectly, and I agree. I just know that she's going to need time to work this through." A pause, a look at me. "It may take a while. She has a lot to work through."

"So what you're sayin' is, politely, she don't want to see me."

A shrug. "She didn't say so, but that was the subtext to much of her ranting last night and this morning. But it's also clear to me that she has feelings for you, or she wouldn't be so upset. So my advice comes from wanting her to be happy. If that includes being with you, she's going to need time to dig through all this, and if I can get her to agree, perhaps even see a therapist."

I sat, and thought, and came to a decision. "Well, Mrs. Goode. I appreciate your time and your advice. I think I'll take it." I stood up. "How and when you tell her you saw me is up to you. I know myself well enough to know if I'm around town, I'm gonna go nuts wanting to see her, talk to her, bug her, make things better, go back on what I said just to be around her. So if she really does just need time to get this shit in her head and heart worked out, then I gotta give her that time and space." I scuffed my foot on the step. "I got a cabin up north of Anchorage a ways. I'm due for a hiatus from things anyway, so I guess I'll just head up there and stay scarce. If and when she wants to see me, tell her my cousin Juneau will know how to find me."

She frowned. "Won't you have a cell phone or something?"

I just laughed. "Well, for one thing, where my cabin is, there ain't even any roads, not so much as a two-track. It's several hours' hike in from the nearest two-track. So, cell phones, even if I was to bring mine, which I won't, sure as shit don't work. Not within fifty-some miles of where I'll be."

Liv nodded. "I understand. Lucas and Ramsey specialize in places like that."

I smiled. "Well, Lucas and Ramsey specialize in getting there, in showing people how to get there. I grew up there." A shrug. "Well, not in that cabin specifically, but a place a lot like it."

She watched me descend the steps. "Ink, I know she's upset right now, and I do think perhaps you could have been a bit more politic but, overall, I think Cassandra is very lucky to have found you."

I shook my head. "Mrs. Goode, ma'am, I'm the lucky one."

She just rested her chin in her hand, smiling. "Good answer. Which means it's mutual." She slid a cell phone out of her purse, glanced at the screen, and put it back. "I have to go, I have an early client meeting."

"Thanks for your time, Mrs. Goode."

"Call me Liv, please."

Another wave, and I walked away, bare feet padding through the dew-damp grass, leaving footprints on the sidewalk.

About thirty minutes later, I was paying a call to Brock Badd—I found him at the slip where he parked his seaplane—tinkering in the engine compartment. He didn't hear me at first, having a small Bluetooth speaker perched on the strut nearby, classic rock blaring from it.

Not wanting to cause him to bump his head, I sat cross-legged on the dock, watching him crank a wrench while cursing floridly and continuously.

Finally, he pulled out, frustrated, smacking the wrench against his open palm with one last vicious curse.

"Problem?" I asked.

He glanced over at me, blinking in surprise. "Ink. Didn't know you were there." He wiggled the wrench. "Damn bolt is stuck like a motherfucker. I like to think I'm pretty strong, but that bitch is on there."

"I don't know much about fixin' shit like that, but I got more bulk to put behind a pull. So I can try, if you like."

He reached in, fit the wrench on the bolt, and waved at it. "Go to town, buddy."

I leaned in, peering at the engine compartment—part of the issue was that the bolt he was trying to loosen was in very tight quarters without much room to maneuver. I didn't think much of my chances, but I grabbed the wrench and pulled, straining as hard as I could.

Nothing.

I tried again, and this time with one hand while smacking at my fist with the other, growling through the strain. I felt it begin to give, just a tiny bit. So I paused, sucked in a deep breath, held it, gritted my teeth, and then put all my strength into pulling at the long-handled socket wrench. Growling through gritted teeth, I felt the bolt give a bit more, and then a bit more, and I renewed my effort until I felt light-headed, and this time I added all my weight.

And then, met with a sudden lack of resistance, I fell backward away from the seaplane and onto my ass on the dock with a thud which made the whole dock shudder. I laughed, stood up, and handed Brock the wrench.

"Well, it's loose. Not sure if the bolt is even there anymore, but it's loose."

He peeked in, snorted. "Damn, dude. I thought for sure I was gonna have to shear it off. Thanks."

I shrugged. "Bein' big has advantages, I guess."

He leaned into the cockpit and snagged a big Thermos, poured steaming black coffee into a Styrofoam cup he produced from somewhere, handed it to me.

"So, what brings you to my slip?" he asked.

"I gotta get inland, and I don't have a car. Hopin' you have some time free today to fly me up as near to Talkeetna as you can get."

He dug in his back pocket for his phone and consulted it. "I have a flight scheduled at ten, should be back by noon. So, if you can wait till around one or so, I can do it for sure."

I nodded. "Fine by me." I combed my fingers through my beard. "Just let me know your rates so I can grab some cash."

He stared at me like I'd grown a second head. "Bro, you new? Family doesn't pay."

I shrugged. "Didn't want to assume, just 'cause my cousin is serious with your cousin."

He just grinned. "Well, no need to assume. It's not about blood or relational distance. I'm telling you, you're family, and family doesn't pay. All you need to do is ask." He pulled a paper chart of Alaska from the cockpit, unfolded it, perused it, found Talkeetna, and examined it for a moment. "I can get you right to town, looks like. I'll file a plan and we'll figure on lifting off around one, one thirty." He eyed me. "What's there, aside from a whole lot of not much?"

"A whole lot of not much is why I'm going there," I said. "Got some shit happening and I need to get away."

He nodded. "Well, just a heads-up—Claire had business cards printed up for me recently, as a kind of joke." He handed me one, and I read it.

Brock Badd: pilot, philosopher, arm-chair therapist.

I laughed. "So you're gonna try to get the story out of me."

"Try? You'll tell it to me and not even realize what's happening."

I held out a fist, and he bumped mine with his. "Challenge accepted." I waved at him. "Well, I'll let you get back to your engine. See you in a couple hours."

He was already looking at the engine compartment, and just waved at me.

I headed home to pack.

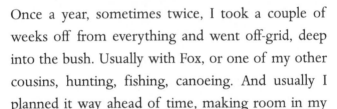

Once a year, sometimes twice, I took a couple of weeks off from everything and went off-grid, deep into the bush. Usually with Fox, or one of my other cousins, hunting, fishing, canoeing. And usually I planned it way ahead of time, making room in my schedule for the time off, saving cash and paying bills ahead of time.

This was...impromptu.

I spent most of the time leading up to my departure with Brock on the phone, apologizing to my clients for the last-minute change, and pushing them all at least a month out. I'd need that amount of time—how I knew that, I wasn't sure, I just knew this wasn't going to be a quick or easy thing.

I told all my clients they'd get their next session half off for the inconvenience of having to reschedule so suddenly, but hey, personal crisis was personal crisis.

I honestly wasn't sure, either, why I was leaving.

I just knew I had to.

Had to go.

Couldn't be here in Ketchikan with Cassie, or I'd hound her. I'd need her. I'd demand her time. Consume her energy. Use her sexually for my own ravenous needs, but I needed an emotional connection. Call me a girl if you want, but sex for me has never been purely physical. It's a bond with the person. That's why what happened with Elise was so damned gutting—I'd thought we had that connection, that emotional bond. I'd assumed she *got* me. But she didn't. She couldn't.

Cassie wasn't ready for that kind of bond. She may want it, but she had to be able to look herself in the metaphorical mirror before she could give any part of herself to anyone else.

And if I was around, I'd just get in the way of that process.

I had to get away, for her sake.

Something told me, too, that I had my own shit to wrestle with, and I couldn't do that here, in the city. The only way I could get quiet enough in my own head was to be out there, in the silence of nature.

So, I packed some gear—real clothes, due to mosquitos and midges and black flies and no-see-ums and bracken and such, boots, binoculars, my self-defense handgun and bear spray, survival knife, hatchet, matches, canteens…all the various paraphernalia of wilderness survival, the packing of which was second nature to me. I packed a second bag with food items to see me through the first few days, knowing I would hunt and fish for fresh meat as I needed it.

Packed, I shouldered my bag and headed for the door.

Then I stopped, for some reason. Bugged by something—wasn't sure what.

My phone—I'd been on it all morning and intended to leave it behind. I'd stuck it on the charger and left it there.

But, for some reason, I pulled it off the charger and shoved it into my pocket. Why, I wasn't sure. It made no sense. I just…had to.

Mystified at my own actions, I shook my head and schlepped my bag across town to Brock's slip. I was wearing a shirt and hiking boots for the first time in months. It felt odd and unnatural, but I knew from experience that I would feel at home again the moment I entered the forest outside Talkeetna.

I tossed my bag into the fuselage, climbed in after it, and used the available straps to tie it down. Then I sat in the open doorway kicking my feet in space, watching Brock bustle through his preflight checklist once, twice, and then a third time before settling into the pilot's seat.

He glanced at me, jerked a thumb at the copilot's place. "Hop in, big fella. Let's get lost, huh?"

I grinned at him. "Sounds good to me," I said, plopping my ass into the chair and buckling up.

With a cough, sputter, and belch of exhaust, the twin propellers spun into life, and within another minute we were streaking across the channel, bouncing on the waves, skidding, skipping, momentarily weightless, and then angling skyward, floating upward, buoyed on the magic of physics.

TWELVE

Cassie

MY PHONE BLARED THE MOST ANNOYING, JARRING, SKULL-splitting song I could think of—"Chop Suey!" by System of a Down. It was my alarm, and it was going off at the ungodly hour of five in the morning.

I groaned and rolled over toward the edge of the bed.

Why had I set my alarm for five a.m.?

Oh yeah. To work out. Mobility exercises. Regain my strength and endurance and flexibility. The road back to dance.

Because…

Why?

Why couldn't I just go back to sleep? Accept my

fate. Let myself go. Just be fat and lazy and stupid and useless the rest of my life. Never dance again. Screw the workouts. Screw the relentless internal drive to move, to follow the music and the rhythm and the movement across the floor as if pulled by invisible strings.

I groaned again.

Why have you forsaken me...

I had to get out of bed to shut off the alarm because I'm a diabolical person and put it across the room so I couldn't talk myself out of getting out of bed. So, I got out of bed, trudged listlessly across the bedroom to the dresser and shut off the infernal noise. I stood there, glaring at the time readout on my phone: 5:02 a.m.

Idiot phone.

Idiot me.

Idiot leg.

Idiot car wreck.

Idiot Ink.

Idiot life.

I couldn't, for the life of me, remember how I'd managed to do this every day of my life for more than ten years—up at five, bike the three blocks from home to the studio, dance until six forty-five, ride home, shower, change, and get on the bus to school by seven thirty.

Then, at college and professionally, I'd often had to get up even earlier, four thirty some days.

Awful.

I stared longingly at my bed, rumpled and probably still warm. It'd be so nice to just climb back in.

But no.

No.

This was the first day of the rest of my life.

Screw Ink and his ultimatums and his rejection.

I didn't need him.

Sure, I wanted him. Sure I needed his heat and warmth and safe arms and his…

Huge cock.

I giggled, because the thought came up, and I had an image of him, naked in the moonlight, on his back, hard and beautiful and sliding easily and silkily through my fist…

My mouth…

My sex.

Stop, stop, stop, fucking stop, Cassie.

Bad girl. Thoughts of his cock won't help.

And he wasn't right.

He just wasn't…wrong either.

And, girl, it's okay to want him, but you can't have him right now, because you have your life to get back on track.

Which means being able to walk without a damned limp, at least. Plus a few other things.

But, baby steps first.

Before I can dance, I have to able to move smoothly. Walk. Run. Bend. Squat. Lunge.

Then I can leap and spin and roll to a handstand and to a forward somersault.

And to do any of that, I need a habit. A pattern. I need my muscle memory to kick in. Something familiar to rely on.

And my whole life, that bit of familiar has been a five a.m. wake up, followed by coffee. Then a few minutes to think and clear my head. Some stretches, some warm-ups.

I'll start there.

For me.

Not for Ink.

It's not for him. It has nothing to do with him, or with anything he said to me.

I'm still mad. And I have every right to be. Mostly.

I think.

Maybe.

Whatever. It doesn't matter. I won't see him till I can dance again. Run, perhaps. Or at least walk without limping. I used to run three or four miles every day—after my first practice of the day—not fast, not super hard, just a decent jog, because it cleared my head and loosened up my tight muscles.

I missed running, truth be told. It was meditative, for me. Time for solitude. I'd put in my earbuds, crank up a bouncy hip-hop playlist, and let my body move without worrying about a single damn thing except the next step, the next turn, the next breath.

I knew that was my next immediate, short-term goal: run a mile.

Just one.

Should be easy.

Right?

————————✖————————

Wrong.

I'd very clearly misunderstood the necessity of working on my basic mobility, of keeping my muscles on a regular schedule. That one mile was brutal. And it hurt like hell. My chest hurt, and my leg was killing me.

I've danced through bleeding blisters and twisted ankles and pulled muscles, but that was nothing compared to this.

Mom came home for lunch and found me lying on the floor, sweating like a pig, crying.

"Cass? What's…what's going on?"

I shook my head. "I can't even touch my toes, Mom! I'm flexible enough, but it just…hurts. One single squat and I'm shaking."

She sighed, and left the room without a word.

"Okay?" I said, to the empty room.

She came back moments later with a towel and a bottle of water. "Here."

"Oh." I sat up, slowly, and took them from her. "Thanks," I mumbled.

She watched me towel off and sip the water, and then her expression shifted to the thoughtful *aha!* expression she got when she had an idea.

"What?" I asked.

"I have an idea."

I rolled my eyes. "I'm *not* seeing a therapist—psychological or physical."

"Cass—"

"No, Mom. Just...no."

She sat on the floor beside me and took my hands. "Cass, just listen."

"Mom—"

She gave me her hardest glare, used her Mom-est voice. "Cassandra Danielle. I am your mother and you *will* hear me out."

I rolled my eyes. "Fine."

She skewered me with another glare. "Try that again, and this time endeavor to sound something like a mature adult instead of a petulant child."

"Yes, Mother," I droned. "Speak on, oh wise one."

She cackled. "Smart aleck." She gave a prim, motherly smile. "Now. My idea is that Lucas has a nephew named Baxter who owns a recreational gym. It's mostly a club for boxers, MMA fighters, and heavy-duty bodybuilders, but I've met Baxter on several occasions and he's a great guy. He's trained me several times, and he's an absolute darling. More to the point, he's an incredibly talented personal trainer. Many of his clients come to him for help rehabbing sports injuries. I know I've seen several people in his gym who were professional athletes. He's one of the best."

"I don't need a personal trainer, Mom. I've been keeping myself in peak professional athlete physical condition, on my own, for years."

She smiled. "I know that, dear. But that's different than getting your body back where it should be after a serious injury. He's not a therapist—well, I actually think he *is*, technically, but he promotes himself largely as an athletic conditioning and recovery coach. He can help you."

I sighed. "Mom…I don't know."

She patted my shoulder. "I do. He's a Badd, which means, as my daughter, you're automatically part of the clan, which means he'll help you for free, because you're family. And he's very, very tough on top of being knowledgeable, so he'll push you past where you think you can go."

"I've never met the man. Why would he consider *me* family?"

She just smiled again. "The men and women of the Badd clan take the concept of family and loyalty very, *very* seriously. I'm all but engaged to Lucas, Baxter's uncle. You're my daughter. Therefore, you're family. He would take a bullet for you, whether he's met you or not."

I blinked. "Oh, come on, Mom. You make him sound like a superhero."

She shrugged. "Wait till you meet him. If he wasn't the sweetest, funniest, warmest person I've ever met, I'd be absolutely terrified of him."

I shook my head. "You must really like him."

Her grin was contagious. "I consider all of the Badd boys the sons I never had. Or wanted. But that's beside the point. They're all wonderful." She tugged at my hand. "Come on. Just trust me."

Trust me.

Mom's magic words. She didn't often ask you to trust her, but when she did you ignored her at your peril. She was seldom wrong, especially when she felt strongly enough to insist.

"Okay, okay," I sighed. "Set up an appointment. I'll go see him."

She just laughed. "That's not how it works with these boys, sweetheart. We go over there now."

"Now?" I gestured at myself—booty-hugging dance shorts, loose tank top, sports bra, cross-trainers…and a sheen of sweat and aura of body odor. "Like this?"

She rolled her eyes at me. "Yes, Cass. Like that. It's a gym, he's a married man, and a former professional athlete. A little sweat won't bother him in the slightest." She sniffed. "Some deodorant wouldn't go amiss, however."

I cackled. "Nice, Mom."

She just popped me on the butt. "Go. De-stink yourself, grab your purse, and let's go."

Within ten minutes we were in her car and heading across town to what passed as an industrial area of Ketchikan. The gym was in a warehouse, and the sliding doors opened all the way to admit the brilliant sunlight and relative warmth. Rock music thudded from surround speakers, and the sounds of a gym floated out to me as I exited Mom's car: the clink and bang and rattle of barbells and metal plates, grunts of exertion, raucous male laughter, the high rhythmic thud of a speed bag, the deeper thwacks and thumps of heavy bags, and the creaks and squeaks and thuds of boxers in the ring.

Clean, well lit. New and well stocked, but not glitzy. Utilitarian—thick mats on the floor, a stretch of AstroTurf against one wall with a power sled on one end and a thick rope running across the space. There were massive multiperson powerlifting cages on three walls, and racks of bumper plates, metal plates, dumb-bells, and kettlebells in between the cages. The boxing ring took up the center of the warehouse with plenty of space around it. A glassed-in office space occupied a far back corner along with the bathrooms, and the locker rooms were beyond that.

It wasn't bustling or overflowing, but it was busy. Most of the power cages were occupied, and a trio of burly, shirtless men took turns using the thick rope to pull the weighted sled toward them and then push it back across the AstroTurf. Several other men, and a couple of women, moved around the open space do-ing bodyweight exercises, or working with dumbbells or kettlebells, and a pair of men danced around the boxing ring.

One of the boxers was young, maybe nineteen or twenty, black, thin and wiry, quick, lithe, and shredded; the other was...I had no words. About six feet, but muscled like something out of a superhero graphic novel. Absurdly proportioned. Shoulders so broad and wide and thick I could probably stand with both feet on one side. He had arms that must have been eighteen or twenty inches around, defined as if carved out of marble, chest muscles you could break a hammer on, an eight pack, a narrow waist, and legs to rival a sprint cyclist's. He had blond hair cut in a wide almost-Mohawk style, the top shaggy, the sides buzzed, with heavy stubble on his jaw. He had the flat practice pads meant for training punches on his hands, and was dancing around the ring avoiding punches and kicks. He was coaching footwork, it looked like, calling out instructions now and then.

Mom pointed at the giant blond god in the ring. "That's Baxter."

I gaped at him. "Well that's just ridiculous. No one looks like that in real life."

Mom laughed. "That was my thought the first time I saw him."

"He looks like he could bench press a Buick."

"Watch how light on his feet he is, though. He's not just muscles."

I watched. He was…well, a dancer, by all rights. No wasted energy, each movement precise, lithe, graceful, and powerful. "No kidding."

"Don't let his looks fool you, either. He's very smart."

I'd seen and met a few other members of the extended Badd family by now, and they were all as ridiculous in their own ways as Baxter. But Baxter was by far the most mind-bogglingly perfect physical specimen of humanity I'd ever seen in my life.

I suddenly felt underqualified to even be in this gym. I was suddenly hyperaware of the extra layer over my abs that hadn't been there a few months ago.

The fact that my ass jiggled a bit instead of being hard as a steel drum was super embarrassing. The fact that I'd already lost a good bit of tone in my arms and shoulders, and the weakness in my injured leg really brought home the knowledge that I was out of shape.

"Get out of your head, Cassandra," Mom murmured to me, yanking me across the gym.

"How the hell do you know what I'm thinking?" I snapped.

"I know what the heck you're thinking because I know you. Whenever you start to doubt yourself, you get this look on your face like you have to poop."

"MOM!"

She laughed, shrugged. "What? It's true."

"And you get on *my* case for being crass."

She just pulled me to a stop at the side of the ring, where we watched Baxter, the Gargantuan God, dance around the ring, letting punches and kicks from his trainee smack and whack, sometimes moving his pads so the trainee missed, forcing him to regroup and find his footing.

The trainee was blindingly fast, but Baxter seemed to anticipate his every move, able to get his glove in place, or move without any effort.

A few more minutes of this, and then Baxter called a halt in a gruff, permanently hoarse voice. "Good work, man," Bax said, whacking the trainee across the shoulder with a pad. "Great footwork. Keep lifting, though. Go heavy for low reps, get that power up. And try to work on not telegraphing your left cross."

"Sure thing, Coach," the younger man said. "That it?"

Bax nodded. "Yeah, man. Get goin'. See you next week."

A wave of a gloved hand, and the trainee ducked under the top rope, jumped down, and headed for the locker rooms, unlacing his gloves as he went. Baxter grinned at Mom.

"Livvie!" He sounded genuinely happy to see Mom. Ducking under the ropes, he removed his pads as he dropped to the floor. "Back for a HIIT session, are you? Been a while."

Livvie? No one called Mom that. Not even Dad. I didn't think even Lucas called Mom *Livvie*.

He picked Mom up in a great, shaking, off-her-feet bear hug, swinging her around until she cackled and whacked at his shoulder.

"Oh my god, put me down, you big lunatic!" Mom didn't seem at all fazed by the fact that he was coated in a glistening layer of sweat, despite not being out of breath in the slightest.

He set her down, and had the unmitigated gall to ruffle her hair like she was a four-year-old girl instead of a woman quite literally old enough to be his mother. "Good to see you, Liv."

I frowned at Mom, wondering when the sharp denunciation of his hair ruffling would be voiced.

Instead, she just fixed it without a word, and grinned at him. "Bax, I want you to meet my second oldest daughter, Cassie."

Baxter nodded, looking me over. "The gimp."

I widened my eyes. "Excuse the fuck out of you!"

Mom just laughed. "Be nice, Baxter. She may not be in the mindset for teasing."

He just shot me a grin, which I assumed had melted a rather comical number of undergarments in his day. "Coupl'a things, babe," he said, hands on his hips, eyes on mine. "One, I'm a merciless teaser. Give as good as you get, and we're golden. Get your knickers in a twist, and we probably won't be friends. I don't mean nothin' by any of it, so don't take it personally. Two, I don't play any sissy fuckin' games in this place. This gym is hallowed ground. The workout is thy lord and master, and I'm the lord and master of the workout. Obey me without question, and all shall go well with you."

I gaped. "I—you—I—"

"Three." He spoke over me. "Weakness is the illness, and I'm the doctor. We're here to heal, so don't hide your weakness. Defeat it. Don't be ashamed of it. Don't mistake laziness or lack of will as weakness—they ain't the same thing. I can fix weak, I can't fix lazy."

I glanced at Mom. "Did you tell—"

"Four, and last, judgment or criticism is utterly *verboten*. Talk some unkind shit about someone else, and we'll have problems." Another grin. "That's it. Welcome to paradise."

I shook my head. "You have some nerve, Baxter."

He just laughed. "You're here, ain't you? Gotta know what I expect so we can make this work." He jutted his chin at me. "Goals and expectations."

I blinked. "What?"

He snorted. "We're establishing baselines, here, babe, keep up." He glanced at Mom. "She always this slow on the uptake?"

"Listen here, gorilla man—" I started.

Mom just patted me on the shoulder. "Go all in, Cassie-Lassie. Give this all you've got. And trust him." And then she left.

What?

"What?" I echoed my own thought out loud. "Mom?"

She waved as she exited the doors. "And have fun!"

I watched her drive away. "Now, what the fuck?"

Bax tilted his head. "She did tell you where she was taking you, did she not?"

I nodded. "To meet you. I didn't know we'd…I don't know. Start before we'd even said hello."

Bax reached out, took my hand, and shook it. "Name is Baxter Badd. Call me Bax. I'm your new trainer and rehab coach. You're Cassandra Goode, car wreck survivor, bum leg as a souvenir, dancer and, apparently, dumb blonde."

I yanked my hand out of his grip and reached out to smack him.

Or, intended to. He caught my hand with a strong but gentle grip, a playful grin on his face. "Ah, ah, ah. We're not in the ring. No hitting."

"You—you—!"

"Just joking. Making sure you're paying attention."

I put my face close to his. "Call me dumb blonde again and I'll rip your dick off."

His grin widened. "Ooh, baby. Talk dirty to me." He frowned. "Well, actually, don't. I'm married, and I love my wife. But, for real, that's how you play the game around here." He clapped his hands together. "So, let's get started."

I sighed, flapped my arms out wide and let them slap against my thighs. "Alright, might as well just go with it. Work your magic, Mr. Badd."

He squatted in front of me, glanced up at me with his hands hovering around my bad leg, but not touching. "Quick look, in a purely professional and therapeutic way. So, you know, don't knee me in the face when I touch your leg, 'kay?"

I shot him a sour look. "I'm not a prude, Bax."

"You're plenty touchy, so you never know." He spoke absently, his fingers now prodding my scar tissue, kneading the muscle.

I frowned. "Touchy? I'm not touchy."

"You're uptight as fuck, babe." He grabbed my wrist and placed it on his shoulder, which felt like putting my hand on a marble statue. "Balance on your good leg, please. Need to test your range of motion."

I rolled my eyes and balanced, without his shoulder, without so much as a wobble. Glad to know I've still got that much left, at least.

"Nice," he muttered. "Solid core foundation."

I snorted. "Mom may have told you I was a dancer, but I'm not sure she qualified it quite correctly. It wasn't a hobby, it was a profession."

I demonstrated, by extending my bad leg in front of me, lifting it toward the ceiling, arching over backward into a full backbend, into a handstand, held there for a beat, and then continued forward, landing on both feet...

And promptly falling sideways as my bad leg collapsed, dumping me onto the mat.

"Well, that was impressive," Baxter said, plopping onto his butt next to me.

"Until I fell," I muttered, staying where I was, lying awkwardly.

"No, it was impressive, full stop. The fall was beyond your control. I wouldn't have advised you to try that until you knew your leg could take the weight, but it was impressive as hell."

He grabbed my leg and massaged the muscles around the scarring, which hurt like an absolute bitch, yet somehow still felt good.

"Number one, Cass," he said, still manipulating and massaging my leg, "you need to give yourself grace. Give yourself the permission to just understand, mentally, emotionally, and physically, that you suffered a motherfucker of a trauma. The muscles, tendons, and joints in your entire left leg were seriously fucked over. You won't get anywhere if you force unrealistic expectations on yourself, or on your poor fucked-up leg."

I felt my teeth clench. "I get it, okay? My leg is fucked up. You don't need to keep hammering it home."

He kept massaging. And despite the fact that he was gorgeous in a superhero, pro wrestler, rugged,

I-eat-mountains-for-breakfast kind of way, I wasn't attracted to him at all. At least not beyond an objective sense of understanding that he was an incredibly attractive man. Not my type, for one thing, and two, knowing he was happily and dedicatedly married cut anything else off at the pass. Besides that, attraction just wasn't possible. My entire capacity for attraction was focused solely on Ink.

But I wasn't thinking about him right now.

Bax met my eyes, his deep brown eyes serious, for once. "Your leg is absolutely fucked. You can barely put weight on it. You ought to have a cane, honestly. It's so fucked up it's a miracle you're able to walk at all."

"I get it!" I snapped.

"Fucked up, fucked up," he sang, "your leg is fucked up!"

I yanked free of him and rolled away, tears pricking. "Shut up!"

He stayed with me. "Accept it. Stop fighting it. Stop thinking you have to be okay."

"And you're going to get me there by ramming home how fucked up I am?"

"Yep." He popped the "P" sound. "You're still trying to insist on things not being as bad as they are. You want to hope some miracle will happen to take it all away."

I ground my teeth. Hissed through them. "Shut the fuck up, Baxter. You don't know shit about me."

"Sure I do. I've trained all sorts of people. Started out helping MMA and UFC guys get into condition, and I still do that. Moved into the PT field, helping athletes rehab injuries. I also specialize in helping elite military combat veterans with injuries and people with loss of limbs learn how to regain their mobility, independence, and give them the ability to hit the gym like they used to." He let that sink in. "You fall into the category of injured athlete."

I eyed him. "So you consider dancing a sport?" I asked, skepticism rife in my tone.

"Fuck, yes! Dancers, especially of your caliber, are some of the most elite and impressive athletes out there." A shrug. "Anything that puts strain on your body and requires physical conditioning to perform is a sport. Dancing sure as shit falls into that category."

"So you're going to get me back on the stage?"

He winced. "I don't know about that. I'm always a hundred percent honest with my clients about that—they have to manage their expectations. Knowing that, ninety-nine percent of the time, the greatest limitation on a person is himself or herself. I helped a SEAL who lost his leg from the knee down get back out into the field as a capable operative. It required him to do a shitload of work along with an unimaginable amount of dedication and suffering, along with a truly intense ferocity of spirit, but he did it, because he refused to accept anything else. So could you get back to professional dance? If you want it bad enough. If you're willing to do whatever it takes. I won't bullshit you—that would be brutally hard—especially since it looks like you're missing parts of the muscle in your outer quad."

I nodded. "It was one of the worst breaks they'd ever seen. Just…destroyed."

"I can tell." He held my gaze. "Here's what I'll promise you. Stick with me, give me a hundred percent effort, have your specific, predetermined goal written down, and I'll get you wherever that is. I won't let you give up on yourself, and I won't let you give less than a hundred percent effort, every session, every day. I will get you there. More importantly, what I'll really do is help you get *yourself* there. You just have to know where *there* is." A pause. "Look inside and don't answer this question until you know the real, true answer, the truth as it exists in your bones, in your blood, in your gut, in your muscles, in your balls."

I snorted. "Female, here, remember?"

"Metaphorical balls. I could say ovaries, if that makes you feel better."

I laughed. "Nah. Just giving you shit." I sighed then turned serious. "So. What's your question?"

"What is it you want? What's your goal? What am I helping you achieve?" A hesitation. "That's one question phrased three different ways."

I blinked hard. "I…I don't know."

He nodded. "That's why I'm asking. Think about it." Another short, but intense silence. "Be real with yourself, Cassie. What do you want? I ain't a shrink, I ain't a psychotherapist, I'm just a muscle-head who likes helping people overcome physical obstacles. But in my experience helping clients who have suffered injuries like yours and worse, answering that question—what do you want?—often requires looking at more than just the physical. It's more than just walking normally again. If that's your goal, just walking without a limp, we can get you there. If it's dancing again, but not professionally, we'll get you there. If it's getting you back to your dance company as a pro dancer, we can get you there." His fingertip tapped the end of my nose. "You just have to know what your goal is."

I started talking, and it was as if my brain and soul took over. "I want to run. I love running. I want to dance. I need the movement, the expression." I felt tears, and didn't bother stopping them. "I don't want to dance professionally anymore. I don't. I lost that— that part of me died in that car, I think. I just…I don't have the will to do that any longer. And…" I sobbed, a hiccup. "And that's okay. I have to grieve it. I have to be okay without that. I just...I don't know what it means for me. Dance is who I am, who I've been my whole life. But what do I want now? I want to put the accident behind me. I want to move normally, like I used to. Run, dance, jump, all of it. That's what I want."

He nodded. "I'll have you walking without a limp, or much less of one, in a couple weeks. Running short distances a few weeks after that. By fall, you'll be dancing and the past'll all be a bad memory." He smiled at me, and something about him just...encouraged me. "Focus on that, on those goalposts. By the time you get there I think you'll know what you want, long term."

———— ✺ ————

Two weeks passed, and I missed Ink worse than I thought it was possible to miss anyone.

I'd learned from Mom that he'd taken a leave of absence from his tattoo shop and was living at his remote hunting cabin somewhere outside Anchorage. To give me space, she said.

Somehow, that made me miss him all the more—it made me care more. Because I did need the space. I needed him out of my life so I could focus on me.

If he was here, I wouldn't be able to do that. I'd want him.

Need him.

Think about him.

Be with him.

Learn him.

Damn him...he'd been right. I'd been using him as a distraction from the work I needed to do on myself.

And then, to give me space, he'd left his home, his job, his family, his friends, and me—for whatever it was I meant to him—so I could do what was needed to be who I needed to be.

I was grateful to him, for that.

But holy *shit*, I did miss him.

I let myself think about him—really truly openly deeply think about him—but only once a day. At night, in bed before I went to sleep I'd bring up an image of him, hear his voice, feel his voice. See his eyes. Feel his hands on my skin. His kiss.

I'd let myself remember his mouth between my legs. His hardness inside me. His kisses drowning me, drugging me.

I'd remember him, all of him, allow myself to want him, let myself need him.

I'd touch myself thinking about him, bring myself to orgasm and wish it were him doing it.

And then I'd fall asleep, wishing his arms were around me.

When I woke up, I'd put aside all thoughts and memories of Ink, and focus on my day. Coffee. Stretching. Testing movement, feeling myself for aches, pain, tweaks, twinges. Walk over to Bax's gym. Work out until I was totally sapped—conditioning, strength, toning, muscle building, flexibility as well as working on rejuvenating my bad leg.

The two weeks became three, and I was able to walk without limping, and could run a mile, almost two before the deep throbbing ache in the muscle and bone started again.

But the more time passed, the more I missed Ink.

And the more I realized how much he'd come to mean to me in a bizarrely short time.

I'd fallen for him.

I'd caught feelings, and I was okay with that.

But now…now I wanted more than just feelings. And I was beginning to understand what he'd told me about not falling in love, that it wasn't an accident, or something beyond control, a black-and-white you-are-or-you-aren't thing.

It was an organic, living thing. You *grew* love.

I had the feelings, the connection, and the attraction.

But I wanted more.

It was going to take work, and it would be a risk. I could hurt him, he could hurt me. We would fight. There'd be times we wouldn't feel love.

But I wanted the process. I wanted the work.

And I wanted it with him.

So, four weeks and three days after meeting Baxter, I sat across from him in his office. "I'm taking some time off my rehab."

He set his pen down, flipped the folder of his financial reports closed, and propped his feet on the desk. "Oh?"

I nodded. "I have to go talk to Ink."

He lifted his chin, hands behind his head, a knowing grin on his face. "About fuckin' time, sweetheart."

I frowned. "I haven't talked to you about him, like, at all. I don't let myself think about him during the day. I focus on me during the day."

He rolled his eyes. "I hope you don't think you're good at hiding your feelings, Cassie-Lassie, cuz you ain't." He just laughed. "I've watched you shake him out of your head at least once an hour every single day for the last month."

I laughed. "You are far too observant for a barely sentient gorilla."

He snorted. "You just wear your entire self on your sleeve." A gentle smile. "It's a good thing."

I let silence wreathe between us—he had quickly

become one of my best friends, which was weird because I'd always thought it was impossible to have a real and truly platonic friendship with a heterosexual member of the opposite sex. But then I'd met his wife, and I understood. Not only was she one of the most ridiculously, extravagantly, absurdly voluptuous women I'd ever seen in person in my life, she was breathtakingly beautiful in a classic, early Hollywood sort of way, and was also the sweetest and most genuinely kind person I'd ever met.

I simply understood that I could never hold a candle to her, and I understood that that was okay, that I didn't have to feel like less of a woman because of that. He loved her absolutely, and she him, and she trusted him. Of course, she still made a point to come by the gym a few times a day to say hi and kiss him and let him rub her round pregnant belly, and to chat with me.

So we were friends, Bax and I.

It was a friendship I valued, and appreciated. He'd helped me find myself again. Helped me center my life. I was running again, slow and not far, but running. Dancing, gently and carefully.

He'd helped me, but I'd done the work.

Now it was time to put Ink back into my life.

Bax was eyeing me, and I recognized the thoughtful look on his face. "Uh-oh," I said. "You're thinking."

He shrugged. "Been thinking."

"About what?"

He set his feet on the floor, waved at the plate glass window and the gym on the other side. "Expansion. Adding another trainer." A glance at me. "Adding classes."

"Classes?" I asked, a pit opening in my stomach, one filled with butterflies and possibilities.

"Yeah. There's a market for..." he paused, chewing on the right phrasing. "A certain kind of fitness instructor. Which I am not. Lots of tourists around here, lots of younger women and certain kinds of men, too."

"Quit waffling and say it, bonehead."

He grinned; he truly did respond best to good-natured but brutal teasing. "Dance classes."

I sighed. "You're creating something to throw me a bone."

He ignored that, rifling in a drawer and coming up with a notebook, battered, dog-eared, filled with Post-It Notes and folded down page corners. He opened it, flipped toward the front. "This is my ideas book. Like a journal sort of, but for shit I want to do and how to get there."

"Okay."

"I date each page, each entry. So I can refer to when I had the idea, because usually there's other shit

I'm thinking about related to it, and I need to refer-
ence it."

I nodded. "Following you so far. What's your
point?"

He rotated the book and slid it to me. "Look at
the date."

I did—it was dated six months before I ever met
him. "Okay."

He tapped a line item, scrawled in messy, barely
legible handwriting that was a mix of all-caps and
cursive: *Expansion ideas—classes. Boxing? MMA? Self-
defense martial arts. Anti-rape defense skills for women.
Dance fitness? Find dance instructor, I don't fucking dance.
Zumba or some shit. Women love that shit.*

I laughed. "Okay, okay. You were thinking about
it before you met me." I rolled my eyes at him.
"What's your point?"

A shrug. "I'm just laying out a possibility. I've
not found the right person, someone who I get along
with, who represents the mentality my gym is built
around. Someone who can dance, and who under-
stands fitness. My thought was, the classes would use
dance to teach flexibility, movement, whole-body understanding, provide aerobic conditioning, strength.
But it has to be the right person teaching."

I swallowed. "Bax."

He closed the notebook. "You could do it. I'd like

it, personally, if you did it. One class a week to start. You create it—it'd be your baby. We could do a thing where people can take just the classes by themselves for one fee, per class or a group of classes, or get a discount if they join the gym to use the weight equipment and get one free training session per month with me, along with access to your classes, and we'd split those fees down the middle."

I shifted on my chair. "I feel like the injured dancer who takes up teaching is such a cliché, though."

He blew a raspberry. "Yeah, and? You love to dance. You're out of the professional world, the competitive world. This lets you dance." An arched eyebrow. "Plus, you're hella fit. You clearly enjoy fitness, being active, being strong. Get certified as a personal trainer, put your shingle out next to mine."

I dragged my hair out of the ponytail, finger-combed it, rebound it. "I've been doing a lot of yoga with my mom since I moved here," I said, letting myself conjecture out loud. "I'm really good at yoga, and I love it. I've been thinking of getting licensed to teach that."

He nodded. "Do it." A wave. "Do the yoga cert, the trainer cert, and while you're getting those, start up the dance class and, as you build a clientele, add more services."

I felt a little giddy. "I would love to teach yoga."

I couldn't help grinning, letting excitement bubble over. "When I lived in Paris, at least once a week I had someone at the gym mistake me for a personal trainer and ask me for advice, and I remember thinking, if I ever stop dancing, I should be a personal trainer."

He nodded. "You'll kill at it."

I eyed the gym space. "Where would the classes go, though? All your floor space is dedicated."

He grinned and opened the folder that he had been working on. "The warehouse next to this one is about half this size, but they're separated by only about twenty feet. That warehouse is for sale for wicked cheap. I put in an offer, super lowball, and they took it. It's, like, a steal. Legit. Anyway. I had a contractor take a look, and he said I—we—could connect the two super easy. Wall off the empty space between each building at either end, roof it over, insulate everything, put in doors, connect the electrical and shit, and bam, I've got two connected warehouses, with a new twenty-by-one-hundred-foot space between them. More lockers. Changing rooms. Some chairs, a TV. Then the new warehouse becomes class space. It could be designed with flexible instruction spaces that could even be rented out to independent teachers, you know like, tap or ballet, meditation, whatever."

My mind was buzzing, and I felt an excitement I hadn't felt since the last time I stepped on stage.

"You know, when I was dancing I made good money. Saved most of it, as my ex-fiancé and I lived in an apartment his parents owned, so I had super low living expenses. Meaning, I've got a good bit saved, since I've been living with Mom and she won't let me help with money. Plus, there was an insurance settlement payout, which wasn't anything to sneeze at."

He just looked at me, waiting for me to continue.

"So," I continued. "What if we go in fifty-fifty on the new space and reno costs?"

He held an open but neutral expression on his face. "So you're all in? No backing out, no second thoughts, don't need time to consider? This is what you want? For *you*? No bullshit. You *know*—you *know* you want this."

I nodded, unable to hide my excitement. I wanted this. I now had a future here, in Ketchikan. This was where I had Mom, where I had my new friendship and soon-to-be partnership with Baxter. This is where Ink lived.

This was home, and the realization hit me like a ton of bricks. In the last few minutes, here in Bax's office, my life had changed and had taken on new meaning. Suddenly I could see the future, and it looked exciting.

"I want this, Bax. I want to teach dance and yoga and become a personal trainer. It all makes so much sense, and I can't thank you enough."

He broke into a boyishly excited grin. Stuck out his hand, and we shook. "Partners?"

"Partners." I laughed. "Don't you, you know, need to consult Eva?"

He pointed behind me—I twisted to see Eva, standing in the doorway looking as if she'd been there a long time. "Duh."

Eva came in, bent over, and gave me an up-side-down and from behind hug. "Congratulations, Cass."

I wiggled, too excited to hold still. "Oh, Eva. I'm so excited. I gotta go tell Mom."

Eva held my hand, kept me from bolting off. "I'm taking you for a girls' night out to celebrate."

I hugged her. "Oh, that would be awesome."

"And not just me—the whole pack."

I cackled. "Pack?"

"We girls of the Badd clan." She grinned. "You haven't lived till you've been out with all of us. It's wild."

I blinked. "How many of you—us—are there? And do I even count? Ink isn't a Badd."

"Ink is an honorary Badd," Bax said. "And you're my business partner, and your mom is shacked up with Uncle Lucas. You're one of us in at least four different ways."

"That's three ways, dear," Eva corrected.

"What the fuck ever," he said, waving. "Three, then. Point is, yes, you're in their pack."

I smiled at their good-natured banter. "So, who's in the pack?"

She took a deep breath. "Dru, Mara, Claire, me, Tate, Aerie, Joss, and Low." A smile. "Plus your mom, and now you."

I blinked. "I've laid eyes on everyone at least once, I think, except for Low. I've not met her."

"Her real name is Harlow Grace," she said. "She's Xavier's fiancé and he's the youngest of Baxter's family."

"Harlow Grace, as in…"

"The actress, yes." Eva shrugged. "We don't think of her that way, though. She's just family. She and Xavier split their time between Hollywood, Silicon Valley where Xavier's robotics startup has offices, and here. So they're only here part of the year, but they're in town right now for a few months. They got in…?" She glanced at her husband for assistance.

"This morning, early," Bax said. "I haven't seen them yet, but we're all supposed to meet at the bar for lunch." He'd been on his phone, which he now put down, and winked at me. "Brock has the plane ready, by the way."

I frowned. "What? Plane? What do you mean?"

"My next oldest brother, Brock is a pilot, and has his own seaplane. He took Ink up north." He shrugged. "I mean, you're not planning to drive to Talkeetna, are you? I hear it's, like, a forty-some hour drive."

I laughed. "Well, since I don't even have a driver's license, no."

He furrowed his brow. "You don't know how to drive?"

I shook my head. "After I graduated high school I moved to New York to study dance, and then ended up in Paris. Just never got a license. Never needed one."

"So Brock can fly you up there when you're ready."

I moved around to hug him. "Thank you, Bax, for everything. You've just changed my life."

He hugged me tight and then gave me a playful shove. "Thank *you*. We're gonna make bank on this, you know. I've had people asking about classes of different kinds for years."

I waved to both of them as I headed for the door. "I'll see you...whenever I get back. No clue when that will be."

"Getcha some, girl!" Bax shouted.

Whack. "Baxter Badd. Don't be crude."

"Have you *met* me?" I heard Baxter reply.

"Intimately, yes."

I just laughed as I stepped out onto the sidewalk. It had been a gloomy, overcast day with low, heavy clouds hanging over the water. And there had been a light drizzle on and off all day. But when I emerged and started jogging, as if to validate my decisions, the sun peeked out from behind a break in the clouds and bathed me in a bright ray of warm sun which stayed with me all the way back to Mom's condo.

THIRTEEN

Ink

BROCK HAD FLOWN ME RIGHT INTO TALKEETNA, situated up north with Mt. McKinley white-capped in the distance, and wild Alaska just steps beyond the town. After I'd said goodbye to Brock, I spent a couple of hours collecting more supplies—mostly perishable food items. And I did what I usually do in such situations: I fell back on my childhood and the week-long hunting trips with Dad, or one of my uncles, or cousins.

I cut some long poles out of fallen branches, and used some of the hemp twine I always carried to fasten smaller branches into a basket between the poles, which I'd crossed into an X at one end. This done, I had a crude but effective travois, a kind of sled which I piled with my gear and supplies. Then I plaited more twine into a long, thick strap and tied the ends together where the poles crossed. I hooked the strap around my shoulders, leaned into it, and started for my cabin.

It took a couple of hours of hard trekking through the forest, sometimes following trails, other times heading off-trail when I knew of a shortcut. It was dusk by the time I reached my cabin.

The cabin was...well, I'd used the word "remote" with Liv. But that really didn't cover it. Unless you had been there with a guide, were well versed in off-trail forest navigation, could hike for several hours on end, and knew how to get there with your eyes closed, you'd never find it. Not in a million years. You could walk right past it and not see it unless you knew what to look for. It had been built at the edge of a little pond, small enough that you could skip a rock across it. There were lots of big, moss-covered boulders ringing the pond, and stumps of old pines stood, like the broken teeth of dead giants, in the water at the far side. All around was forest, deep, heavy, dark, chaotically thick. The pond had no name, unless one of the local tribes had named it, but I'd never heard about that.

The cabin was sort of a family heirloom—the

history of it was murky, though. I knew it had been built several generations back on my father's side—a great-great-grandfather, or uncle. Something like that. The point is, it had been built a long ass time ago.

The logs were mossy and had grayed with age and weather into a color that blended in with the rest of the forest, and the rocks used to make the chimney were equally mossy and aged. The windows, such as they were, were so old and dirty that they didn't reflect sunlight. Meaning, unless you knew you were looking at a cabin, you'd likely miss it. The chimney was positioned directly beneath the thickest layers of coniferous branches, so even when a fire was burning in the fireplace, the smoke would dissipate before it left the tree cover.

There was an outhouse about thirty feet from the house, and once a year I hauled up lime to maintain it. There was no indoor plumbing, although there was a well pump inside the house, and another near the outhouse. No electricity.

Definitely not for the faint of heart, and it took "roughing it" to a new level.

But it was paradise, for me.

I came up here to recharge, to get in touch out my wild creative bents—as a tattoo artist, I tended to fall into predictable patterns and subjects and styles, and rarely had time to pursue styles and mediums.

Coming up here was a chance to flex those other muscles.

I kept all sorts of art supplies up here, and every time I came I would bring up new stuff: oil paints, pastels, charcoal, a manual camera and hundreds of rolls of film—I could block off the already dirty windows and use the cabin as a darkroom. Years back, I'd gone to the effort of hauling up a full darkroom kit, including an enlarger. I had an easel, rolls of canvas that I stretched and framed myself.

I would spend days on end just geeking out in whatever medium caught my fancy. I had bins full of photos, both framed and not, old rolls of film kept in airtight storage. Stacks and stacks and stacks of paintings—pastels and charcoals—some framed, some just the canvas.

When I got up here I did have a tendency to go full artist and just zone into my project, forgetting to eat or sleep for forty-eight or seventy-two hours at a time.

But this time?

This was different.

The entire first four days I was here, I'd stared at my phone and wondered why I'd brought it. It didn't work out here; I had no charger and no way to charge it when it did die. Why had I felt such an odd pull to bring my phone with me?

It had baffled me the whole way up here.

I had no one to call—Juneau knew I was up here, and she knew the only way to get me in case of an emergency was to just come out here. She was the only person—outside of my immediate family who, never came here—who even knew where the cabin was, or how to get here.

My client list had been postponed indefinitely. My voicemail and website had been updated to indicate my leave of absence. I had plenty of money saved for supplies, and could live off the land indefinitely anyway.

Cassie was back in Ketchikan, and I was just operating under the assumption that either I'd get tired of being up here and go back home eventually, and would figure it out with her then, or she'd come find me.

So…why did I bring my damn phone?

Finally, a week in, I picked it up, turned it on, and…

What?

I had no photos, couldn't access the Internet.

I tapped the photos icon. I'd brought it to a family get-together last year, so I had a few photos of baby cousins and my parents and shit, but that was it.

But wait.

The "Photos" tab at the bottom just showed the

family reunion shots and an album file. Then under al-
bums, I scrolled down. Down, down. To the bottom.

And there, at the very bottom, was a little
line—"hidden."

That was not there last time I looked, and I hadn't
put it there.

So, I tapped it.

Fuck me running.

When did Cassie do this?

Dozens of photos. A hundred, maybe.

All of her.

Ho-ly. Shit.

An array of thumbnails. Cassie clothed was the
first one. I tapped on it to enlarge, and just stared.
This made me miss her even more.

Only a week had gone by, but I missed the shit
out of her.

And here she was...in my bathroom, in my
house. So. She'd taken photos of herself, hidden them
in a secret album, and not told me.

Hoping, probably, that I'd find them when I least
expected to, as a fun, sort of kinky little surprise.

You little minx, you.

God, I loved her.

Whoops. That was unexpected.

But true.

I swiped right: the next one was of her clothed,

again, but a different angle. Ripped tight light wash blue jeans, the ones she'd been wearing the last night I saw her.

I swiped through, slowly, savoring.

The next one was of her in jeans and a black bra. Oof—the hard-on seeing that was instant and painful. And it only got worse when I got to the topless shots. Shit, she was perfect. I wanted her, so badly. God, I wanted her.

Those delicate, dainty, pink little breasts, darker pink areolae, brownish nipples. Perfectly round breasts, tight and high, the tips pointing just slightly toward the sky. Plump, pert.

Fuck.

I kept scrolling. Topless again, but without the jeans. Just those lovely little tits and her in a pair of light gray briefs, the kind where the leg holes are cut way up high past her hipbones. God.

Then, ohhhh lordy.

In the last few she was totally nude. In the first, she was tastefully turned to one side, showing me the outside of her thigh, the phone, her breasts, eyes on the camera, platinum hair loose and draped around her shoulders.

The next was less tasteful and more scandalous. Hot. God, so hot. Facing the mirror, hiding nothing. A small smile on her lips. Looking in the mirror and at the camera—at *me*—as if begging me to come through the photo and make her feel good.

God, if only I could.

In another shot she showed me her ass, high and round and taut. Toned, muscular, with just enough delicacy and softness to make me nuts.

I knew why she'd done this.

It was for me.

Because she wanted me to embrace my sexuality.

Giving me clear and undeniable permission to use her as fodder for my imagination. For my needs.

It wasn't as good as the real thing, in my hands, but god did I need release. I'd spent the last week in agony, waking up thinking of her. Dreaming of her. Remembering her. Wishing she was here, yet still refusing to let myself think of her like that.

Even though she'd told me to, that I could, that I *should*, old habits die hard; ingrained resistance is difficult to overcome.

The visual stimuli helped.

A lot. A *lot,* a lot.

Instead of giving in and letting myself use her as release, I turned to art for expression.

There was only one medium for this—my oil paints. I stretched half a dozen canvasses, chose my palette of paint colors, and went to work.

In the first one I reproduced a photo as directly

as I could, going for photorealistic—I started simple, her in those faded ripped jeans, pale skin showing in tantalizing glimpses, shirtless, wearing just the black bra, a full coverage functional piece, showing just enough cleavage to make me hard, make me imagine what lay beneath.

I set that one aside and kept going. Another photorealistic transcription of a photo; in this one, I allowed myself to represent her topless, in just those high-cut briefs.

I spent hours and hours painting, each one taking several hours, and even that was blasting through at a reckless pace, sacrificing technical precision for the passion of just gettin' the paint on the canvas, getting the images out of my head.

I painted for forty-eight hours straight, ate a full day's worth of calories in one go and then slept—fitful, restless, dreaming of her, seeing her writhing naked on my bed.

I took my canvasses and paints and easel outside, by the pond.

I painted her on a boulder, in a bikini, head turned to smile at me, a sultry, sexy, come-hither grin, hair spilling over her slender serpentine back.

When I lost the light, I went inside again.

I painted her naked by the fireplace, on the floor. Sated, sweaty, on her back, feet pointing at the fire, eyes closed, breasts peaked and nipples hard, a scrim of blonde fuzz around her core. One arm tossed across her belly, the other extended out behind her. The viewpoint was from behind her, standing just above, gazing down at her.

It was a furious time—hours spent painting becomes days, days become weeks, and I was running out of paint. Running out of places to stack my drying works.

I couldn't stop, though.

I was obsessed.

It was frantic, a frenzy. A need to paint her, see her, a way to put my mental images of her out into the world. Express my need for her in a visual context.

I lost track of time. I ran out of paint. I made the trek into town to resupply paints and canvas materials.

Hunted for meat. Fish. Hiked the wildest places, clearing my head, thinking.

When I got back to the cabin I started working on a new piece right away.

How many portraits have I done? Ten? Twelve? I was barely eating, barely sleeping. When I was exhausted and fried, I would pack a bag and head out for more hunting, more fishing, more trekking through the forest, recharging my mind and soul and body.

Finally, I just literally passed out on the floor of the cabin. I was beyond exhausted, emotionally burned out from putting so much energy into feeling her, seeing her, painting her, wanting her, needing her.

Cassie...

Where are you?

FOURTEEN

Cassie

I CAN FEEL HIM, THE CLOSER WE GET.

Juneau, Remington, Ramsey, and Lucas were all with me. Guiding me. I'd never felt so much like a helpless city girl in all my life—we were miles from the nearest trail, dozens of miles from anything like civilization. I'd peed in a bush, wiped with a leaf. The mosquitoes were the size of crows. The temperature was cool, but I was hot.

I had no clue where we were. If Juneau and the boys left me now I'd die, for sure. Juneau led the way, marching unerringly...recognizing specific landmarks, individual trees. She would touch a tree, stroking a trunk, as if recognizing an old friend. We would pause in a clearing, at a boulder or a downed tree, and Juneau would examine them carefully, looking for clues. At one place she smiled as she overturned a huge rock, finding a small cache that included a small hide bag that had a knife and a flint inside. She looked at everything and then replaced it, simply telling us we were heading in the right direction.

She glanced at Remington, at one point. "I haven't been up to the cabin in a couple years. Funny how the old landmarks jump right out at you."

Remington nodded. "Go somewhere enough, it gets ingrained."

"I need to come up here more. Ink and I used to make trips up here all the freaking time. Then life got busy and I just...stopped." Juneau sighed, a sound somewhere between relief and joy. "I feel more alive, being up here."

He just squeezed her shoulder and we continued on deeper into the wild.

Further, deeper. Wilder.

Then, suddenly, we were in a clearing, and there was a small cabin and a pond. I barely saw the cabin at first, as it was well camouflaged to look like part of the landscape. The pond was tiny but lovely, a pastoral scene of elegant, wild beauty. A crow perched on the stump of a dead tree poking up out of the water, cawing. A dragonfly flitted across the surface, pausing and darting in unpredictable patterns.

I glanced at Juneau. "This is it?"

She nodded, grinning with pure giddy joy. "The Isaac Retreat." A sigh, gusty and happy. "For a while, this was my home away from home."

Lucas glanced around, nodding. "Quite a place. Looks like it's been here a while, huh?"

Juneau shrugged. "Since the seventeen or eighteen hundreds, we're not sure."

"How far around does the property go?" Ramsey asked.

Another shrug. "I dunno. I don't know that we actually even own anything. It's just always been here. We come up, we hunt and fish and hike and read and relax. We don't harm the forest, we don't leave anything and we don't take anything we don't need. We leave it stocked and unlocked, and if you know about it and are in the area and in need, you're welcome to it. Just respect it, and the land."

Ramsey nodded. "De facto, grandfather clause sort of ownership."

"Yep."

"He's in there," I whispered, staring at the cabin. "I need to see him."

The men and Juneau all exchanged glances.

Juneau bit her lip and said to the guys, "Um. If

you guys are game to keep hiking, I know of a great spot for a picnic on the way back to town."

A chorus of agreements and goodbyes and, within moments, they'd all trooped around the far side of the pond and up the hill. Leaving me alone in the forest, breathing slowly, raggedly, summoning my courage.

I walked up to the door of the cabin.

The door handle was nothing but a small metal lever lifting a latch—I lifted, pulled.

I stepped inside into…a sanctuary of me.

I was everywhere. Paintings of me on every surface. So, so many versions of me. He'd found my little gift, clearly.

I was stunned breathless for several minutes, just staring. The talent…god, the talent. He was a genius. In one, I was at the pond's edge. Nude. Facing away from him, stepping into the water. I was partially bent, one hand extended to ripple the greenish-brown surface of the water. He'd captured me in motion, somehow frozen an instant in time, a fictional instant.

Another was a close-up, just my bust, a hint of cleavage propped up as I lay on my side, smiling at him with soft tender love in my eyes; tendrils of hair wisped across my face, paused in being blown by a breeze or his breath. My eyes were utterly *me*. It was like looking in a mirror, writ large. Seeing myself, the way I…the way I would look at him as I lay in his arms in the afterglow of making love.

I teared up.

There were stacks and stacks of paintings. God, he must have been painting me over and over the entire time he was gone, the entire time I was healing and strengthening and giving myself a future.

I moved forward, into the cabin, scanning around quickly. The inside was chaotic—one room, a bed in the corner, kitchenette in another, one wall contained the fireplace which currently glowed with the amber-orange light of a dying fire. The windows were grimy with age, keeping it dark inside. Everything else was art—paintings, darkroom equipment, boxes of film, several old manual film cameras, rolls of canvas and lengths of wood for stretching the canvas, framing supplies, paints, brushes, knives and scrapers and god knows what else. A window was open for ventilation, but it still reeked of oil paints, and Ink.

Then I saw him on the floor, passed out. A palette lay to one side, a brush to the other. His hair was loose, all over the place. He was…a mess.

He had paint crusted on his hands, wrists, in his beard, on his legs. He was coated in old crusted paint.

An artist, lost in his art.

Lost in his mind. His heart.

Lost in me.

I was filled with tenderness, watching him sleep. A frown furrowed his brow. I knelt, and then sat beside him. Smoothed the frown away with my fingertips, and he stirred. Rumbled wordlessly in his chest. Stirred again.

His eyes fluttered, opened, fixed on me. "Cass." His voice was so low I could barely hear him, but I felt the sound of it.

"Hi." I reached for him, and he shifted toward me. I pulled his head into my lap, stroked his hair.

"You're here." He wrapped an arm around behind me, cradling my waist.

"You've been busy, I see," I said, letting humor fill my voice.

He snorted. "Yeah. Found your little folder of goodies."

"I'm not sure what came over me. I've never done anything like that before. Never taken a single nude or even a partially nude photo of myself."

"I'm glad you did." He glanced over my hip at the nearest painting—a photorealistic version of one of my photos, me in nothing but underwear. Instead of holding a phone and taking a selfie, though, he'd made it so I was just gazing at him, one hand gathering my hair at the back of my head, the other at my side. Sensual, sultry. I felt sexy, in that painting. Looked like…a strong, powerful, lithe warrior goddess. Fearless, bold.

I swallowed hard. "You're so talented, Ink. You could put these in a gallery."

He hummed. "Some of them are pretty intimate and personal."

I laughed. "I mean, maybe not the fully nude ones." I frowned, my fingers dancing over his temple, through his beard. "I don't know. I'm not an exhibitionist, but I...they're incredible paintings, Ink. Truly remarkable."

He shifted to sit up, facing me. "I couldn't display you like that." He got up, pulled one out from the middle of a stack—I was kneeling on a bed, upright on my knees.

Naked. My weight was on one side, as if I was in the act of sliding off the bed. My hair was down and loose, and I wasn't looking at the viewer, but off-screen so to speak, laughing at something. Joy suffused me. It was an intimate moment, private. It had the air of us, Ink and me, post-sex. I was clearly climbing off the bed to clean up, to pee, wash my hands, whatever. Laughing at Ink. It was just...*private.*

But there was something that just drew you in. It wasn't sexual, and even my nudity wasn't the focus. It was the moment that was being captured—it was a beautiful, private, delicate, joyful moment.

I wondered how I would feel letting strangers see it. See me, like that.

Oddly, it was okay. It was art, and I was confident in myself.

Even with the fact that he'd lovingly and, in exquisitely personal detail rendered the scars on my leg.

"Sell them," I said, abruptly. "They deserve to be seen."

He blinked, shocked. "What?"

"Unless you don't want to."

He shook his head. "I did them for me. To express...I don't know. How I feel. How I see you."

"But they're too amazing to just...sit up here collecting dust." I sighed. "I don't mean that as anything about me—it's you. It's your art. It deserves to be seen." I met his eyes. "I'm okay with it. I want you to show them."

He rubbed his jaw. "Wow. I wasn't expecting that. I thought you'd be creeped out by how many different times and ways I painted you."

I shook my head. "I'm not."

"It was... I *had* to. I saw those photos you took, and I just...had to paint you."

I stood up, faced him. Took his hands. "Thank you, Ink."

He tilted his head to one side. "For what?"

"Giving me time."

He just shrugged. "I should've...I don't know. Not been so harsh with you. I'm sorry."

I stepped closer. "No, don't apologize. I was angry for a while, yes. But I realized it was what I needed. I had to be pushed. And then I needed to be left alone to deal with myself. To figure my shit out." I dragged my fingers through his tangled beard. "So, thank you, Ink. For giving me what I needed when I didn't even know I needed it."

He gazed down at me, and his hands captured my hips. "So, did you?"

"Figure myself out?" I nodded. "Yes, I did."

"And?"

I stepped back, out of his hands. Crouched, leaped, landed in a plié, straightened and did a series of turns, spotting on him.

"You're dancing again." His grin was contagious.

I bit my lip, feeling overcome by emotion. "Yeah. Not all the way back, but mostly."

"And what are you going to do?" He was happy for me, overjoyed, proud. "Go back to Paris?"

He managed to suggest that without any hint of worry or fear.

I shook my head. "No." I sighed. "That season of my life is over, Ink."

"So...what, then?"

I grinned even more widely. "Well, I'm going into business with Baxter. I'm going to teach dance and dance fitness classes at his gym, and eventually yoga, and do some personal training. We're buying the building next to his, connecting the two, and renovating it into a facility for classes."

He let out a breath I hadn't known he was holding—and I got the impression he hadn't known he was holding it either. "So you're staying in Ketchikan?"

I nodded, returning to him, putting myself in his arms. Gazing up at him. "With you." A pause, as I swallowed fear and doubt, letting hope bubble and rise. "If you..." My voice caught. "If you still want that. Want me. Want us."

"You're staying for you? Because that's what you want for your future?"

I nodded. "I'm crazy excited. I'll get to dance again, but no pressure. No stress about staying at the top. No more living out of hotels and suitcases. No bickering with the other girls. Just...dancing. Teaching. I'll get to be in the gym all day, every day, and I love working out and being in the gym almost as much as I love dance. This lets me do both, and make money at what I love, but without the stress of the troupe." I bit my lip and stared into his eyes. "I'm also staying because I..." I lost my breath, my courage. Summoned it, and used it. "Because I love you. I want to grow a love with you. I want to be your muse every day of our lives. I want to do life with you."

His eyes were dark, wild, boiling with tumultuous

emotion. "Cassie, god, babe." He wrapped his hands around my hips. "Say it again."

I grinned up at him. "I love you." I lifted on my toes, whispered against his lips. "That part?"

He picked me up, his hands cradling my ass and gathering me against him. "Yeah. I like hearing that."

"You want to know how it'll sound even better?" I asked, reaching down to find him over his shorts. "If you bring me over to that bed. Make me scream, and I'll scream how much I love you."

He snarled. Turned. Took two long steps, and deposited me on the bed. Knelt over me. "You gotta hear it from me, though, Cass." He planted his huge arms beside my head. "I love you more than I know how to say, Cassandra. Truth is, I spent the weeks up here painting like a crazy man because it was the only way I could stay up here and give you time and space you needed without losing my goddamn mind. And I may have lost it a little bit, I don't know. I just know I need you. I fuckin...I *need* you, Cass."

Lying on my back with my big beautiful Ink above me, all around me, I drew his shorts down. He was bare underneath, as usual. Hard, he angled toward me. Bulbous and rigid. Beautiful, god, so beautiful.

I took him in my hand and closed my eyes in bliss as I caressed his length. "God, you don't know much

I've missed this." I stared up at him. "I dreamed about you every night. Fell asleep every single night, dreaming about *this*," I squeezed him, "inside me. I masturbated every single night, thinking about this, about you. Wanting you."

He hissed, his eyes fluttering, meeting mine. "Shit, Cass. Feels so good to have your hand on me. I want you so fuckin' bad. I'm crazy for it."

"I'm here, Ink. I'm here, and I'm all yours. Take me. Whatever you want, however, as long as you want. I'm here for you. All yours, baby."

He kicked his shorts off, and then knelt on the bed and made quick work of stripping me naked. Boots, socks, jeans, sweatshirt and T-shirt, bra, underwear, fell into a haphazard pile on the floor, and then he was between my thighs and tasting me, nuzzling me with his nose and smelling me, flicking his tongue against me, and I spasmed at the first wet slither of his tongue at my sex, whimpered when he licked me, and came within seconds. A little one, a precursor. He knew that, and didn't stop. Each movement of his tongue drew me up to wilder heights, made me shake and spasm, quake and shiver.

And then, when I was an instant from falling over the edge a second time, he slid a finger into me and sucked my clit into his mouth and I came with a scream.

True to my word, I screamed his name.

He kept going. Didn't stop. And I didn't ask him to.

I went with him, let him take me where he wanted me to go. He went slow, this time. Slow, lazy, fat circles of his tongue. Licks, flicks. Bringing me there lazily. Up the slope to shaking hips and quivering thighs, buttocks off the bed with my heels dug in, spine arched, fire in my belly and stars in my eyes. I shook, and I forced my eyes open, stared down my body at him, stretched out beneath me, his mouth at my core, my thighs framing him.

His eyes met mine, and I saw them smile.

This time, just as I reached the thrashing crescendo, he stopped.

I knew why, didn't go crazy asking him why, or beg him to keep going.

He pulled away. Crawled up my body. "I can't wait anymore."

I clasped him, stroked him to full hardness. "I know." Pulled him closer. "I can't wait for you anymore either."

He frowned. "I...I don't have any condoms. Again."

I pointed at my small pack. "I do."

He grabbed it, opened it, and pulled out the box of condoms I'd bought. Ripped a square away and tossed the rest of the string on the floor. I took it from him and opened it with my teeth, pulled the latex ring out and rolled it hand over hand down his length, my eyes on his the whole time.

He was kneeling. Facing me.

I needed something else, though. I guided him to his back, and climbed astride him. Kneeling on him, reaching between my legs I grasped him. Took him to me, fit him to my opening. I kept my eyes on his, my eyes widening and my lip caught in my teeth as I filled myself with him. Glutted myself on him, impaling him deep inside.

I was drenched with need, slick and ready for him, taking all of him inch by glorious inch, until I was sitting on his hips. He filled me so full I felt split apart by him in the most amazing way possible, aching to take all of him.

I let myself fall forward, catching my weight on my hands, braced on his huge chest. "Watch me, Ink. I want you to see what I can do. I want you to see what I *want*."

"Cass, I—"

I drew my hips up, sliding him out. Hesitated. "Pay attention, Ink. This is how I want you."

I slammed my ass down, hard, taking him all the way in with slapping, shocking force.

He groaned, and I screamed through clenched

teeth. I was burning with him, shaking already. He hit everything inside me, sliding past every stretched nerve ending.

"See, Ink?" I pulled up. "See how perfectly I fit around you? I can take you. All of you." I bent, touched my lips to his. "I can take everything you have…" I slid down him again, "…and still want more."

"Fuck, Cassie."

I laughed. "Yeah, Ink. Fuck Cassie. Fuck me. Let go."

He caressed my breasts, hanging and swaying between us. Then grabbed my hips and held on as I moved, not guiding me or controlling my movements but rather following along. Feeling me move.

I lifted, sank. Again.

Faster.

He groaned, head tossing back. Hips pushing up to meet mine on my downstroke. "God, god, god, Cassie."

His thickness was battering against something inside me, sliding past a nerve that made me wild. Ohhh god, that was new. It made me crazy. Insane with hysteric need. Screaming, unintelligible and hoarse.

I involuntarily slammed down around him, sucking in a breath as that nerve sang, and I twitched, shaking, my fingers curling into claws in his chest, my ability to move rhythmically gone, now. I felt the heat blossom inside me, felt it rising, felt myself riding it.

"Ink," I whispered, meeting his eyes. "Oh god, what are you doing to me?"

He groaned, shook his head. "I...god, Cass. I feel you squeezing around me. So fuckin' tight, Cass. I'm so close, can't hold out much longer."

"Don't, Ink. Don't wait for me." I shifted, moved my weight forward, lying prostrate on his hot skin, my face in his throat, breathing him in.

I moved only my hips, then. Slamming backward into him. Faster, and faster. No technique now, nothing but wild abandon. Taking him with all that I had, taking him hard and taking him fast, and it felt like heaven.

"Ink, god, please, please—" I wasn't sure what I was asking for. Just that I was on the edge, riding the razor edge of climax. Unable to fall over...yet.

"What, Cass?" He had my ass in his hands, holding me apart, guiding me on the downstrokes, lifting me up.

"Show me how you like it, Ink," I murmured. "Show me."

He growled, groaned. "Cass, I'm—you..." A sighing growl again, as he buried up into me. "Ohh fuck."

"Show me, Ink. Take me. Take it. God, *please*, show me."

"Cass, you don't know what you're—"

I snapped my eyes open, held his gaze as I felt raw furious need blast through me. "Yes, I do, Ink. I know exactly what I'm asking."

He shook his head.

"I can't come till you do," I said. "I won't."

"Cass…"

I gathered his head in my arms, wrapped him close, put my lips on his and whispered, desperate, frantic. "Trust me, Ink," I hissed. I slammed down hard. "Feel that?

"Ohhh god, Cass." Ragged. Still holding back.

I pulled up, drew a few slow shallow strokes around the tip, and then drove down so my ass clapped against his hips. "Like that. Feel that? Feel me take you?" I did it again. Harder, faster. "Feel me? Feel me taking you? I *like* it. I *love* it. I want more, Ink. *More*. Give it to me harder, Ink. Let go." Again, and again, and he was growling nonstop, pushing up into me, matching me, nearly. "Let go, Ink."

He whimpered, a quiet, raw sound.

His eyes flew open, met mine.

Fierce.

Wild.

"Yes, Ink." I saw it in him.

He grabbed my hips, lifted me so he nearly slipped out.

"Yes," I gasped, tremoring with anticipation. "Yes!"

And then he drove in, and this time there was no restraint. Not hard, necessarily, but I felt him give it up, felt something inside him break.

He started moving me, lifting me up, drawing me down, meeting me with harder and harder thrusts. Our bodies slapped together, and I screamed each time our bodies touched, gasping in desperation as he withdrew.

What followed then were the most beautiful moments of my life.

He held my gaze and he let go.

He fucked me with total abandon, and it was intimate and surreal and vulnerable lovemaking, pure and wild and primal and delicate.

He surged into me, and I fell down around him, crying with the bliss of him inside me.

I came with him driving in, came around him, and in the moment of my orgasm, he unleashed. I felt him shudder, and our eyes held as he gave himself to me, nothing left inside to hold him back. Each movement was pure and liberated love.

When we finished, I fell asleep in his arms.

A day later—after we'd spent the previous twenty-four hours eating, fucking, and sleeping, and talking.

Fucking.

That's what Rick had called it, what my brain wanted to call it out of habit.

But it wasn't that, not anymore. This was new, this was ours.

Silly and saccharine and old-fashioned, perhaps, but I liked to call it lovemaking. Because that was the most accurate term. It was our souls joining. Our hearts merging.

Sometimes, though? It was just good plain old raw fucking.

And that was beautiful and intimate, too.

Today, though, we'd finally left the cabin. We were hiking through the forest, and I knew exactly where we were going, even though I'd never been there before.

His waterfall.

I followed him, my hand in his. He wore a shirt for the first time since I'd met him, and huge, expensive thick-soled hiking boots, and he carried a big backpack.

It took an hour or two of walking, but we reached the river about noon, and after another thirty minutes upstream we went around a bend, over a hill, and then there it was…exactly as he'd described it.

A thin river meandering through the forest, and then descending abruptly over a break in the hill, a fall of only about ten or twelve feet. It splashed down into a pool, swirling and bubbling, a picturesque, storybook setting. Surrounded by the dense forest, the waterfall roaring and splashing, it was…a spiritual place.

He sighed as we settled on the edge. "Love this place." He looked at me. "Love being here with you. Never showed anyone this."

"No one?" I asked.

He shook his head. "Nobody."

I smiled. "Stay here."

I recognized this spot as the precise location of his first drawing of me, where he sat now was where he'd placed the viewpoint of that sketch.

I stood at the edge of the pool and stripped naked. Slowly, for him.

Stepped into the water, squealing in surprise— cold at first, but then warming to a tolerable temperature as I waded in. I doused myself in the spray, scrubbed my hair. My body.

I turned to look at him, intentionally taking the pose he'd drawn me in: one thigh drawn and bent against the other, an arm across my breasts. He laughed, recognizing what I was doing, and I laughed too.

"Literally making my fantasy come true," he said.

I crooked my finger at him. "Anything else happen in your fantasy?"

He laughed. "You are absolutely insatiable, you know that?"

He shucked his clothes and stepped in, wading in up to his waist. Drawing near to me. When he reached me, I gathered him in my hands. Brought him to life.

"So." I caressed him, eyes on his. "What's the fantasy of this place?"

He laughed, and took my hand. "Come on, let me show you something."

He led me to the waterfall, and we both got soaked in the plunging spray. To one side, there was a little nook. Not quite behind it, but off to the side was a patch of forest floor right up against the side of the fall. In the noise and white spray of it, wet and mossy and soft—sun peeked through, creating a million rainbows in the water.

"Here," he whispered.

The pool swirled and bubbled, the forest stood dark and trackless beyond it, the falls a wonder of wild power. I knelt, facing the falls, standing on my knees. He moved behind me, buried his face in my neck.

Pressed up against me. Inhaled me.

I reached around behind me, took his waiting manhood in my hand and plunged my fist around him, once, twice, and he gasped at it, and I knew it was time. I pressed him to me, and he groaned.

"Bag is over there," he muttered.

I slid my knees apart, pressed my lips to the soft part of his cheek just above his mustache and beside his nose. "I don't care," I whispered.

I held my breath as I nestled his thick fat round head inside me.

"I just need you," I whispered. "Here, now. Bare."

"Cass…"

"I've been on birth control for nearly a month," I said. "I got on it the day after that talk. The last time we talked."

He breathed a slow, tremulous breath. "Ohhh god, Cass. Are you sure?"

I sank down on him, and he groaned. "Yes," I gasped. "I'm sure."

He drove up, meeting me. And this time, bare, it was heaven, even more, even better, it was everything. Utterly everything.

I turned his face to mine, kissed him. We moved together, in perfect synch. "So perfect, Ink," I said. "You're absolutely perfect."

"God, Cass," he moaned, breathless. "How can

something I thought was already perfect get even better?"

"I don't know," I whispered, gasping, "but it is."

We moaned together, gasping, moving. His hands cupped my breasts and I fell back against him, and he did everything, moved for us, and I just writhed on him, let him dictate the rhythm and speed and took all of him, took him as he gave himself to me.

"I love you, Cass," he moaned. "I love you."

"I love you, Ink." I felt him shake as he moved into me. "God, I love you."

"Cass, I'm...I have to—" a growl. "I have to come."

"Now, Ink!" I sank on him. Drove down hard, taking him as deep as I could. "Please, now!"

"But we're—"

"I want it like this, Ink," I said. "I love you, I love you, that's all that fucking matters..."

He palmed my breasts in one hand, and pressed his hand across my belly and hips and where we were joined together, pressing me against him, pinning me there.

I whispered and chanted and screamed his name as he snarled and thrust his way to climax, and this time, I *felt* it. Hot and wet, a powerful rush of him into me, filling me, and I came with him, his fingers helping me there, and I came around him and he moved into me and I cried to feel it, to feel us, to be bare and naked with him, filled with him, sated on him, utterly sated on everything Ink, completed by him, and in him, with him and for him.

He held me as I lost all control, kissed me as he filled me.

Later, we lost each other in the waterfall, again and again.

And each time was better and wilder and more than the last.

He'd brought a tent and a sleeping bag in his pack. After setting it up, he made a fire by the pool. We ate out of cans heated on the fire. Wrapped up naked in a sleeping bag.

Made love deep into the night, bare every time.

I knew the risks, but with Ink, I didn't care. The only risk was pregnancy and, crazy as it sounded, I wasn't afraid of that either. I just needed *Ink,* needed this with him, needed to feel him. Feel us.

I wanted to feel and be loved by him—and know that my love for him was enough for him. That we were everything to each other.

We lay in the tent, drowsing near dawn.

"Build a love with me, Cass. Build a life with me." He dug in his bag. Pulled out a small crimson velvet bag. Produced a ring—a tiny diamond solitaire.

"This was my great-grandmother's. Supposed to go to my mom, but Dad insisted she have his. So I have it. Had it for years. Just held on to it, carried it around with me."

I swallowed hard. "Ink…" I gazed at him in the gray soft light. "Really?"

"I want to grow this love with you, Little Sparrow." He touched my hand, lifted my finger. "Say yes."

"Yes, my love. Yes, a million times yes," I whispered, choking on my own emotion, my tears, my love, my words.

He stared at me, almost shocked at my answer. "Yes?"

I flexed my finger. "I want to love you forever. I want your grandmother's ring. I want us. I want to live in Ketchikan and dance and make babies with you."

"It'd be a miracle if we already haven't," he said.

I stared at the ring, marveling. "I'd be okay with that, honestly."

He marveled. "You would?"

I laughed. "I'm all in, Ink. All in, all the way."

He wrapped me up. "What did I do to deserve you?"

I laughed as we found each other yet again. "I don't know, but I'm excited for our future."

"Me too."

Our future held love, days of it.

At the waterfall, at the cabin. In the woods. Outside by the pond.

His home.

My home.

Our home.

Home.

I was home.

EPILOGUE

———⁓✄⁓———

Charlie

Mʏ ᴘʜᴏɴᴇ ʀᴀɴɢ. I ᴘᴇᴇʀᴇᴅ ᴀᴛ ɪᴛ, ɢʀᴜɴᴛɪɴɢ ᴀɴ unladylike curse. 3:33 a.m.

Lexie.

Why was she calling me at three in the morning?

Why was she calling me at all?

She never called.

I answered it, rolling to my back, putting it on speaker and tossing the phone on my chest. "Lex? What is it?"

"Charlie, god, thank god you answered. I…I'm sorry. I couldn't call Mom. I didn't know who to call."

"What's wrong, Alexandra?"

A sniffle. "I'm in trouble, Char. I…I need help."

This from the most independent human being I've ever met. The girl who was cooking herself breakfast by four, packing her own lunches by kindergarten, had a job at fourteen, a car at sixteen, and despite her ostensibly hand-to-mouth existence, better credit and savings than me.

She never needed help. Had always refused it.

"What kind of trouble, Lex?"

A sob. "Not over the phone."

"Oh geez, honey. It must be bad."

A sob. "Yeah. It's bad. I'm a terrible person. I'm a sinner, and I'm going to hell, and I'm in serious trouble."

"Drugs, the law, or babies?" I asked.

"Charlie, *please.*" I've never heard such a raw, broken plea from anyone before.

"Where are you, and what do you need?"

"I'm at college. But I need you to…to…to come get me."

"It's not close, sweetie."

"Please."

"Now?"

"Can you get here any sooner than right now? I need to get out of here. I can't stay here anymore."

"What the *hell* happened, Alexandra?"

Another sob. "I'll tell you everything when you get here."

I put her college into Google Maps on my phone, and it spat out a drive time of around three hours. "I'll be there by seven. I'll call you when I'm close."

She sighed. "Thankyouthankyouthankyou!"

"This had better be a life or death thing, Lex. I'm dealing with my own crisis."

"It is. I mean, I'm not going to die, but I'd half like to. Thought about it."

"Alexandra!"

"Truth, Char. I did. I thought about it."

"That bad?"

"I've just transferred to Sarah Lawrence. And now I have to leave." She sniffled. "God, why?"

I sighed. "Be safe, be smart. I'll be there by seven a.m., okay? Just hang tight. Big sis is on the way."

"What would I do without you?" She sounded utterly relieved. "And Charlotte?"

"Yeah?"

"When I tell you my story, will you...will you promise to not judge me? Or, not judge me too harshly?"

"You're my sister, Lex. Whatever it is, we'll figure it out. You and me, okay?"

"Promise you won't hate me?"

"I don't make promises, Lex. But you're my sister. I won't hate you."

"You don't know, Char, you don't know what I've gotten myself into."

I sighed, roughly. "If you want me to come get you, you have to let me go so I can get dressed and drive all the way there from Boston."

"Okay, okay. Just…just call me on the way? I can't be alone."

"My god, Lex. It's going to be okay. I promise you."

"I wish I could believe that."

I got up and started getting dressed. "Lex, believe it. We'll…" I thought of Mom, and my last talk with her. "We'll have a road trip. You and me. New York to Alaska. We'll go see Mom and Cassie and their new boyfriends. We'll drive, take our time. Slow and easy and fun. We'll talk it through, and we'll figure it out. Sound good?"

She hiccupped. "Yeah, it does. That'll take weeks! It'll be great."

"It does and it will. So pack your crap, sis, we're going on a road trip!"

Ready for Charlie and Lexie on an epic
cross-country road trip?

NOT SO GOODE

Coming soon!

Also by
Jasinda Wilder

Visit me at my website: **www.jasindawilder.com**
Email me: **jasindawilder@gmail.com**

If you enjoyed this book, you can help others enjoy it as well by recommending it to friends and family, or by mentioning it in reading and discussion groups and online forums. You can also review it on the site from which you purchased it. But, whether you recommend it to anyone else or not, thank you *so much* for taking the time to read my book! Your support means the world to me!

My other titles:

Preacher's Son:
Unbound
Unleashed
Unbroken

Delilah's Diary:
A Sexy Journey
La Vita Sexy
A Sexy Surrender

Big Girls Do It:
Boxed Set
Married
On Christmas
Pregnant

Rock Stars Do It:
Harder
Dirty
Forever

From the world of *Big Girls* and *Rock Stars*:
Big Love Abroad

Biker Billionaire:
Wild Ride

The Falling Series:
Falling Into You
Falling Into Us
Falling Under
Falling Away
Falling For Colton

The Ever Trilogy:
Forever & Always
After Forever
Saving Forever

The world of *Wounded:*
Wounded
Captured

The world of *Stripped:*
Stripped
Trashed

The world of *Alpha:*
Alpha
Beta
Omega
Harris: Alpha One Security Book 1
Thresh: Alpha One Security Book 2
Duke Alpha One Security Book 3
Puck: Alpha One Security Book 4
Lear: Alpha One Security Book 5
Anselm: Alpha One Security Book 6

The Houri Legends:
Jack and Djinn
Djinn and Tonic

The Madame X Series:
Madame X
Exposed
Exiled

The Black Room
(With Jade London):
Door One

Door Two

Door Three

Door Four

Door Five

Door Six

Door Seven

Door Eight

The One Series
The Long Way Home

Where the Heart Is

There's No Place Like Home

Badd Brothers:
*Badd Motherf*cker*

Badd Ass

Badd to the Bone

Good Girl Gone Badd

Badd Luck

Badd Mojo

Big Badd Wolf

Badd Boy

Badd Kitty

Badd Business

Badd Medicine
Badd Daddy

Dad Bod Contracting:
Hammered
Drilled
Nailed
Screwed

Fifty States of Love:
Pregnant in Pennsylvania
Cowboy in Colorado
Married in Michigan

Standalone titles:
Yours

Non-Fiction titles:
You Can Do It
You Can Do It: Strength
You Can Do It: Fasting

Jack Wilder Titles:
The Missionary

JJ Wilder Titles:
Ark

To be informed of new releases, special offers, and other Jasinda news, sign up for Jasinda's email newsletter.

Made in the USA
Monee, IL
18 June 2020